Praise for
K.M.TREMILLS

"Readers will be inspired by Gabriella's journey into the heart of darkness and her triumph over those who seek to diminish her. *Messenger* is a terrific debut novel!"

– Elizabeth Stanley, *The Dark Path Chronicles*

"Full of mystery, suspense, beauty and courage. *Messenger* made me fall in love with reading again! I had forgotten how much fun it is to get lost in a story."

– Megan Barker, Empowerment Coach

"Well-written and entertaining. The *Great Lands* series gets it all just right. The characters were strong. I had a great time reading it and was sorry when it ended."

– Joe Gazzam, *Uncaged*

"A beautifully crafted story of a young woman gifted with unusual talents and tasked with a quest. There are fairy tale qualities to *Messenger*, reminding me of Aesop and his fables."

– Judith Nappa, Amazon Review

"This enchanting series is so visual that you feel at one with the characters and plot line. K.M. Tremills has a true gift for transporting you into the world she creates."

– Desiree Daniel Miller, OP Media Group

"*Messenger* is an absolute treasure and a fascinating story. The storytelling and the cast of characters are unique and make the novel a true joy to read."

– Renee Alarid, Associate Director of Creative Services

"K.M. Tremills is the gold standard for strong, independent and feminine heroines. *Blue Moon* is the start of a wickedly clever series!"

– Kathryn Cottam, *The Shoemaker*

"I fell in love with these vibrant characters. The *Fated* series is a delightfully dark blend of quirky, flirty, sarcastic, and charming."

– Vanessa Mayville, Vanessa Mayville Designs

"The ancient wisdom in the engaging story of Gabriella comes through in the eloquent words of K.M. Tremills. The *Great Lands* series can be read on many levels, all of which are entertaining."

– Jen Clarke, Executive Director at One to World

"The *Great Lands* series is brilliant ... a fantastic journey that steps into a realm of mysticism and fantasy. K.M. Tremills causes the reader to ponder their own beliefs."

– Barb Weston, Inner Focus Holistic Healing

"K.M. Tremills finds balance between page-turning plotlines and ethereal story-telling. Time well spent!"

– Roberta Cottam, *Bluebeard's Bride*

MESSENGER

K.M.TREMILLS

ALSO BY K.M.TREMILLS

Warrior *The Great Lands Series*
Queen Isabel *The Great Lands Series*

Blue Moon *The Fated Series*
Assembly of the Gods *The Fated Series*

FEATURED IN

Fabled: 17 Tales You Think You Know
Red: Three Short Tales of Red

MESSENGER

BOOK I
GREAT LANDS

K.M.TREMILLS

Messenger
© Kate Tremills 2013

Ebook Edition: September, 2013
ISBN: 978-0-9921042-0-7

First Print Edition: April, 2013
ISBN: 978-0-9921042-1-4

Second Print Edition: March, 2017
ISBN: 978-1-987818-04-8

Cover artwork © Roberta Cottam, 2017
Cover photography © Kaspars Grinvalds/Shutterstock.com

Published by RavenHeart Press
www.kmtremills.com

To the lovers of myth and beauty:
May you awaken to your power in the world.

THE GREAT LANDS
N
W E
S
GREAT MOUNTAINS
ASTERIA WOODLANDS
GREAT FOREST
GRANAMORE
INFINIMARE

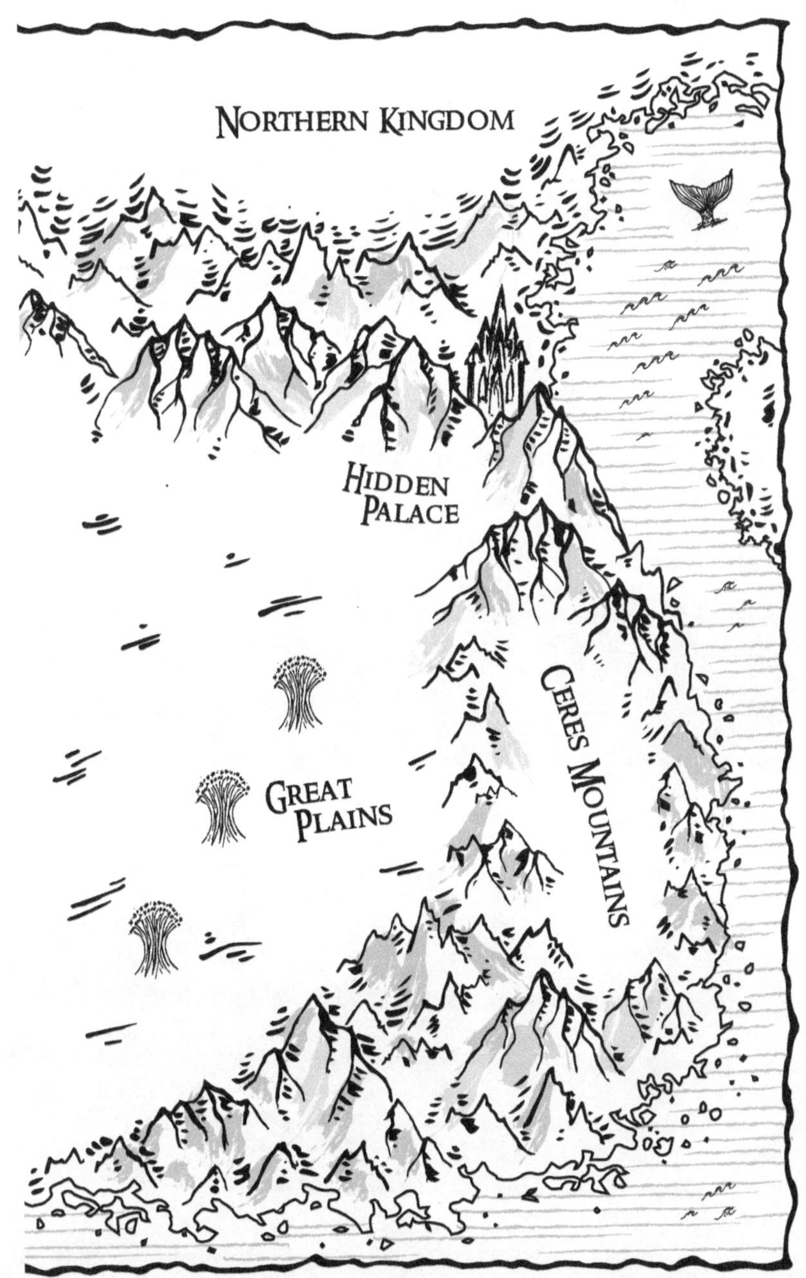

Northern Kingdom
Hidden Palace
Great Plains
Ceres Mountains

PART I

THE
MESSAGE

PROLOGUE

MANY STORIES ON THIS EARTH have never been told. Tales lost in the sands of time. Lands left undiscovered and worlds not ever sought. This is one of those stories.

Long, long ago, all beings were part of the tribe. No matter their form. Human, animal, or stone. All were brothers and sisters. And all were welcome.

No one can recall what caused the tide to turn.

A wind shifted. And darker times came. Over time, fewer people sensed the change. People grew numb to the way things were.

Trust wore away. Help was no longer freely offered. And gates rose up around every home and every heart.

Until, the day came, when one man, a violent and vengeful man, chose to make the whole world his own.

And there was no going back.

ONE

MY WORLD IS DYING. And I am on the run. The others cannot see it. In fact, they are fighting for the very world they need to let go. But my father could see it. He knew that life was about to get tenuous and I had to be hidden.

When life gets frightening, people act out. They take their fear and they send it into the world. They burn. They rape. They pillage. They chase away the very thing that holds hope in the tender palm of an open hand.

I cannot blame them. It makes me angry. But I cannot blame them. People have forever crushed the things that scare them most.

And nothing is more frightening than a thing not understood.

This is what has brought me to the church. A tiny church. Filled with kind, brave souls who understand what I feel. They do not speak the words out loud. For to do so would call the monsters to their door.

But they know. They know I am what these times need. What they have prayed for over many decades.

And they have agreed to give me shelter until the time comes that I must leave.

They know I am a Messenger.

I see it in their eyes. They understand that a Messenger, by her very nature, cannot stand still.

She can wait. She can rest until the Message is ready...but once she has received it, she cannot hide anymore.

To do so is to forsake the gift of the Message.

That would be the most dangerous thing of all for her. And for the World.

TWO

THE CHURCH WHERE I AM HIDING is far on the edge of my father's lands. Others call it his Kingdom. Though my father would never claim ownership. He believed he was a steward. A guardian of the land. Appointed by the Divine to care for those within the reach of his authority.

There was a time when this was the common opinion. When all believed that the land was a shared gift that no one owned.

But this is not the view anymore. In their fear, people want to own things. To lay claim and carve their names into buildings and archways.

In their fear, they grasp, they clutch, they hold.

They became infected by the suspicion that spread across the land. A fear that was less palpable as the years wore on. But even then, it was making its way across all the Kingdoms.

By the year when I was born, Queendoms had ceased to exist. People could not comprehend a woman on a throne alone. Or with a King as her consort.

The fear had taken root. Pushing out the old ways.

I cannot lay the impetus of this change at the feet of the Great Prince. For no one remembers the source. Or what brought the fear to our shores.

What I do know is that the older the Prince became, the stronger the winds of hatred and suspicion grew.

The more the idea spread that, instead of many smaller Kingdoms, there should be one Grand Ruler. A single man who knew what was best for all. No matter how foreign their ways or how remote their villages.

A truly strange notion. And a dangerous one.

For placing power in the hands of one man has only ever left all at the whim of one man's thoughts. Fears. And every strange notion.

Power is balanced in the sharing. In trusting that others are as capable of holding your heart with care. A notion now deemed perilous.

Trust has become that foreign to us.

As suspicion spread from village to village, and Kingdom to Kingdom, lands were closed to one another. Neighbours became guarded. And the slightest difference was perceived to be a threat.

Life went from a beautiful mystery to a beast that must be wrestled, conquered, and kept safe in a stockade.

This is why the church where I am hiding is precious.

The wise ones who were once the gateways to mystery became gatekeepers. Clutching the key to a magical realm that is no longer deemed safe for the average being. In fact, they deny the mystical unless it suits their needs.

Amidst fear and uncertainty, anything that challenges the rule is heresy. Treason. And something that must, immediately, be extinguished.

That includes me. You see, I have always been different...

Wait. That is not true.

In truth, I am like everyone else. Yet this truth has been lost. Buried. Crushed under the burden of suspicion and doubt.

Kept from the common person in order to keep the wheels turning.

So that now, the very thing we all share, has become the thing that stands me apart. That marks me as different.

Different. Frightening to some, and special to others. A line in the sand that draws people into two camps.

When all it means is one thing is not like the other.

And this difference that I must hide? I feel the connection to the Gods and Goddesses. I am their hands on this earth. I know that the very things I touch, say, do, need – are extensions of the Divine Ones.

This is true of us all.

And this, I am told, is heresy. Except... I know in my heart of hearts, that the Great Prince also knows it is true.

He denies it. Sending his minions to strike the thought from history.

Cutting the words from people's mouths. Burning it from their bodies. But this does not negate the truth. In fact, it makes the truth stronger.

For the truth is like a whisper on the Wind. Living on forever and carrying for miles. No one knows when that whisper may turn the corner and whirl back into her life.

Like the Wind, a truth has many seasons. And stands the test of time. A truth is carried by many. And owned by none.

And when a truth has been forced to lay dormant for too many years, the whisper awakens in a being asked to make this truth her essence. Her mission. Her reason for walking this earth.

For a whisper does not exist unless it is shared.
This is my whisper to you.

For a whisper does not exist unless it is shared.
This is my whisper to you.

THREE

I SPEND MOST OF MY DAY on a hard wooden pew, watching. I keep the soft brown hood around my face. For though I feel safe with the patrons of this church, I never know who might enter the doors.

The brothers and sisters go about their work, softly and diligently. They tend to this ancient place with the devotion of children caring for their elders.

They practise an art that has been lost. Their daily attendance is a kind of offering.

A devotion not to a God that looks down on them. Rather, a simple gesture to a Divine Being that holds them in the embrace of life.

They tend to this space as their home.

Not only for themselves. This is a space they hold for all. Understanding that we are each a unique expression of the Divine. Every being that enters is God. Every creature is the Goddess.

What do you offer when you enter the home of someone you love?

To clear the table. Wash the dishes. Tend the fire. You wield your being and effort for the benefit of all. By doing so, you leave a little piece of yourself with your loved one. And the entire home flourishes.

This is the tenderness the clergy bring to their church. A place they love and have opened to me. Despite the risks.

The sister looks up. Her face on full alert. Her body attentive.

A stranger is coming.

Her gaze brushes over me as she turns to pick up her dusting cloth. Our gaze connects and I immediately see what she sees. Hardened boots. Dusty clothing. Forceful steps.

A chill runs down my spine. The stranger is no friend.

I stand up. Pull the soft hood over my face. Turn my gaze downward.

And move swiftly out of the line of sight. If I have mastered anything, I know the art of moving silently from a place. As though I had never been there.

Just in time, I merge into the shadows of the church pillars. Leaving the pews. And watching the strange man approach the doors.

Though his fine clothes give me pause, this is not what troubles me. For the Great Prince commands all his people to dress in a manner befitting his status. No matter that this man spends most of his day astride a horse.

My concern goes deeper. Beyond what may be seen on the surface. To the core of the message he carries into the church. Punishment. Arrogance. Unbridled rage.

This man believes he can balance the world by removing the elements that do not suit his master. The pieces that do not fit.

The unruly ones. Like me.

Focused on his mission, the stranger moves down the nave. He does not pause. He does not consider. He only sets his sights on his target.

The brother and sister tending the sacred womb of the church.

Watching him approach, they stiffen. Their movements are subtle. Trained to be hidden. Their gaze levels on him. And they focus.

The mercenary walks toward them like he owns the very ground. That no person stands in his way. And he need never ask permission.

My eyes fall to the curved dagger on his belt. Displayed for all to see. Housed in a white casing as though this could negate the rivers of blood that have flowed from the blade. I cannot let this man harm the ones who have sheltered me.

Pulling deeper into the shadows, I watch closely as the mercenary confronts the sister. I feel her fear. And yet, I also know her peace.

The mercenary may play with death. Wield its weapon. But he still thinks he can win. That if he takes enough lives, and covers enough miles, he will cheat death.

In a flash, I can see exactly how he will die. And how many lives he will take before that day. My throat closes and I must fight the urge to leap from the shadows.

To protect the ones I love. To wield my own dagger of truth and retribution.

But I swore to my father that I would not jeopardize all that he has risked to send me on my mission. And when I sought refuge here, the sister made me swear to protect myself above all else.

For she knew this day would come. And the only thing that would keep me from endangering all we love would be my word.

Holding me, tight to the shadows.

In this moment, I loathe being a Messenger.

FOUR

THE DIVINE HAS PUT ME here before. Two short years ago, my life was beautiful. I lived with my family on our ancestral estate. Though the tide was turning, my father still believed there was hope.

He was sure the ruling kings could be convinced that this new way, this belief that they owned the land and dictated the fate of the world, could be changed.

As king of the ancient forest lands, my father – King Algor – held tremendous sway in the region. Those who held to the old ways, deemed the forests sacred and filled with magic. And revered anyone who spoke for them.

For those who no longer believed in anything sacred, the forests were a coveted resource. One that every person needed to survive.

So when my father sought discourse with the regional kings regarding the changes sweeping the land, every ruler accepted his request. And gathered at our home.

They smiled. They drank. They discussed the ever-changing tides of politics. And still, held fast to the belief that they now owned the land.

The kings did not come alone. The queens held their own communion.

They gathered. And talked. And shared news. All the while, I could feel our land calling to them. Asking them to speak, to save the old ways. To champion the connection that was in grave danger of being lost.

But the queens pretended not to hear. They chose to remain silent. Their voices stolen long ago. They refused to fight to get them back.

I could not believe their cowardice. I knew if they dismissed nature's wisdom, the day would come when we would all pay. And, at sixteen, I only had time for passion. And the honourable fight.

I asked my mother, Queen Isabel, "Why do these women hold their tongues?"

My mother sighed. A tremendous sadness filled her being.

For though she had a loving relationship with my father, she knew this was rare among queens. I knew she mourned a time long gone from this earth. And unlikely to return in her lifetime.

She smiled at my youthful indignation and admired my courage. She did not expect me to grasp what she had to share.

And yet, in her wisdom, she knew the words were important to say. That one day, I might recall them and understand their meaning more deeply.

In a soft and reverential tone, my mother spoke of a time when women were powerful. Even worshipped.

A time when men and women steered the course of humanity together.

Then a shift began, not unlike the shift occurring now, that changed the course of history. She could not explain why. Or what the catalyst might have been.

Moment by moment, our voices became harsh in the ears of men. They did not wish to listen. And we grew either too talkative. Or stopped speaking.

She paused. Taking a breath.

"Silence does not," she explained, "come gently. To steal another's voice takes persistence. Violence. And unrelenting hatred."

Her face grew dark with a shared memory that she carried in her heart.

She sighed. Consciously shifting her energy. Choosing compassion for the queens who knew no better than the fear and shame that had been handed to them like a dark and unbidden inheritance.

"Before judging another too harshly," she said, as though speaking to herself, "always consider the path that led them to the place they stand."

I was, however, a fiery and unrestrained youth. Patience and understanding did not hold my interest.

I wanted freedom. I longed to roam. The practised gestures of the court looked ridiculous to me. I escaped the claustrophobic walls of the palace as often as possible.

For I knew the day was coming that I would be expected to wear the mantle of rulership. And I took full advantage of the dwindling days of unbridled autonomy.

I danced in fields that towered above my head. I sprinted down paths that ambled forever. And climbed trees to peer across the top of the world.

Nothing filled my heart with joy like roaming the lands.

When I was done exploring, I would burst through the palace doors to report my discoveries to my beautiful and refined twin sister, Hannah.

If ever the goddess of desire was embodied on earth, it was in my sister.

She was refined and beautiful and sweet and strong. She learned everything my mother asked her to grasp. She spoke five languages, dressed in silk, and smiled at anyone who crossed her path. Hannah was a beam of sunshine.

Two more different twins could not have been woven together in the world. And yet, we adored one another. Hannah spoke. And I, Gabriella, listened.

She recounted the stories of the castle. I relayed the gossip of the woods. Hannah preferred the comfort of four walls. And I soared in the space of open fields.

Together, we felt complete.

As the oldest, by seven minutes, she was the first to be placed on the auction block of marriage. In keeping with our different views of the world, Hannah was excited. Marriage was a new adventure. A new home. A chance for love.

I knew it was a trap.

Not by nature. Marriage was once a sacred ceremony between two lovers. An alchemy of souls to birth new possibilities into the world. In truth, I believed it was the very foundation of a kind and understanding community.

But the recent changes in my world had also changed the ancient rites. And now marriage had become, for most women, a cage. Four walls to keep you from straying too far or exploring too deep.

This was even more so if you came from a lineage with means. For nothing breeds independence like wealth. And so, we were expected to be silent. Forgiving. And demure.

Traits I never seemed to master.

I knew Hannah's betrothal would not go well. I said as much to my father but he felt it was his duty to the kingdoms to follow through with the ancient ways.

My father still believed that a marriage could heal the ill will that had been blowing across the kingdoms for many years. That, according to the ways of his elders, all it took to set the world right again was one union.

One alliance strong enough to hold everyone together.

I told him he was blinded by duty. That the world no longer functioned by the rules he held so dear. And we would pay the price.

He insisted a solution could be found. That placing Hannah's hand in the palm of the right suitor was just the offering to bring peace.

Though his gesture came from the heart, I could feel it was beckoning another force altogether.

I begged my father to see a dark storm was on the horizon. That he mistook the threatening clouds for nourishing rain. When what was coming was Darkness.

But my father was deafened by hope.

He refused to listen.

FIVE

WHEN THE SUITORS CAME, they sent their soldiers first. A deep foreboding entered my bones. I sat at Hannah's side and watched. I would not leave her unguarded. If my father refused to see the truth, I would protect my sister. Hannah smiled and curtsied and offered her hand to be kissed.

Prince after prince. They presented themselves. Full of rehearsed promises. Not a single one worthy of the prize they sought.

My mother attempted to tempt me from my sister's side. Insisting that this was for the best. As a queen, her words were convincing. As a mother, her eyes spoke otherwise. I knew my mother felt the storm.

As each moment passed, the queen's hope faded. She could feel no love from the aspiring men. No reverence for her daughter. Nor even a faint whisper of unity.

All she felt was each kingdom's desperate quest for wealth.

After all offers had been heard, in a gesture befitting his pride, the Great Prince sent his men. They entered our palace as though the decision was made.

My foreboding turned to dread.

The Great Prince led the charge for all the recent changes. He may not have been the instigator. But he was the champion.

Every tree mowed down with indifference. Every child imprisoned for speaking the truth. Every village burned for keeping the old ways.

The Great Prince had marked the path of their devastation.

And now he sought my sister's hand.

I begged my father to listen. I pleaded with my mother. I spoke words of desperation I never imagined would cross my lips.

All while Hannah sat silent. Refusing to speak for herself.

Would no one say what was truly happening? Were they all too afraid to say it out loud? For fear the truth would instantly materialize?

I did not care what anyone feared. I knew, in my heart, that the Prince had ulterior motives. Ones we could not yet see. Perhaps even he was not sure yet, what they were. But I would not pretend they were not there.

My words no longer effective, I wielded my silent fury like a weapon.

Eventually, my mother could not deny the truth of my feelings. Her eyes filled with tears. She turned to my father with streaks on her cheeks.

Her eyes pleaded with him. What are we to do?

It was in that moment, I suddenly understood. My father was trapped.

He did not want to give Hannah to the Great Prince. But if he were to refuse, he would be accused of treason. The Prince would lock us in prison and take Hannah, anyway. If, as daughter of an imprisoned king, he deemed her of any value.

My father was forced to give his first daughter to a man he did not trust. More than that, a man he feared would tear the kingdoms apart.

King Algor was in the worst position a father could bear.

The court fell silent. Witnessing my father's pain.

And understanding the truth.

Even Hannah, who bore the brave face of a future queen, knew she was a lamb being offered to the slaughter.

No one speculated why the Great Prince had sought out my sister. She was, indeed, a rare beauty. And as educated and demure a bride as could be found.

But these did not strike me as qualities the Great Prince valued. So why choose our family for his betrothal? Why not a closer and more allied kingdom?

I believe he was threatened by my father's wisdom and standing. The other kings revered his words too deeply. And the Great Prince did not brook opposition.

Not that my father openly opposed him. But King Algor stood firm by the old ways when the Prince insisted that a new wind was blowing. A conquering wind. A wind of domination.

And now, the Prince had come to claim his price for my father's determination.

Despite fanfare and announcements, when the Great Prince entered the court, the air filled with a chill. His presence only ever brought violence. Though everyone felt for my family, they did not wish to draw the demon to their door.

But this was the man laying claim to my sister. And I would look. I would know what future he intended for her.

I searched his eyes, his hands, his feet, and finally his heart for some tiny drop of tenderness. Proof that my sister would not be killed. Or worse, tortured.

I sensed fear. Layers of fear. And beneath that, shame. Then, finally. Cowering in the corner, like a child that had been abandoned for years, was trust. A tiny, drop of hope in an ocean of despair.

I immediately locked my gaze on the floor.

If the Great Prince knew for a moment that I saw he possessed vulnerability, I would be dragged to the dungeons. Tortured. And left there to die.

My parents would not recover from losing both daughters.

And so, at the tender age of sixteen, I took my first step on the path of maturity. I breathed deeply. Controlled my thoughts.

And placed my vision of the Prince in the heavenly cradle of an ancient oak tree.

Hold me, I whispered in my mind. Hold me and protect my thoughts. Or all will be lost.

And true to her ancient promise, the Divine listened.

SIX

I HAVE NOT HEARD FROM MY SISTER in two years. Nor has she heard from me. At least, not in letters. I reach her during the dreamtime. But I refrain from speaking about it. In the waking hours, I even keep her from my thoughts.

For these days, it seems, even thinking about such things gets you killed.

Two years ago, my sister was betrothed to the Great Prince and carried away to his lands. The next morning, my father began preparations for my security.

The veil of denial had fallen. King Algor knew that this was no ordinary betrothal.

The presence of the Great Prince in our court was an act of war. And he would not stop until my father's kingdom was decimated.

All this time, I thought my father had been oblivious.

In truth, he had hoped. He had faith in the other kings. Perhaps faith that was misplaced. But he held them as his neighbours and allies. And hoped that one of them would share his vision and the alliance could be a foundation of strength.

The moment the Great Prince appeared, everything changed. There was no other option. When the Prince took my sister away, my father knew.

The wheels had been set in motion. And King Algor would do his best to protect the people and the ways that he loved.

Even before all that happened with Hannah, my father knew that I had the sight. He believed the Divine would not bequeath such a gift without reason.

And so, he prepared me for what he called the greatest mission of my life: survival.

Until now, the king had allowed me to seek my own path. To learn from nature. To build abilities from teachers that I discovered.

Trusting my inherent power to guide me. He could no longer afford that luxury.

Under the cloak of darkness and through the secret ways of the ancient Messengers, my father called in the greatest sages of his land.

Claudius, elegant master of the sword, was tasked with teaching me the art of weaponry and battle. Every day from dawn until lunch, Claudius owned my time, my muscles, and my mind. At noon, I was allowed to fill my belly.

Then I was handed to Serafina, my guide into the mysteries.

The afternoon was spent learning the ways of the sacred. I had always shown an aptitude for reading the hearts, minds, and bodies of people. Serafina taught me how to read the elements, the animals, the past, and the future.

She knew that my survival was not for me alone. My survival was, ultimately, to protect me as a vessel of wisdom.

There would come a day when this would be needed. When the wisdom would save not the world, as so many believe. No. This wisdom would preserve the essence of the Divine in human beings.

Serafina would say, the world does not need saving. The Great Mother has wisdom beyond our comprehension. Humanity is the creature that needs our help. For we have been given feathers to build wings and, instead, we use the quills to draw blood.

After dinner, my mother would guide me to the stables. She would prepare me for riding. Covering me in a soft, brown cloak that matched the colour of my horse. My mother would whisper the wisdom of the animals to me, hand me a map to the kingdom, and bless me with the protection of angels.

Every night, it fell to me to find the secret shelters nestled deep within our lands. To unearth a new nook, another place to hide.

For we all knew the corners of our land would fall into enemy hands. And when those lands were gone, I would need a new place to go.

This was my nightly task.

My mother hated this part of the day. She knew it was essential to build my confidence. To allow me to explore and trust my own instincts while I still had a home. When the day came that I was sent out never to return, I would forever be relying on wits, instinct, and adrenalin to keep me alive.

And she desperately wanted me to know love and safety as long as she could possibly offer them.

SEVEN

I TUCK BEHIND A PILLAR in the church. The stranger of the white blade is speaking to the brother and sister. He does not give the impression of inquiry. Rather, he stands with an air of intimidation.

The brother and sister are not shaken. They know when they take their vows that death is their constant companion. They, unlike a soldier, do not fear death. For a soldier can charge into battle pretending to do so without fear. But the stink of fear touches everything on the field.

A person of faith lives with the presence of death every day. A person of faith makes death her friend. Invites her to lunch. And offers her a seat at the table.

The faces of the brother and sister do not show fear. I can feel that this angers the man with the white blade. Though, his anger is deeply hidden and I have to be careful. For in searching through another's emotions, there is always the potential of detection.

And detection is my greatest enemy.

I feel the sister pushing me away. Her eyes have not moved from the stranger's face. Nor has her body shifted. But she pushes me toward a small hatch at the back of the church.

I move silently in the direction she indicates and find the promised exit.

The door is just large enough to fit my body. I open its filigreed cover and slip inside. I wait for a moment. Wondering whether further direction will come.

When nothing enters my consciousness, I keep moving. At this point, all I know is to follow where the passageway leads. I keep my focus sharp. And trust that the next decision will be clear when I am presented with the end of the tunnel.

The tunnel is dark. And I have no way to know where it will go. I could choose to see where I am headed but I cannot spare the time or the energy at this point in my journey.

There are moments when we simply have to trust that our fate is in good hands.

And be present to the choices available.

We humans love to complicate matters. With all of the skills I have learned, I now know the most precious one is stillness. In stillness is the truth. You cannot hide or run from what you know to be true. The trick is in cultivating your ability to listen.

I continue down the tunnel until I can sense movement and noise at the other end. There is a sharp smell of hay and feces. I know that I am headed toward the stables.

I smile inside.

Though I am still within the clutches of danger, I delight in knowing the sister directed me to an escape route. Out of the church and in reach of a steed. Or, at the very least, a place to hide until the coast is clear.

At the end of the tunnel, I sit for a moment by the hatch. Hearing only the soft neighing and crunching of horses, I gently open the door. Push away the straw covering my exit and tumble out quickly. Then spin to catch the door before it clangs shut.

Stepping carefully into the stables, I lift a blanket from the wall and place it on Casmire's back. I slip the bridle over his head.

With the basic preparations made, I enter the doorway of choice.

These are the painful moments. Leaving the place that has become my home. No matter how short the stay, I am always grateful and attached to the safety.

Fleeing brings uncertainty. Sleepless nights. Loneliness. I know these companions well. But I do not choose them lightly.

With a deep sigh, I feel I have no other option. I swing silently onto Casmire's back and ease him cautiously out of the stables.

He takes this change of plans in stride. Stepping softly, knowing the ways of stealth. We learned these tricks together.

I often wonder whether either of us will recover the ability to make noise with a light heart. But this is a question for another day.

This moment requires presence of mind.

And focus on the path ahead.

EIGHT

DEEP IN THE WOODS, I feel we are being tracked. I have ridden Casmire eight hours away from the church. And now the cover of darkness has fallen.

I might wonder if we were only being followed by an animal. This is the perfect time for the night ones to hunt. But I was trained by Serafina.

And her voice tells me that this is no animal. This is something with skill.

Somehow, our tracker protects its essence. Keeps me from sensing what it is. And where it is from. That kind of skill is deeply frightening.

Breathing slowly, I control my response. Fear is not my friend. Never mind that any loss of control on my part will only spook Casmire. Sending twice the signal to the tracker.

I weigh my options.

We're deep enough in the trees that flight is not easy. Two hours ago, I chose cover over exposure. And now I must live with that choice.

Casmire knows a decision is coming. We have travelled together long enough that he picks up on the kind of tension that foretells a choice.

He moves patiently forward. Until I am ready, he follows the present course.

Softly stepping on the fallen needles. Cushioning the sound of our movement as he waits for my signal.

I manoeuvre Casmire onto a side path, stepping deep into the cedars. If flight is not possible, I will plunge deep into cover.

He flicks his head to express his discomfort in being so close to the trees. Their bark scratches his sides. Their branches poke his haunches. But he refrains from sounding his displeasure. Knowing our lives hang in the silence.

I slip off his back and back him further into an aging thicket. The colour closely matches his coat and my hood. I crouch down and gesture for him to stand still.

Watching the path, I cannot find the tracker. I reach out gently with my senses. Probing the energy field for a unique pulse. Nothing.

This fact does not give me comfort. The absence makes me more nervous.

A foreboding chill goes down my spine.

I will not let things end here. In the middle of the woods. When all I have done for the past two years is run and hide.

Fury ignites in my belly.

Losing my family. Abandoning my home. Swallowing fear at every turn.

I have turned away from defending every person who has helped me on the path. I have honoured my father's wish and my mother's prayer. I have even kept silent for the sake of my sister. All for what?

To cower in the woods and beg the trees to protect me? I am supposed to protect them!

I stand up. And step directly onto the path.

If my mission is to survive, then tonight, I choose to fight. No more hiding.

My muscles are ready. I hold steady in a soft stance but my muscles burn with the desire to spring. To tackle. For once, to do anything other than run.

I feel a soft shift in the wind. Like something has arrived. I just cannot see it.

My skin prickles. Goosebumps raise on my arms.

All of my senses are on high alert. I feel Casmire's fear, though he holds tight to his position. I send him a soothing message from my heart and assure him that if he needs to run, he should run.

Immediately, he is insulted. But his irritation cannot mask a practical recognition that this course of action may be necessary.

Taken off guard, before I can react, I feel a forceful surge enter the glade where I stand.

Instinctively, my muscles brace. But the flash of light and blaze of heat is too intense. None of my training prepared me for this sensory onslaught and sheer force of power. I use every ounce of my will just to stay on my feet.

Temporarily blinded, I grapple to control my fear and sustain my wits.

Without sight, I must compensate with my other senses. The birds continue to chirp. And have not fled. This gives me hope that pure destruction is not at hand.

I smell and taste the air. No hint of sulfur or bitter rage. Instead, I can smell hints of lavender and lemon. My muscles relax a notch. Enough to bend like a willow. This is a good. The blood still flows and I have, at least, a chance at running away.

Though, if this creature can control the sun, I have little chance against its power.

I try opening my eyes. Tears flood my pained irises.

I catch only a glimpse of a brilliant shape before me. The force of its light pushes the lids back over my eyes. Sending the tears down my cheeks.

How am I to defend myself against such a creature?

And yet, I do not feel threatened. The moment I realize this notion, my legs crumple. I land like a child on the soft ground. Defenseless and senseless.

I pray that this creature is not manipulating my feelings. If that is true, all I have struggled for, all my parents have sacrificed, is lost. In one humbling moment.

I struggle, but cannot regain my stance.

"Nor do you have to," the creature speaks directly in my mind.

"How do I know you are not deceiving me?" I whisper back.

"Search your heart," the creature states. "Indeed, search the heart of your companion. Beasts are harder to deceive. They do not rely so heavily on their intellect."

Despite the creature's wisdom, my immediate reaction is to protect Casmire. At least, until I recognize that I cannot manage even to stand.

I reach gently out to Casmire, and discover that not only has he not fled. But he has exited his hiding place. Contentedly sourcing and chewing on any available flowers.

"Traitor," I think, infuriated.

Casmire snuffs his objection at my quick and summary judgement. Especially, when he has given me precisely the answer my heart wants.

"Fair enough," I respond. And turn my attention back to the blinding creature.

"What is it you seek from me?" I inquire, fearful of the answer.

"Given that you perceive yourself to be a Messenger. Have you never wondered what, in fact, is your message?"

I should be dismayed that this creature knows I am a Messenger. And has called this to my attention.

Instead, I find myself annoyed. Faced with an otherworldly being, I, Gabriella, do not bow in awe. No. I take it to task.

Summoning what minimal dignity I have, I find my feet. Standing up, eyes closed. Tears drying on my cheeks. And proceed to give this sacred being a lecture.

"If you knew anything about Messengers, fair creature, you would know that I cannot command the message. A Messenger can only wait until the message is ready and presents itself. Therefore, do not lecture me on appropriate behaviour. For I know full well what to expect of my mission and comportment."

I try not to huff at the end of my diatribe. I can feel the being is amused. In fact, the entire forest seems, suddenly, to be sharing a joke at my expense.

This confuses me even more and brings a heightened colour to my cheeks.

"And what would you, in your infinite wisdom, perceive to be a sign that the message has arrived?"

Suddenly, I realize what is happening.

My knees shake but I manage to stay on my feet. Whether through fortitude or sheer humility, I cannot say.

Standing before me is a Divine Messenger. The one I have been waiting, since my first breath, to encounter. And instead of being gracious, I have proceeded to lecture the voice of the ancient stars.

Oh, Gabriella. Thank the Heavens and the Deepest Seas your mother is not here to pay witness to this moment.

I bow my head and apologize, silently, with every fragment of my being.

The Angel chuckles. "No. Do not be ashamed. I admire your spirit and your honesty. Without these, you would not have the fortitude or character to be a Messenger. The Divine Ones have chosen well."

"Do you have a name I may use?" I ask, cautiously. "Mine is Gabriella."

"Oh, I know, little one. I have known you since long before you breathed this earthly air. You may call me Astriel."

"Astriel," I whisper. Amazed by the infinite beauty of the name.

I can feel the angel smile. And the trees rustle their leaves in appreciation.

The sound like gentle applause drifting on the wind.

NINE

Astriel guides me to a sheltered spot out of the path's sight. I settle into a nook between two enormous oak trees. The brilliant light fades to a soft glow and I am, for the first time, able to see her sacred form.

I say her form, for she feels more feminine to me, though I know that is highly inaccurate. Likely, she has chosen an energy that puts me at ease rather than makes me nervous.

While I do not feel aligned with most women, I have always felt safe with my sister and mother. And Astriel projects a similar protective and loving energy.

I have no doubt, however, that the message she has come to share with me will not be an easy one to hear. For while we all fantasize about being chosen or given some great mission, these are, inevitably the most dangerous times of our lives.

Forsaking the old to birth the new. This is a frightening prospect, as I have well found out.

Fantasies about great missions and daring deeds are the fodder of children's stories. They are true, despite that we belittle the audience. But it is rare that the authors genuinely convey the chasm of deep terror that must be traversed in order to arrive in the land of courage.

The baby bird that leaps from the nest to test her wings for the first time faces equally the prospect of death as much as the potential of flight.

Having barely passed the first test for my wings, I lean against a tree to gain some of its strength. Thank the Goddess for the wisdom and generosity of trees. I would have perished months ago without their support.

To ease my anxiety, Astriel takes a seated position. The fact that she hovers several inches above the ground, slightly undermines her attempt to calm me.

"The time has come," she says, "for us to have the inevitable conversation."

I nod, solemnly, in reply.

No one has truly prepared me for this moment. I have read stories and discussed possible scenarios with Serafina. The catalytic moment is, however, different for every Messenger.

And I have often wondered how well words could convey such an experience.

My entire body feels suddenly alight with fire.

I shift away from the sacred oak's trunk. After my ungracious diatribe, the last thing I need is to set a forest on fire in the presence of an angel.

Astriel smiles. "The heat you feel is an alchemical shift," she explains. "Your essence is responding to my energy but also preparing for a shift in your being. Every part of you is readying itself for the Message."

She glances up with reverence at the ancient oak twins. "You will not set the sisters on fire. You can rest easy."

I glance at the two trunks, noticing for the first time these two magnificent trees are connected below the earth. Two separate beings sharing the same root system.

Sadness enters my heart and I ache for the companionship of Hannah.

I involuntarily see an image of her, locked in a bedroom. Alone. Peering out a window. Her face filled with sadness. Like mine.

"Yes," responds Astriel, as though I asked a question out loud. "Your sister is connected to your message."

In an instant, she has my full attention. I sit up, waiting.

"You, like these trees, were born of one seed. Two beings as intimately connected as possible on this plane of existence."

Astriel watches my face, as though to gauge my reaction. I hold my tongue. Eager to hear more.

This, it should be noted, takes all of my concentration. Not merely because I am naturally impatient. But the mere mention of my sister has filled me with a furious need to launch her rescue.

"You are blessed. The connection you feel with your sister is both a great gift and a great burden. Yours is as sacred as any union under the stars."

Astriel continues to watch me carefully as she speaks. "You are too young to know this, but the connection of being a twin is not always a blessing. As many grow up with resentment and hatred in their hearts as ones that feel kinship and love."

I cannot help myself. Astriel's words have awakened the burning wound present in my heart since my sister was wrenched from my life.

"Why then," I challenge, "was she torn from me? If her existence is such a blessing? Why does the Divine punish us through this unkindness?"

Tears stream down my face. But my fists are clenched.

Astriel has every right to chastise me. To put me in my rightful place. Instead, I feel her tender reach, wiping a tear from my cheek.

"Why would you assume that this act is an unkindness?"

She waits. Opening a moment for the possibility of a response. I have no words to offer. Only quiet tears.

"This terrible event in both your lives bears the mark of a catalyst. If the Great Prince had not come to claim your sister, you would both have forever remained at home."

Suddenly, the words seem to find my lips.

"And this would be such a crime?" I demand, filled with righteous fury.

"Not a crime," Astriel assures me, "but a tremendous waste of talent. You know in your heart that you and your sister are here for a more profound journey than playing in regal fields."

I feel the challenge in Astriel's tone. Everything around her has shifted. Even the air.

She has transformed into the Divine Flame. The fire that incites us to change.

As angry and broken as my heart may be, I know she speaks the truth.

I get a sudden flash of Hannah with her head tilted as though she, too, is listening to our conversation. She likely does not know what is happening, but her face is serene.

This gives me courage.

I take a deep breath. "What is it, Astriel, that you have come to ask me?"

She smiles, serenely.

And waits.

TEN

NIGHT HAS FALLEN. And still we sit. Looking at one another. The most frustrating thing about Divine Beings is they have all the time in the universe. I have no choice but to wait until Astriel and the Message is ready.

Though, to be fair, this is only a guess.

Only the spheres know what makes an angel wait.

After passing through all the stages of impatience – fury, aggravation, judgement, annoyance, guilt, and reluctant acceptance – I land on the realization that this is the first time I have had a guardian since I left home.

For two years, I have slept with my senses on high alert. Even when sharing a roof with others, I could not allow myself to relax.

Here, in the middle of the deep woods, I actually have a guardian angel. Within moments, I am asleep. The kind of restful, dreamless sleep I have not had in years. Every element in my being recharges.

Until the deepest hour of the night. When the earth is completely still. The night ones are finished hunting. And the creatures of the day have not yet alerted to the dawn.

This is the threshold hour.

Suddenly, I am awake. Not clear what has roused me from so

deep a slumber. But I am up on my feet before my mind registers that Astriel is gone.

I look around as though an angel could possibly be missed. She cannot be gone.

Then the panic hits. Did I sleep through the moment? Did I offend her? Has she forsaken me?

Am I no longer a Messenger?

This question fills my soul with anguish. I've never considered that I could be stripped of my purpose. There are tales of beings who so deeply offended the gods that they are cast adrift for the rest of their days.

This cannot be.

Suddenly, and strangely, I am filled with deep calm. I close my eyes. And breathe. There, in the inner sphere, is Astriel.

No more lights. No more fire. In their stead, is a resonant silence. Full yet empty. Simultaneously.

I feel connected to every filament in the sky. The darkness and the light. The infinite web of life holds me in her arms.

Astriel steps forward in my vision. "The time has come, Gabriella. To hear your Message. And to be given the first stone on your path."

"The first?" I ask, within my mind.

"Yes," she replies. "The rest are essential to your journey."

"And must be discovered by me."

Astriel nods.

I can feel the impatience and irritation rise up in me. I both acknowledge their honesty and marvel at the way we humans always want the easy path.

Is that some subterranean memory from a time when things

were simple? When the gods handed us everything on a platter? Until the day came when we took it for granted, and craved something else?

I am suddenly aware of the truth behind the day of reckoning. The moment we were pushed out of the Divine Garden.

While many have used this to create an image of a wrathful god, the truth is we grew bored. We craved a harder, more challenging road.

Like rams that seek the highest peak on a mountain. They are wired to keep climbing. For far above everything else on earth, is a view over all creation. And, for a brief moment, the ram feels like a king.

He forgets that he climbed the back of a beautiful mountain that forever and a day has the same view. Or, perhaps, he climbs to remember.

Astriel watches me. Paying close attention to the dance of feelings that comes with this body. She seems fascinated and bewildered at the same time.

I completely understand. And I wonder whether she is merely being patient. Waiting for me.

And so, I calm my inner being. I bring myself to as close a moment of silence as I am capable of achieving.

She smiles at the effort. Then grows serious.

"Yours is not an easy road, Gabriella. You must know, I have debated your mission with many of my peers."

A question surfaces in my heart. I quell it. Now is not the time for inquiry.

"This debate did not find its roots in doubt," she assures me. "I am confident in your honour and ability. I only feel compassion for your tender age."

Astriel pauses. I can tell she wonders whether to have surrendered the debate. No matter. She is here with me now. And so, shakes off the unchangeable.

"These, as you know, are times of great transition. Times filled with two equal forces: great fear and great courage. These forces are not, as some would say, enemies. They are, in truth, partners. Fear and courage must, by necessity, come together. For each activates the other in the great dance of expansion."

I nod to acknowledge this truth.

Astriel looks at me with infinite kindness. "I know you understand this. And have even tasted its wisdom."

Her gaze intensifies. "You are, however, about to embrace the fire of this truth. For every truth burns. Some of us are born to love and crave this burning. Others run from the fire for every day of their existence."

I blanch. An image of the Great Prince flits across my consciousness.

"You, Messenger," she continues, "have been selected to carry the flame. To burn with the truth of existence. And to light this fire in as many individuals as you can. This is not an easy task and comes with great consequence. Of this, you must be made aware, before you accept the mission."

"Accept?" I ask. The question flies into the ether before I can keep it in check.

"Yes," Astriel says. "A secret that no Messenger is told until the day of the Message. You have a choice." Astriel's presence intensifies in my consciousness.

As though to emphasize the point.

"You do not have to accept this mission. There is no shame in walking away," she pauses. Allowing the notion to sink in. Knowing that I would find turning my back on anything a challenging concept.

"In fact, there is honour in both paths. You must not take on a mission with half a heart. If you are to accept, and I have made it clear how heavy this burden is to bear, you must do so with all of your being."

The searing truth of Astriel's words takes my breath away. I feel, suddenly, as though she is giving me a taste of this path. And how much is being asked.

Until now, I admit, I felt the call to be a Messenger made me special. Despite the caution, the running, and even losing my family, I took comfort in being chosen.

And perhaps it does. But that does not make it easy. Nor does it mean I will be adored. Or even appreciated.

I am deeply humbled by this realization.

I know also, in my heart of hearts, that to refuse this mission would be to dishonour everything that has been sacrificed on my behalf. Every action my parents —

"No!" Astriel interjects. Her expression stern and commanding. I wish I could close my eyes to her intensity. Her fierceness explodes in my mind. All I can do is bear the pain and listen.

"You cannot make this choice based on the actions of others," she insists. "Those choices were theirs to make. You do not own them. Nor can you use them to justify your decisions."

Her being alights with the full Divine fire. I wince at the sheer force of the flame.

"Make this choice for your own heart."

In that moment, as though struck by a bolt of lightning, I feel the command issued from my soul.

I fall to my knees. My arms cross instinctively over the core of my chest. And my hands land lightly against my shoulder blades. With my head bowed in reverence.

"I accept," I whisper out loud.

Astriel appears, suddenly, before me. Standing still for a moment. Lending honour and acknowledgment to this choice on the sacred path.

She places two hands of brilliant light on the crown of my head.

"Now," she commands, "You are a sacred Messenger."

ELEVEN

As THE SUN PEEKS her first rays over the horizon, Astriel accompanies me through the heart of the woods.

Casmire follows. Pretending not to listen. But his attentive ears belie his interest in our conversation.

No wonder, I think. As every word affects his journey as much as it affects mine.

"The road you have chosen," explains Astriel, "is a long and winding one. Most days, you will not be able to see around the next bend. That is to be expected."

I raise my eyebrows. "Will I be blindfolded for the entire journey? Is this a test?"

"Some days, yes. It is a test," she admits. "Most days, however, this is merely a factor of the journey. Many decisions carve a road. I cannot say what will happen. Neither will you be able to see it."

I fall silent. Realizing the intensity of faith and trust being demanded.

"This is the reason, among others, that we only give you the first stepping stone. I can point you in the right direction and reveal the first challenge. After that, the path is yours to walk."

"Will I not be given any help along the way?" I cannot stop myself from asking. Though I know I sound like a child. Echoes of being exiled from my family, lead to thoughts of abandonment. And a tumult of emotions unleash in my chest.

Astriel stops on the path and steps in front of me. I force myself to look at her, though I expect to be chastised for my insolence.

"Gabriella," she says softly. "When have we ever forsaken you?"

Tears well in my eyes. The depth of her compassion breaks my heart, and fills it with love, all at the same time.

I can only lower my head in apology.

Astriel touches my cheek. "I know the motives of the Divine are mysterious. This is as much for your protection as it feels like a source of frustration."

I raise my eyes to her, grateful for the understanding.

"Always remember, little one, that we are at your side. Never more so than when you feel most deeply abandoned."

Feeling my heart has lightened, Astriel admires a beam of sunlight bursting through the trees. Then silently, resumes our journey. The far-off edge of the forest is visible and I know that she will not walk with me much longer.

I allow myself a brief moment of unguarded joy.

Watching the birds dance through the trees. They follow us out of curiosity and gossip. For few others love to talk the way birds do.

I smile to myself. Grateful that, in these tenuous times, humans do not listen to the whimsical chattering of the winged ones. Otherwise, I would have been discovered months ago.

Astriel's voice breaks through my thoughts. Shattering my reverie.

"You know the one they call the Great Prince," she says.

It's not a question. Before I can reply, my body reacts. Bracing for battle. I do not trust myself to speak. So I stay silent.

"Your life has already been touched by him," she adds.

"Touched is not the word I would choose," I growl. "But that is true."

My mood shifts and I have to shield my heart from the revenge my mind has already envisioned. The birds stop singing and fly high to the tops of the trees.

They know all too well the danger of an angry human.

"Your instincts to protect yourself are wise," Astriel offers, "But you must know that your destinies are intertwined."

She pauses, allowing me a moment to search my heart. I cannot deny that I always felt the Prince and I would inevitably meet.

But I can tell now it is a greater connection than a single encounter.

Astriel seems pleased. "The things we notice in others, no matter the concentration, we cannot deny exist also in ourselves."

"You speak of hatred," I admit. "And revenge."

"Yes. But also love and tenderness. You have seen these in him."

"Barely," I grumble.

"Barely matters." She looks at me. And I know she is right.

The edge of the forest inches closer. I feel the time for her to reveal my first stone approaching.

I get a sudden flash of my sister at a long dinner table, far across from the Great Prince. She does not appear happy. Nor does she mask this fact.

The Prince glares down the length of the ancient wood. Willing her to say something. Hannah does not oblige. I feel the silent battle waged in each moment of silence. I shudder.

And return to the soothing embrace of the trees. The kindness of birds singing.

Astriel knows what I have seen. "The first stone on your path is to seek and find the Hidden Palace of the Great Prince. This is where he holds your sister."

My heart leaps. Finally! The freedom to launch the quest I have wanted all along.

Ready to jump on Casmire's back, I reach, instinctively, for his reins. Excited and elated all at once. Not needing another word to be on my way.

"But first," Astriel interjects, "you must know this is not to rescue your sister."

I stop, shocked by her revelation. The blood rushes from my head and I suddenly feel dizzy. Casmire feels my altered condition and instinctively steps behind me.

Ready to brace my body, in case I should stumble.

"Why else would I go?" I gasp.

"That question is the essence of your journey," responds Astriel. "I cannot reveal the answers to you."

Fury engulfs my body. I pull my dagger from my belt and thrust it deep into the ground. Casmire backs away. Giving my rage the space it needs to burn.

"How could you ask me to go there if not to rescue my twin?" I rant. Walking in circles around the dagger as I puzzle over her cruel request.

"What could you possibly want of me?" I ask, not expecting an answer.

"Am I to take her place? No. You would deem that a rescue. Am I going to watch the Prince torture her? Is my mission merely sport provoked for Divine entertainment?"

I can tell I have crossed a line. Familiar with, though not comprehending the whims of human emotion, Astriel waits.

Casmire lowers his head. Slightly abashed that I would speak this way to a sacred being. Yet understanding the need to protect a member of my clan.

Struggling to regain composure, I yank my dagger out of the earth. Wipe it angrily on my cloak, and shove it back in its sheath. Astriel patiently gives me a moment.

Then asks, "Have you not heard a word I have said?"

I grumble to myself, still pacing. Trying out scenarios. Venting my frustration. Not ready to let go of the thoughts whipping back and forth.

Until I stop. And realize what she is saying.

"You're asking me not to assume why I am being sent to the Hidden Palace. Rather, to be open to the path that appears."

Astriel smiles. Seeing the burden fall from the young Messenger's shoulders. Releasing her to walk in the moment.

"Yes. And with that understanding, my dear Gabriella, you are ready."

A blinding light pulses between the trees. Blasting through my being like an ecstatic wave of love. As the force abates, I pry open my eyes.

Peering all around. Already knowing the truth.

Astriel is gone.

And my journey has begun.

TWELVE

My first steps beyond the shelter of the forest are hesitant. I have grown so accustomed to Astriel's presence that I feel unprotected not having her with me. I am like a young child attempting steps for the first time. Timid and uncertain. Wondering whether the earth will help me or hinder me.

Casmire nuzzles my back. As though to remind me that I am not in this alone. Incredibly, I had forgotten he was there. How can a person so hard-wired for survival get so lost in her own thoughts?

I stroke Casmire's muzzle with gratitude. At least one of us seems to be paying attention. Taking his reins gently and swinging myself up onto his back, I am gifted with an expansive view of the terrain.

The rigid line between the great forest and the open plains we now traverse is sudden. As though designed to avoid any confusion between the two lands.

Indeed, the forest has always been deemed wild and open to any who risks its crossing. These plains, however, are the land of the Great Prince.

I have stepped into enemy territory.

My senses are on guard and my body tenses for a fight. I guide

Casmire forward. But he, too, knows we must be ready for anything.

Neither of us has traversed this land before.

The territory is far from where we were both raised. In truth, few cross the Great Prince's land without an entourage.

Vast numbers are wise when you are in violation of the Prince's property. For that is how he views anyone on his land. Until they prove their worth and purpose.

I am a traveller alone. The runaway daughter of a rogue king and a resistant princess. This is how the Prince views me. And by extension his minions.

So, the faster I am out of view, the better.

I gaze across the horizon. Achieving that task is another matter entirely. For at the edge of the Great Plains, there is hardly a tree for miles. The view is so revealing, I can actually see the boundary of the first town in the far distance.

Which, I quickly realize, means they can just as likely see me.

I have no choice but to slip off Casmire's back. The way may be slow but if a horse is spotted without a rider, he is a curiosity. A horse with a strange rider is decidedly a threat.

As I take my first steps by Casmire's side, I realize I have a more urgent problem than being spotted.

I have no idea where I am going.

The Great Prince owns vast tracts of land. His Hidden Palace could be anywhere. Everyone knows the location of his ostentatious Great Palace. This is why, when the Prince is feeling paranoid, he retreats to his Hidden Palace.

These days, it seems, he is always paranoid.

With not a soul in sight for miles, I determine my options. Mumbling out loud. Weighing variables including supplies, distance, protection, and weather. Never mind, the foreign nature of this land.

Casmire keeps an eye on me. Even though he knows that this strange behaviour is part and parcel of my working out an issue. He's very patient for all his strength.

He could easily force me in a direction. Use his instincts and pull me along against my will. But, thank the heavens, he seems to have respect for me and my mission.

And I am sure Astriel's appearance profoundly helped my case.

Casmire has adopted me as his family. He feels responsible for my welfare and my lessons. Even if that means letting me make the decisions. Likely, he knows there is no other way for a stubborn child to learn.

Given his intelligence and instinct, his faith in me is deeply generous. And I am forever grateful.

Still, I mumble. Puzzle. And am no closer to a solution.

Exasperated, Casmire nudges me. I wave him off. He nudges me again.

When I ignore him a second time, he nickers softly. Clearly annoyed.

Finally, I look up. He flicks his nose in the direction of the horizon. Fixing his gaze far off toward what appears to be the faint foothills of a mountain range.

But the mountains are not the big surprise. Rather, it is the strange, blurry snake in front of them that causes me to stop in my tracks.

Casmire stops beside me. Either anticipating my next need or simply conserving energy. I suspect the former given that he knows me better than I ever seem to know myself.

I shove my hand into a hidden saddle bag and pull out a spyglass. A parting gift from Claudius and I treasure it deeply. I haven't retrieved the spyglass since it was packed. But if there were ever a moment to use such an item, I would say this is it.

Gently opening the glass, I pull it out to its greatest length. Peer through the end.

I gasp. And look at Casmire. He flicks his ears at me. As patient as he can be, he knows we must get moving. And that relies on my decision.

I look back through the glass. The long, slithering snake is actually a caravan of people. Whether they are together or not, I cannot tell. But they are clearly heading in the same direction. Carrying more than the basic needs.

They appear to be on a very long journey. Though I cannot imagine to where.

"Whatever could it be?" I say to Casmire, as much as to myself.

"The annual pleading," a deep voice replies.

I fold the glass, pocket it, and whip around into defensive stance. All before you can say my full name.

The stranger stands, calmly. Knowing that his voice would provoke such a reaction. He waits for me to make the next move.

This man does not seem concerned, even though I am ready to fight. His casual air more than disturbs me. It assumes I am not a threat.

Until I recall Serafina's teaching: that my appearance is my greatest weapon.

"Being a woman will cause the foolish to assume you are weak," she explained, with clear disdain. "Do not feel this is a bad thing. For in truth, it is a fierce weapon. They will treat you as inconsequential. Use this against them. And they will fall every time."

"What do you want?" I demand. Keeping Casmire within reach. Ready to flee, if necessary. But curious to examine the stranger more closely.

He is not old, nor is he young. I would guess him to be thirty-six years. Though his rugged appearance suggests years of travel. Despite his well-shielded gaze, I know he is younger than he looks.

I am still unsure what led me to tune in to his essence. For in not knowing this man, the risk was far greater than the gain. I could not restrain my curiosity.

The moment I sense his age, I have to disguise my shock. He is only twenty-eight years. What has this man seen to hold the burdened energy of a man almost ten years older? I want to know more. To hear the stories.

When my instincts remind me that his story does not make him any more likely a friend. As though intuiting my questions, he responds.

"Would you not rather know who I am?" he asks.

Evading the question. Or so I assume.

"I have no need for your name," I reply abruptly. "Only your purpose. I do not anticipate we will travel the same road for long."

His head tilts. Taking me in. I notice his emerald green eyes for the first time. Their contrast to his dark brown hair is striking. And the sudden rush of attraction takes me by surprise.

Struggling between the inner ambush and my embarrassment, I compel my body to restrain itself. I reprehend her for her basic human needs. Ones I have never been permitted to let run wild.

For fear of my safety.

As though talking to my only long-term friend, I demand: Can you not see this is entirely the wrong time to notice the appeal of a man? On the edge of the Great Plains with not a single ally in sight?

Despite my admonition, my body refuses to listen. She deems the young man attractive. The lack of competition, timely. And the ample space in every direction, convenient. In short, she declines to relent.

A slight smile appears on his lips, adding to my annoyance. For the second time today, I feel naked. And I do not relish the feeling.

I picture myself encased in jousting attire. Head-to-foot in solid armour. Satisfied, I think to myself, "There! Get past that."

The stranger makes a clicking noise. Luckily, before I launch a sharp and offended response, I notice a stunning white mare respond to his call. She appears by his side and waits.

Unabashedly evaluating Casmire, as he returns the favour.

"My name is Adrian," the man offers. Clearly, expecting a response.

"How do I know that is truly your name?" I inquire. Buying time, as much as I am curious to hear his answer.

"The same way you determined my age," he replies.

Revealing more about him, and me, in a single instant than most people figure out in a year of acquaintance. My mouth opens. Then closes. I am unsure what to say.

I have never encountered this scenario.

So few people believe in my gifts. Let alone understand their subtleties. Most consider the ability to read another's essence a mere rumour of the past. And feel comforted by that assumption.

"It's okay," he offers. "I deserved it. I took you by surprise instead of revealing myself to you more directly. I just…"

He pauses to consider his words, concealing his energy as he thinks.

Despite understanding his need for caution and privacy, this action makes me wonder about his true purpose. And his full arsenal of skills.

"You surprised me almost as much as I surprised you," he finishes.

"I doubt it," I reply, flippantly. Though I quickly sense that he is telling the truth.

I release my defensive stance. Standing tall. But still not ready to tell him my name. I take the conversation in another direction. One better suited to my moving on as quickly as possible.

"What is the annual pleading? And why do they carry so many goods on such a long journey?"

Adrian gazes at the line on the horizon. A sadness flickers across his face. Then disappears as quickly.

Making me wonder whether I am imagining his emotions.

I cannot let my guard down with a man I have just met. No matter how attractive. Despite my body's traitorous protestations.

Adrian's face is inscrutable. Whatever memory passed through his mind has been tucked firmly away. Though he still answers my question.

"Once a year, people are permitted to make a pilgrimage to the Great Palace. They must follow a designated path. And bring a significant offering to the Great Prince. And in exchange, they are given a brief audience with the Prince."

"Why do they do this?" I ask, though I already have a few

guesses.

"Many reasons," replies Adrian. He watches the line shimmer in the distance.

"Most common is the need to be pardoned for a criminal act. Or requesting the return of their land. Some even make the journey because they believe the Prince's blessing is good luck."

Adrian's contempt leaks through as he speaks, even though he tries to keep it hidden. I suspect he considers the Great Prince an enemy.

Which both intrigues me and reminds me to be careful.

I am already an active concern for the Prince. To be travelling with another enemy of the realm makes me doubly vulnerable.

"You have no love for the Prince," I state bluntly.

Adrian sighs. He shoulders relax a little. As though he has laid a burden down.

"It's true. And I know it is the same for you," he adds, looking directly into my eyes. The honesty of his gaze takes me off guard.

Instead of reaching for my dagger, I nod.

Catching my indiscretion, I immediately ask, "How do you know this?"

He pauses. Considering his reply. Holding me in his gaze, I can tell he is assessing my trustworthiness. And my propensity to strike first and ask questions later.

His gaze is penetrating. I begin to feel uncomfortable.

"Answer or let the question be. Either way, stop staring!" I demand.

Casmire takes a step forward. Standing at my side, protectively. He snorts at Adrian. Echoing my sentiment to declare his intentions one way or the other.

Adrian nods his head, respectfully, at both of us.

"Come," he adds, gesturing as he walks toward the base of an undulating section of plain.

He pulls a piece of woven cloth from a saddle bag and lays it on the ground.

"Let us share a meal. And I will answer your question."

THIRTEEN

ADRIAN BUILDS A SMALL and contained fire for cooking. I sit at the side and watch as he creates a better meal than I have eaten in months.

Fresh meat, herbs, a dash of oil. All from his saddle bags. I marvel at the quality of his supplies. And the care he takes with the preparation.

I cannot help but wonder. Who is this man? And what is his story?

I may be only eighteen years of age, but I grew up in a revered and established court. I have met thousands of people. Many who possess unique gifts.

And still, Adrian is a puzzle.

He looks up, catching my gaze. I do not move my eyes from his face. He knows I have been studying him. There is no need to cover the fact.

That does not mean, however, that my study should cause him discomfort.

I lower my eyes. And tousle Casmire's forelock as he crunches the dry prairie grass, next to the blanket.

"I believe you promised me an answer," I offer, to start the conversation.

Adrian smiles. And hands me a small bowl of food. My stomach growls, appreciating the generous offer.

He takes a seat not far from me, but keeps the fire between us. As a sign of respect and an acknowledgement that we are still determining our level of comfort and trust.

Adrian takes a bite of food. Savouring the moment. Appreciative of the small victories when each day can seem like an endless battle.

I do the same, though my hunger brings me to eat a much larger mouthful. I am transported to heaven. Amazed how delicious such a simple bowl of food can be.

"How..." I begin. "What..." I stop talking. And savour another bite.

He smiles, pleased. "The secret is the quality of the ingredients. You don't need much if what you have is extraordinary."

He pauses, brow furrowing. "But we can talk food another time."

I am relieved I don't have to speak. This way I can focus on my meal. Though, I'm aware that this skill has added to the complexity of the Adrian puzzle.

Just as I am contemplating the possibilities of his past, he ambushes me again.

"I know you are no friend of the Prince because I have seen your sister," Adrian states abruptly. I lower my bowl. My body has grown cold. I stare at him.

"I do not know her name," Adrian continues quickly, "Nor do I know yours. But the resemblance is striking. Enough to call you twins."

He considers my face, "Though you do not look identical."

I exhale hard. Relieved that he does not know who I am. I watch him closely. Like an animal that's unsure for the moment if she is the hunter or the prey.

"When I saw her – your sister – I could tell she was deeply unhappy, yet somehow resigned to her fate."

Adrian looks directly into my eyes. "Like she chose it for the sake of many."

My gaze drops to the ground. I struggle between wanting to scream and wanting to cry. I choose neither. I force myself to take a deep breath.

"And what were you doing at the Hidden Palace?" I finally ask, accusingly.

The moment the words exit my lips, I realize the gift the gods have offered. My eyes lock onto Adrian's face. He's been to the Hidden Palace. He can lead me there. To my beloved sister.

I force my heart to stay calm. And my face to stay straight.

I need to hear more of his story. To gauge the kind of person he is.

But I already know that, regardless of the conclusion, this is too beautiful and rare a coincidence to be a mistake.

Adrian plays with the food in his bowl. Making his own assessment of what is safe to share. Gauging just how far to trust me.

He takes a deep breath. "I was there to determine its defenses."

I'm intrigued, but conceal my reaction. "For yourself or for another?"

"Both," he replies cryptically. Avoiding my gaze.

I have many questions firing in my mind. But I must walk this maze carefully. I neither want to get lost nor frighten the creature offering to show the way.

"Did you make contact with anyone at the palace?" I ask, guardedly.

He looks up. His true intention as hidden as my own. "If I did my job well, no one saw me. Including your sister."

"Convenient," I respond. "For no one can validate the truth of what you say."

My heart sinks a little. Realizing, for the first time, that this could just be a grand story designed to impress.

I consider the risk of probing past his defenses. He's adept with his emotions. He would know. And I might lose his confidence forever.

"Is not witnessing your sister enough?"

"You could have easily seen us —," I stop. Realizing I have one foot over a bear trap. I gently pull my foot back.

"No. It is not."

I level the challenge. Angry with Adrian that he caught me off guard. Furious with myself that I almost jumped in. Offering too much information.

Regardless, I revealed that I care more about his story than I should.

Adrian sighs. Setting his bowl aside. "You mistake my intentions. I do not wish to ensnare you."

I'm startled. For I could swear I had guarded my feelings well.

"Nor," he continues, "do I mean to boast of my exploits. Or talents." He lifts an open gaze to mine. Offering a truce.

"I merely wanted —," he catches himself.

Then clearly decides to finish the statement. "I merely wanted you to know that your sister is safe. And well. If not happy."

He picks his bowl back up. Though he no longer appears hungry, he forces himself to eat. I stare at him. Confounded.

"Please," he says. "Let us find another subject to discuss. Or, preferably, eat in silence."

I take a bite and chew slowly. I am mystified by this man and have significantly revised my estimation. I consider Adrian more than a worthy opponent. More than a mere puzzle. I believe he is a master.

Not since Serafina have I dueled energetically and verbally with such an alert presence. Indeed, I assumed I had the upper hand.

An immediate and fatal error had Adrian been bent on destroying me.

I ponder my situation.

Within seconds, I make my decision. For rarely have I found in battle, or in life, that delaying a decision changes the truth.

Here, in front of me, is exactly the person I need. No matter how dangerous he may be to the realm.

Adrian is to be my guide.

I will make sure of it.

PART II

THE
JOURNEY

ONE

THE FIRE CRACKLES. Flames flickering softly in the silent night. For the moment, Adrian has decided to stay with Gabriella. Watching over the camp as she gets a precious few hours of sleep.

He looks over the terrain. Sensing any movement near enough to be of concern. Or far enough away to be of no harm.

Adrian loves the darkness.

The curtain of shade affords him cover and silence to think. The day hours are filled with motion and thought and too much energy. The night has movement but is much more serene in her approach.

Why anyone thinks that the darkness is deceitful is beyond him.

He finds the night to be clear and true and much easier to read. The intentions are honest. Most of all among the beasts that want to eat you.

The daytime holds all the deception.

Gabriella shifts and growls in her sleep. As though picking up on his thoughts. He watches her for a moment. Taking in the youth of her face.

She is more beautiful than she realizes. Likely because she has always been compared to a refined sister.

Gabriella possesses a fierce and fiery beauty. One of mission and clarity.

He allows himself a moment to admire her. Knowing well that this is a delicate path to walk. She may sense his gaze and awaken.

Gabriella stirs and tosses under her cloak. Shifting sides. Adrian raises his eyes to the horizon. Moving his thoughts to other matters.

He has no hold over Gabriella's destiny. She must go where she is called.

He frowns, slightly. Though he does take exception that the Divine would send her into battle at such a young age.

Adrian sighs.

Knowing that this is forever how it has been and forever how it will be. Those called to service do not get a choice as to when or where or even why.

They are simply called.

And to deny that call is to ask for a life filled with anguish.

TWO

THE FIRST RAYS OF DAWN peek over the horizon. Adrian glances at Gabriella, still asleep. He smiles slightly. Clearly, she feels safe in his presence. Even if she will not admit it to him. Or to herself.

Gabriella. She does not remember that they have been in the same room. He has been to her home. This is where he first saw her and her sister, Hannah.

He was one in the long line of suitors.

But the moment he laid eyes on Gabriella, he had a vision. He saw that their fates were tied. And he was not meant to be presented to either sister. Not on that day.

The vision was clear that he would need to live in the shadows for a time. That he could not show his face. The day would come soon enough for them to meet.

Until that day arrived, they could not know who he was or where he came from. Though there was no shame in his past. Or in his lineage. But he could not risk the disclosure. They might assume too many things.

Just as he assumed too many things about Gabriella.

He must forget who she was and embrace who she is. For the place she came from no longer plays a part in where they must go.

At least, not yet. Not for a long time.

They are both castaways on the sea of destiny. And they must hope that the skies stay clear enough to present the North Star.

Adrian feels the melancholy that inevitably appears when he thinks of the sea. He has not seen his homeland for many years. He misses the sharp wind, the salty air. And when looking across the vast expanse of water, the comfort of perspective.

Most of all, he misses the company of the ocean. Whispering her secrets. Calming him with her rhythmic grace. Reminding him that life moves steadily.

No matter whether you fight the tide or flow with the waves.

Returning to the moment, he gazes at the brown grass covering the Great Plains. The people of this land often compare the plains to the ocean. Saying the grasses move in graceful waves. The wind sweeps the grain in a constant tide, as the moon pulls the waters of the sea.

There is no comparison for him.

He sees beauty. And fire. And a vast expanse of landscape. But no ocean.

Gabriella stirs. Then sits up, suddenly. Ready for her attacker. As though someone already pulled a weapon and holds her at his mercy.

Realizing she is mistaken, she calms a little.

Grabs her cloak and orients herself. Looking at the campfire. Feeling the blanket beneath her. Taking in Adrian. Slowly, she remembers where she is.

Adrian pokes at the fire. Giving her time to adjust.

He understands the reaction and the confusion. Knowing she was far enough away that returning to the harshness of her present surroundings can be tough.

Gabriella is a traveller. She wanders in the day and she ventures in the night.

For though Adrian knows this earth is the path they chose to walk during the daylight, he does not deem the far-off travels of the night any less important.

Those are the deep and transformative hours that reveal our deepest yearnings and greatest lessons. The challenge is to remember them on awakening. And bring the wisdom of the moon into the realm of the sun.

The path of the moon shows us the deep work our soul has chosen.

If this world is to change, travellers such as Gabriella must strengthen their ability to bring forth their night training. Over a bridge others cannot see.

His heart is suddenly filled with compassion. She walks an exhausting path.

As though sensing his kindness, Gabriella fixes her eyes on him.

What does he want? What has he been doing all this time she's been asleep? She dons her cloak and crouches by the fire. Eyes full of suspicion.

Adrian regards her, evenly. And makes a mental note.

She needs to guard her feelings better. Whoever taught her the arts of protection either did not have time to finish the lessons. Or had an area of blindness in their skill. Either way, the omission puts her in danger.

Adrian catches himself. He is not this girl's teacher. Nor has there been any agreement that he should guide her or make up for her lack of training.

He holds Gabriella's gaze. Reminding her silently, he is no threat. Though her eyes stay guarded, her shoulders relax a notch.

He returns his focus to the fire.

All Adrian knows is that he and Gabriella have been united two times by the hand of fate.

And when fate casts the same number twice, you pay attention.

THREE

GABRIELLA STIRS THE FOOD in her bowl. Takes a bite. And peers over the spoon at Adrian.

He continues eating, not making eye contact. He knows she wants to ask something. She has been approaching and retreating, sourcing her courage through every mouthful.

For whatever reason, she cannot convince herself to say the words.

Adrian decides to look up. Catching her gaze. Gabriella drops hers to the grains in her bowl. He frowns.

Troubled by this behaviour. Despite her age, she cannot afford to act like a schoolgirl. Adrian restrains his frustration. Keeping it from Gabriella.

There is no time for silly games! She must step up to her destiny. If she does not, realms will be lost. How can she not recognize how much rides on her shoulders —

His spoon freezes in mid-air.

The thought catches him by surprise. He has never been offered that knowledge until now. This is the first time his guardians have shared that she is a person of deep consequence.

A chill runs through his body.

Adrian looks at her. Really taking Gabriella in.

Realizing, that he is in the presence of a world-changer.

His reasoning mind tries to shrug off the occurrence with a bevy of facts. Anyone can change the world. Everyone has the ability to make a difference. No one person is more special than another.

All of which is true.

But. His body knows that Gabriella is walking the path that has been laid before her. She has the capacity and the will to bring the vision to reality.

A second chill runs down his spine.

His body cannot be fooled as easily as his mind. Adrian can feel now that he is in the presence of a being of tremendous power.

And she has no idea yet just how powerful she is. Why, then, is he here? What part has he to play in her unfoldment?

Nothing. His mind is blank.

Adrian feels the anger burst up like a flame. He allows the feeling passage, and instinctively sends it on to the sky.

While he honours the fiery, protective emotion, he cannot afford to be distracted. He has already wasted too much time on questions the Divine is not yet ready to answer. A mistaken and costly detour.

All the while, the sun has risen in the sky, and they are exposed in a hostile land.

Adrian quickly swallows the last bite from his bowl and wipes the container clean.

He packs the bowl away. Grabs a handful of dirt and casts the dry soil over the fire. Stamping down the embers for good measure.

Gabriella understands the signals of departure. And quickly gathers her things. She moves efficiently. Placing her few belongings in the bags on her horse and readying his reins.

An adept traveller, Adrian clears the site. Covering the ground carefully. Making the trail difficult for all but the best tracker to tell they spent the night.

He strides calmly to Ginetta.

Placing a palm on her neck. Respectfully letting her know the time has come to leave. She flicks her head in acknowledgement and glances at Gabriella.

Adrian nods almost imperceptibly.

He knows a question waits in the wind. He listens for a moment. Then realizes the question is not his to ask. He stands with his hand on Ginetta. Knowing he cannot leave before the question arrives.

Ginetta flicks her ears, ready to move. She does not like waiting. Adrian assures her silently, that the time is at hand.

A throat clears behind him.

Adrian turns gently toward Gabriella. Waiting.

"I was wondering —," she starts, a little too loud. Gabriella coughs. Scuffs her foot in the dirt. Embarrassed.

She corrects her volume and tries again.

"I was wondering if you would consider … being my Guide?" she blurts. Unable to find a more elegant way. Desperate to cast the words between them. They land somewhere between the command of a Queen and the urgency of a Novice.

Adrian watches her for a moment.

On the one hand, she is royalty. Used to people simply doing what she asks. Her confidence has, however, been mitigated by her time spent on the run.

And now, she no longer knows who she is.

That is not quite right. Adrian can tell she senses who she is.

She just does not know how to embody her natural power.

Gabriella shifts uncomfortably.

The question has hung in the air too long. He knows the silence is cruel. She has revealed her hand. And shown uncharacteristic vulnerability.

And yet, Adrian is not completely sure how to answer her request.

He knows he is meant to help her. But is this the way? Adrian allows a moment for his guardians to weigh in with their infinite wisdom.

Except, for some reason, the angels chose today to be coy.

How can he know they want him to help if they refuse to give him a sign? He exhales sharply in frustration. Sure they are enjoying a good laugh at his expense.

Gabriella tenses at the sound. And automatically takes his reaction as a no.

Before he can blink, she has grabbed the reins of her horse and is on his back.

Now, she most decidedly looks like a Queen. A scorned Queen. The most dangerous kind. And the most susceptible to attack.

"Fine," she asserts. "I do not need you. I can easily find assistance elsewhere."

Adrian reaches out to Gabriella's horse with his mind. Swiftly asking the impressive animal for permission to block their way.

Recognizing the honourable request, Casmire allows Adrian room to prove himself. And, just as swiftly, lets him know that should he endanger Gabriella, Casmire he has no recourse but to crush him.

Nodding, Adrian steps to Casmire's haunches. Ready to

address Gabriella directly, when he is hit with a flash of insight.

His body lights up with the speed and power of the vision.

Knocking the breath from his chest. And forcing him to use all his strength to remain upright. Clearly, he underestimated the heavenly messengers.

Gabriella senses the shift in energy. She knows exactly what it means.

A message has been conveyed. But not to her.

Recognizing the significance of this moment, she calms her adolescent reaction. Sitting quietly on Casmire. For once, waiting with patience and empathy.

Gabriella recognizes the look. And the anguish. Understanding the physical toll a message can take. And seeing that she was right. Adrian is no ordinary man.

When Adrian looks up, he knows the scenario has changed.

Gabriella appears mature and regal. Casmire calmly chews the grass at his feet. Adrian attempts to speak, when Gabriella holds up her hand.

Saving him from the exertion.

She swings off Casmire. Landing gracefully in front of him. "I apologize," she begins. "I spoke hastily."

In her mature and elegant state, Adrian is taken aback. She stands close enough that he can fully appreciate her beauty. Her power. And her intense gaze.

Never before has he laid eyes on a woman like this.

His breath catches in his chest. And he has to control his energy by force.

The fire of attraction has sparked. His mind reels in protest, thinking, "She's still a girl!"

But his gaze and body dispute the argument. Gabriella is more breathtakingly mature than any woman he has ever met.

Gabriella speaks. Saving Adrian from the battle between his mind and body.

"You spoke of the Hidden Palace," she offers.

"Yes," Adrian responds. Speaking out loud, forces him into the moment. And reminds him of the decision at hand.

"I require a Guide to this place," she states simply. Deciding that avoiding the truth would cost both his assistance and more valuable time.

Adrian considers what she is asking. He knows in his bones that this is what he must do.

But he also knows the journey may cost them their lives.

"I can do this," he begins. Gabriella beams.

He feels her stop herself from embracing him in gratitude. Despite holding back, the energy relays between them. Adrian reels from the sheer force of her power.

"But," he adds quickly, regaining some composure. "You must understand how dangerous this path is. We would be walking directly into the arms of the very man who wants us both dead."

Gabriella sobers at his blatant honesty.

"We don't know that for sure," she offers. Though her heart speaks otherwise.

Adrian's tone softens a notch. "You are right," he concedes. "But for our own safety, we must assume it."

Gabriella nods. She deeply appreciates how much he has risked by having this conversation. Never mind that he has just agreed to take her to the most dangerous place in the realm.

Adrian takes a step back and clicks to Ginetta. She approaches, assessing their travel companions with a new scrutiny. Adrian's choice does not just risk his life.

He waits. Knowing he can continue without Ginetta. And hoping she agrees to accompany him.

After several moments, she lowers her head. Agreeing to the journey. He places his hand gently on her head, silently expresses his gratitude.

As he takes the reins, something occurs to him.

He turns to Gabriella.

"Do you know why you are going to the Hidden Palace?"

Gabriella swings onto Casmire. Looks Adrian directly in the eye.

And says matter-of-factly, "No."

Closely followed by the most devastating roguish smile he has ever seen.

FOUR

Gabriella canters next to Adrian in silence. She keeps her gaze forward. But cannot help wanting to examine him. Her mind craves answers to this puzzle.

First, he appears mysteriously on the edge of the Great Plains. Then he cooks for her and stands guard over night. And now, a mere sunset later, he is escorting her into treacherous territory.

Never mind, that he received a vision right before her eyes.

"You should really keep your attention on the terrain," Adrian admonishes.

"I am," she replies. As though she has no idea what he is implying.

She scrutinizes the acres and acres of grasslands ahead. The tiny line of mountains in the distance grows larger. But not as fast as she would like.

Adrian wants to find them some cover as soon as possible.

But pushing the horses in the hot sun when they have minimal water is not realistic. Especially when there is no prospect for replenishment in sight.

"What mountain range is that?" Gabriella asks.

She needs to get acquainted with the physical terrain. And, with any luck, the conversation may prove fruitful beyond mere waypoints.

Adrian appreciates the offer of simple conversation. The last twenty-four hours have been more than a little disorienting.

And nothing soothes his soul like a lesson in terrain.

"They are the Ceres mountains. Beautiful, rugged, and always full of challenges," Adrian explains. "The closer we get, the more opportunities we will find for water. The Plains are easier riding, but more exposed and punishing."

"Than mountains?" Gabriella inquires. "How is that possible?"

"Mountains," Adrian explains, "take a toll on the body. They ask you to be strong and focused. Responding to their challenges with due respect. In return, they offer copious resources. Like water, shelter, and game."

Gabriella squints at the far off mountain range. She is unfamiliar with such territory. And the unknown makes her nervous.

She has learned, however, that unfamiliar ground is her constant now. Since she left her homeland, comfort is the foreign state. She does not mind being nervous. But she also knows, with the unknown, comes the possibility of death.

Adrian notices her silence. And feels her assessing the future of their journey.

"Do not be concerned yet with the mountains. First, we must cross the Plains."

He takes a mouthful of water. Then nods for Gabriella to do the same.

"Exposure is our most significant risk," he continues, squinting at the harsh sun. "Not to the elements. Though they are daunting."

He looks at her with intensity. "We should discuss what to do when we are discovered."

"When?" she asks, as though insulted by his assumption.

Gabriella looks around. Seeing no one for miles.

Adrian calms his reaction. Wanting to reprimand her harshly for such a ridiculous assumption. Remembering that his role is to instruct rather than scold.

He breathes. Focuses on the mountains. The soothing rhythm of Ginetta's gait.

"We are alone now," he acknowledges, "but the risk in crossing the Plains is that anyone can appear in an instant. As I did with you."

"You used magic," she announces, defensively.

Gabriella blushes the moment she utters the words. She has shared a truth that was never meant to be said out loud. And regrets her impulsiveness.

Adrian looks at her sharply. Offended by her accusation.

"You think I used tricks to gain your confidence?" he reproaches.

Gabriella drops her gaze. She expected anger. Not indignation and hurt.

She avoids his eyes. Never knowing what to do with a teacher's disappointment. Failure is much easier to handle than regret.

Adrian waits for an answer, refusing to give her the easy way out.

"Not exactly," she offers, "I just..." She stops. Remembering Serafina's wisdom.

Particularly apt in this moment. "Halt your tongue until you are sure of the words you wish to share," Serafina instructed her, hand gripping Gabriella's jaw, for emphasis. "Every word set loose from these lips has the power to change the world. For better or for worse. So choose wisely."

Gabriella remembers that she wished for this. A chance to get to know Adrian.

She looks at him, with respect. Finishing her original thought, she selects her words carefully.

"I just know you are much more than you appear," she states.

Adrian examines her. Taking a moment to understand what she has said. Both in the words she has chosen and the ones she left out.

He knows intuitively that Gabriella is being honest. A precious trait these days. Especially given all she has endured. And everything yet to be asked of her.

He cannot fault Gabriella for her curiosity. But he must pace what she needs to know with when she needs to know it.

This is the greatest challenge of any Guide.

Gabriella is the toughest of students. Sharp and observant. Yet with too much to prove.

He does not know why. Given her parents. And her upbringing.

Nor, ultimately, does it matter.

Likely, her family both adored and was hard on her. And her royal blood allowed her the rope to hang herself with her curious and insightful observations.

Adrian sighs. He turns his gaze forward.

Giving Gabriella the space to lift her own eyes. And feel safe to look at him.

He feels her relax. Understanding she is not being punished for her transgression.

"Not magic," he offers, "Not exactly."

Adrian strokes Ginetta's neck. A gesture that soothes him as much as the horse.

"You are correct. And astute to perceive that I have more talents than might be obvious to the casual observer."

Gabriella sits taller in her saddle. Pleased with the compliment.

"But you are quick with your tongue," he adds, "and it will be our undoing."

Adrian feels the intensity of Gabriella's defensive anger. She desperately wants to respond. To defend her honour.

But she knows this will prove him right. And disappoint Serafina in the bargain.

As Gabriella battles her inner nature, Adrian breathes a sigh of relief. He has evaded her inquiry. For the moment.

Adrian used the oldest trick in the book.

Nothing distracts faster than unleashing someone's internal dragons. The exciting prospect of treasure fades quickly in importance, when fighting for your very life.

He smiles to himself.

She does not yet realize an essential truth of life.

The two quests are bound together with a deep and sacred bond.

FIVE

THE MOMENT ADRIAN has been dreading has arrived. Far on the horizon, but not as far as he would hope. Other riders. And they are headed in this direction.

Within seconds, Gabriella's eyes are trained on the intruders.

Her entire system goes on alert. She does not seem to realize, this is like a bonfire for anyone with skill. "Breathe," insists Adrian.

Gabriella shoots him a look. Not understanding what he is saying. She has taken his instruction as an insult.

"Being on full guard," he explains, "sends a beacon to anyone who has the ability to read your energy."

Gabriella is ashamed. And flabbergasted. "How did you –," she begins.

"I will explain at a more opportune time. But for this moment, I need you to breathe deeply. And assume that the riders approaching are our friends."

Gabriella scoffs. Causing Casmire to tense in response.

"Now," Adrian adds, annoyed, "You have doubled the size of the fire by provoking your steed."

This gets her attention. Gabriella immediately focuses, calming her reaction.

She strokes Casmire's haunches as a form of apology. He visibly relaxes. And his gait transforms from a horse marching into battle to a casual walk.

Adrian discreetly observes the interaction.

When he draws Casmire into the conversation, Gabriella learns quickly. Her deep loyalty toward her companion gives her the required perspective to make wise and deliberate choices. Rather than reacting from a defensive stance.

Watching them, he realises that Casmire has been Gabriella's only constant ally for two years. And the sole connection left to her family.

Adrian softens. Reminding himself, she is only eighteen. And this has been a hard road. One that will only get more treacherous.

"Excellent," he responds. "You recovered beautifully."

Gabriella watches the approaching riders. Remaining calm and focused. "Why do you suggest they may be friends? You must know that is unlikely."

Adrian can see now that she was trained by an adept hand. Likely, her reactive instinct is a product of age and spirit. And an abbreviated window of instruction.

"However true that may be, you must assume they are friends for two reasons."

Before continuing, Adrian quickly assesses how close these friends are. If they are on well-fueled horses, they may make contact before nightfall.

In which case, the situation may require some recalculation.

"First, making the most optimistic assumption keeps your energy calm and fluid," Adrian listens to his own advice as he speaks. "When you are in the flow with everything else, others will not notice you."

He monitors their energy fields. Pleased with the adept shift.

"Be a wave rolling with the ocean. As opposed to one kicked up by a storm."

She levels inquisitive eyes at him. But does not speak for fear of sounding foolish. Adrian realizes his misstep.

He forgets how sheltered the life of royal children can be.

"Have you ever seen the ocean, Gabriella?"

"No," she responds, "though I have heard tell of it from –," she catches herself, "a teacher."

Adrian does not fault her for being careful. His respect for her deepens, knowing she withheld the name for the teacher's protection rather than her mistrust.

He nods. "My apologies. I will remember to use riding analogies."

And forest metaphors, he thinks. Recalling the land she once called home.

"What is the second reason?" she asks. Gabriella appreciates that Adrian did not push for more personal information.

Though, to be truthful, a small part of her wishes he would.

"Second, locking in to an assumption is the most dangerous thing a person can do," he states. "You invest in your own opinion. Your assumed superiority. Always leave room for the possibilities."

Gabriella smiles. "Like you."

Adrian is silenced by her response. Surprised by her playfulness. He has not seen this Gabriella. And is unsure what to say.

She blushes. And looks away. Adrian watches as Gabriella seeks control. Clearly frustrated with her body's reaction. She refuses to meet his eyes again until the colour in her cheeks fades.

Finally, she looks up. Gazing at him with composure.

"Yes," Adrian responds. Unsure of his feelings. "Like me."

He had expected resistance. Frustration. Even anger. He had not expected…

Adrian knows. But he cannot bring himself to acknowledge it. For fear of adding fuel to a spark.

He focuses on the riders. Using every skill at his disposal to hide his reaction.

They ride in silence. Eyes on the horizon. Neither sure what to say.

Gabriella suddenly understands every confusing conversation Hannah tried to have with her when they turned sixteen.

Her sister would point out boys in the castle. Waiting for Gabriella to respond.

When Gabriella ignored her, prattling on about some new discovery in the forest. Hannah cast her hands up in despair.

"How will you ever find a man if you refuse to even look at them?" Hannah groaned.

"Since when do I care about catching a man," Gabriella replied. She was focused on a cache of seeds from deep in the woods. Dismissing her sister's attempts to civilize her.

"Oh, you wait," Hannah warned her. "You will care when, suddenly, there is a man you like. Who does not notice you."

Gabriella had laughed. "When that day comes, you will be the first to know."

"Just see if I help you then," Hannah teased her. And the two sisters fell into chasing one another around the castle. Until their mother protested.

With her sister's words ringing in her ears, Gabriella wonders, if Hannah has the gift of prescience.

Her gaze falls to Casmire's beautiful coat. For the first time since they were separated, she feels something stronger than missing her sister.

And she dare not look at Adrian for fear of another blushing fit.

Gabriella gasps, suddenly. Catching Adrian's attention.

"What is it?" he asks. Pushing their most recent exchange from his mind.

"Nothing," Gabriella responds, quickly. She does not want to say it out loud. To do so might make it true.

"Gabriella," Adrian insists, "If you have realized something about our journey, I need to know. For you risk my life. As well as Ginetta's. "

She avoids his piercing gaze. Gabriella knows he is right. But this revelation is not hers to share. What if she is betraying her sister?

Adrian can feel she is in the midst of a moral dilemma.

Yet instinct tells him this is relevant to their destination. And how events may evolve. He hazards an educated guess. "It is related to your sister?"

Gabriella stares at him. Piercing him with her fierce eyes.

The look knocks the breath from his chest. For the second time in one short hour, he is forced to steady his response.

This time, he acknowledges what is happening. Though he is mortified. For it goes against the essence of the mentor's code.

All he can imagine is that a spark of attraction has caught the dry tinder of solitude. The loneliness that he and Gabriella have carried too long in their hearts.

And a bonfire has been lit.

He longs to stare forever into the beautiful and dancing flames.

To lose himself in the glory of their force. But he cannot. He must not.

To do so would put them both at great risk. Through the vulnerability of affection.

Adrian controls his breath. Reminds himself that he is only Gabriella's guide. He is here to take her to the Hidden Palace. And, at that point, he must leave her. For both their sakes.

She will continue her journey. And he will continue his. That is what has been laid before him, and that is what he will honour.

"My sister is prescient," Gabriella blurts out. As though she cannot trust herself to share the truth if she tries to make it subtle.

"How do you know this?" Adrian inquires. Knowing that Gabriella holds something back.

Gabriella's regal nature asserts itself in defense of her sister. And herself.

"That does not matter. What does matter is that I believe that is the real reason the Prince wanted to marry her."

"Not for her beauty?" Adrian asks instinctively. Quickly realizing his insensitivity.

Gabriella's eyes drop to her horse. Then immediately lock on the horizon. Her emotional armour springs into place in less than a second.

"No," she responds, coolly. "The Prince is a calculating man. He prizes power above all else."

"And if he knows this about Hannah," adds Adrian, gently, "he may force her to show him whatever he needs to see."

Suddenly, Adrian's heart sinks. He states the obvious hanging in the air. "Including us." Gabriella nods.

The joy and excitement she felt only moments ago, extinguished. Dowsed by the realization that Hannah is, very likely, a prisoner in her own home.

And that the first man whose attention she truly wants…

…may have feelings for her sister.

SIX

THE LOWER THE SUN FALLS, the closer the riders come. Adrian knows he must figure out a solution. Or at least a story. He is confident they are not the Prince's men. But that does not mean they will simply ride on.

Gabriella has been quiet for miles. And, truth be told, he has been grateful for the absence of conversation.

Adrian put himself in this situation. And he must rectify it. If he keeps his feelings in check, he can starve the fire of its fuel.

And, at the moment, they have more pressing concerns.

Adrian breaks the silence. "When riders meet in the Plains, it is customary to exchange a greeting."

Gabriella tilts her head in acknowledgement. Keeping her eyes forward.

"With any luck," he continues, "they will be eager to move on. They may make polite inquiries about supplies. This is only custom. Most likely they are as low on water and food as we are. So we should not expect assistance."

"I understand," Gabriella states, her attention focused on the riders.

Adrian feels a twinge at her coolness. But quells the response immediately. This is perfect. The cool air is exactly what is needed.

"From what I can read, they are not from the Palace," he

explains. "But this does not mean they are not in its employ."

"They could be informants," she infers. "Or mercenaries."

Adrian realizes just how much Gabriella has seen. The twinge returns. Accompanied by a need to protect her.

No! Adrian commands his emotions. Furious at his lack of control.

Ginetta spooks at the shock of his fury. She tosses her head in indignation. He whispers to her directly to her mind. My humble apologies, Ginetta.

Adrian breathes. And allows himself a moment of shielded frustration.

Who is this girl that she reduces him to the tumultuous emotions of a teenager? Unravelling years of training?

What power does she wield that provokes such a strong reaction? And what game does the Divine play bringing them together, only to light such a fire?

There it was. The truth laid bare.

A flash of insight so bright, he reels in pain.

Gabriella and Adrian, create a power unlike the realm has ever seen. Their energy causing alchemy beyond the simple combining of elements.

Together, they are a sum greater than the parts.

His mind scoffs. Mocking him for his illusions of grandeur.

But Adrian knows better than to listen to the critical nature of his intellect. His entire body is alight with the knowledge that he and Gabriella are an essential combination.

A chain reaction that could unseat a Prince.

All the more reason to keep the relationship professional, his training counters. His honourable nature concedes the point. This is true. For both their sakes.

Adrian exhales and focuses. Raising his gaze to the approaching riders.

"We need a story," he states abruptly. Surprising Gabriella with his sudden return to the conversation.

"Okay," she replies, "What do you recommend?"

"We are brother and sister," he replies. Avoiding her gaze.

Gabriella winces. Then recovers. Her heart constricts. But she refuses to let Adrian know her pain.

"So be it," she responds. She pulls her shoulders back just enough to feel her regal blood. To remind herself that she is a Queen and he is her Guide.

They have been brought together for a mission. She must never forget that fact. Her heart twinges. And her mind responds harshly.

Romance is the plaything of schoolgirls and damsels. I am a Messenger with a mission. I do not get the luxury of dalliances.

"Do we have aliases?" she inquires. "I suggest something similar to our real names. So we can recall them effortlessly."

Her professional tone stings. But he commends her instinct.

"Yes. I will introduce myself as Andrew. What name do you choose?"

"Gemma," she replies, without thinking. Somehow, the childhood nickname brings her comfort in this moment of mixed anguish and danger.

"Gemma," he whispers softly. But she does not hear him. Her mind is lost in another world. A familiar and kind world.

He must be the one to bring her back to harsh reality. This is to be his role.

He sighs. There are days when Adrian is not convinced of the kindness of the Divine. Not that the Great Wisdom promised kindness on this journey.

We humans seem to have told ourselves that tale. We are promised expansion, growth, and even joy. But not necessarily kindness. At least, not the way we think.

"We are a brother and sister on our way to the Annual Pleading," Adrian constructs the story quickly. For the riders seem to have increased their pace. "We lost our way and are trying to catch the caravan before nightfall."

"Agreed," says Gabriella. Pulling her hood over her hair.

She tilts her head, and dons a submissive expression. Making it clear that Adrian is expected to do the talking.

He would be offended if the decision were not so wise and effective.

Adrian sits tall in his saddle. Embodying the role of older brother. And preparing to greet the riders as they quickly approach.

"Good day, fellow riders," Adrian begins formally. Quickly assessing the three men. Their laden horses. And the cut of their clothes.

They appear to have wealth. But appearances can be deceiving. They are often, in fact, deliberately intended to put one at ease. Adrian senses this is true.

These men pose as wealthy merchants to gain the trust and confidence of other travellers. Possibly even play on their greed. Then, when the travellers are sound asleep with visions of powerful alliances and overflowing purses, these men steal whatever is of value and —

Adrian covers his reaction quickly. As Gabriella surmised, the strangers are mercenaries. But they kill for their own gain. Possibly even their own pleasure.

"Good day," the lead man replies. Playing the part of a nobleman well. Though Adrian can feel the dripping arrogance and lack of honour on his words.

"Where are you headed and do you need assistance?" the second man pipes in.

This one is smaller and clearly the brains of the operation. His wiry body gives him the look of a mantis waiting for the moment to bite off their heads.

"Thank you for your kind offer," Adrian replies, in the traditional way. "But we are sustained and can reach our destination without burden. And you?"

Adrian occupies the men with, what she assumes is, the formal call and response of the Plains tradition. Gabriella focuses her energy on assessing them. She recalls the wisdom and guidance of Serafina.

Keeping her gaze sheltered under her hood, she regards their clothing. Gabriella sees that the garments give the impression of wealth but are structured for quick and decisive movement.

Not, typically, a concern of men who have guards and knights to fight for them.

Watching the large one, she sees he is the best actor. He knows his lines well. And enjoys the ruse of playing a nobleman. Except while enthralled by his role, he reveals the weapon concealed under his cloak.

The second man – the one with the beady, watchful eyes – wears a distinct odour of superiority. She can tell he believes his companions are beneath him. But they were born with the gift of brawn. And, so, he must bear their company.

The third one – the quiet one – is the one of grave concern.

Gabriella knows well that the silent, watchful ones are the most dangerous. Like a dog that does not bark, this man's only mission is to strike.

His task is simply to be patient for the appropriate time. And he is willing to wait.

She can feel the quiet one's gaze on her. Assessing her size and her weight. Gabriella controls her urge to shudder. For she knows his only purpose is to kill.

Before she can panic and wonder if Adrian knows the danger they are in, his gentle presence touches her mind. She would have expected her consciousness to react. To instinctively fight an intruder.

But her whole being is calmed. Like she has been waiting for his touch her whole life.

Gabriella immediately blocks her emotions. No one gets to know what she is feeling. Least of all one who provokes them so easily.

Adrian can access her mind but she'll be damned if he sees into her heart!

"We are in danger," Adrian speaks directly to her. "I know," she responds.

Adrian recognizes how brilliant Gabriella is when she is focused. He does not know why he should be surprised. She has kept herself alive for two years with little help.

Gabriella marvels at his ability to communicate to her and converse with the men, simultaneously. Even if the conversation is a practised dance.

She must ask Adrian to learn this skill. One day.

"We can reach the caravan by nightfall," Adrian replies to the leader, "This is no hardship for us."

"Please," the clever one responds. "Allow us to accompany you. For five riders is much safer than only two when crossing the Great Plains."

"Thank you for your kind offer," Adrian says, "But we do not wish to distract you from your destination."

"This is no distraction," the large one says, too loud. Causing the clever one to wince with aggravation. "Accompanying such a duo would be our honour."

His flourished gesture takes the performance completely over the top.

So much so, that his hidden dagger drops to the grass. Spooking his steed. And flummoxing his companions.

The conversation goes completely silent. And the breeze of destiny blows between the two parties.

Waiting for one of them to respond.

SEVEN

"GABRIELLA, RUN!" Startled by the use of her real name. She looks sharply at Adrian.

His eyes are still trained on the leader. She realizes, too late, that he yelled into her mind. And her response has given them away.

Her legs tense sharply. Sending Casmire off like a shot. He bolts straight through the men. Knocking them off balance with the sheer force of his size.

She hunkers down. Tucking her body tight to Casmire's. Knowing that doing so will allow them to work with the wind.

And avoid any flying daggers.

Casmire's hooves pound the grass into submission and kick up dust all around them. Creating a clear path for the men to follow. She squeezes harder.

Urging Casmire on at top speed. Not sure where they are headed, except away.

The fleeing is so instinctive that she has covered miles before realizing that she has abandoned Adrian. Her sacred companion, she hears.

A voice, not her own, states this in her consciousness.

Gabriella is startled by the message. And she yanks the reins. Without thinking of the consequences.

Casmire rears up from the sudden pull against his intense forward motion. Gabriella uses all her strength to stay on his back. With both of them reacting, the odds are high that she may end up crushed under his powerful body or hooves.

He paws at the air. Unsure for a long moment, whether he is going to end up on his back—and kill them both.

Casmire struggles with all his might to tilt their powerful motion forward. Forcing his terror into the earth. So he can focus on staying alive. And working with the forces pulling him in the direction he wants.

He gains his footing. Relieved, they are both alive. When Gabriella's muscles seize from the strain. She shifts abruptly in the saddle, with no strength left to catch herself.

And lands – smack! – on the ground.

Her hard fall releases a large cloud of dust. Irritating Casmire. And sending a clear signal to the sky.

Gabriella thumps the ground. Furious. The force of the landing hurt. Her steed is angry. And she abandoned her —

She cannot bring herself to think the words again. Even if it was a message from the Divine.

And she knows it was. Which just makes it worse.

Gabriella yells in frustration. She already made enough of a scene. What does a little extra volume matter?

How dare the Divine bring her a man – a sacred companion – that has no interest in her? Other than to lead her to the place of her bidding then leave?

Or worse.

Fall in love with her sister. If he is not already in love with her.

Gabriella stands up, abruptly. Smacks the dust off her cloak.

And reaches for Casmire.

He pulls his head from her. So she cannot take the reins.

"What?" she asks, offended. Clearly not thinking.

Casmire snorts and paws the earth with his left hoof. Definitively indicating that she needs to get her emotions in check before expecting to get on his back.

"I'm sorry, Cas," she replies. "I reacted without thinking." She whispers, humbled by the thought of harming the one she holds most dear.

"I could have killed us."

She drops her head and extends her palm to him. In a gesture of deep apology.

Casmire moves forward. He nuzzles her palm. Accepting her offer.

Gabriella gently takes the reins. She swings onto his back, and turns him toward the direction they recently deserted. She breathes deeply. Centring her energy.

She calls out, like a battle cry, "Take me to Adrian!"

Gabriella hunkers down and Casmire plunges forward.

They bolt back across the Plains, even faster than before. Heading toward the cloud of dust in their direct vision.

Gabriella prays silently in her heart that Adrian is alive. As they fly across the terrain, she does not care whether she must relinquish him to another.

She cares only that the Divine spares his life.

EIGHT

GABRIELLA AND CASMIRE arrive back at the scene they deserted. Waiting for the dust to settle, she wheels Casmire around. Looking in all directions.

High on her steed, she can see the men's three horses. Standing serenely in the distance. Grazing on the prairie grass.

Gabriella is confused. The three men lay below her, unconscious.

Casmire circles them twice before she can be absolutely sure that they are not going to awaken. At least, not anytime soon.

She jumps off. And approaches the men with care.

They are, indeed, unconscious. And yet, she sees no mark of a fight on their heads. Nothing that would indicate a blow sufficient to knock them off their feet. And send their spirit soaring into the sky while they sleep.

She looks to Casmire. Who has no answers to offer.

Gabriella gazes at the men's horses far on the horizon. They still bear their saddles. Their gear. Their reins. Nothing would seem amiss.

Except for the startling fact that these men have been knocked down. And Adrian is missing.

She whirls around, furiously. Looking in all directions. To no avail.

"Casmire. Where could he be?"

She looks to her friend, desperately wanting answers.

But Casmire can offer her no more than she observes. She sees that the horses are quiet. Even these treacherous men seem peaceful.

And yet, she cannot help but feel panicked.

Gabriella paces in a winding pattern, swerving between the bodies. She searches for clues. The quiet one was able to draw his weapon. But it lies at his side.

She stoops down and checks the blade. No blood. Or sign of recent battle.

She continues past the clever one. Doubting he even carried a weapon. Clearly believing he could outwit any opponent.

Gabriella cannot help but smile to herself at that thought.

Finally, the leader. He fell hard. And possibly first. Given that his fallen weapon is in the same place it landed during his preposterous display. Nor was he able to pull the weapon tucked in his boot.

She crouches, admiring the blade. Contemplating taking the extra weapon.

Then dismisses the thought, knowing she does not want to carry the burden that weapon must hold in its metal. So many innocent lives, taken for greed.

Gabriella rises back up to her full stature. Looking out over the miles and miles of grass and knolls.

"There is nowhere to hide on the Plains," she muses out loud. "Only slight hills that could not shelter him for long."

She muddles through the possibilities. "He could have ridden in another direction. But I would see him."

Frustrated, Gabriella glares at Casmire. Every inch of her body aggravated by the current situation. He gazes back at her. Remaining dignified. Impervious to her fury.

Casmire learned a long time ago that Gabriella is a feisty being that must work things out for herself. He cannot intervene. She is the foal that attempts the fence again and again. Until the day comes that she can leap gracefully over.

This is how she builds her strength. And nurtures her determination.

Staring out over the Plains, a painful thought crosses Gabriella's mind.

What if this was a way out of what she asked of him? A ruse designed for the opportunity to flee?

Her heart sinks with the weight of this possibility. And her mind dances with torturous images of betrayal and humiliation.

Feeling her anguish, Casmire places his soft muzzle against Gabriella's face.

She lifts her eyes from the spectres of abandonment. And places a grateful palm on the side of his face. His essence calms her. Bringing her back to centre.

"What am I to do?" she whispers to Casmire. Aching at the thought of her loss.

"How will I find my way to the palace now?"

"Is that your worry? No concern at all for my life?" a voice states behind her.

Gabriella whips around, dagger in hand. Ready for battle. Until she sees Adrian's bemused face.

She casts the dagger aside. Launching herself at him. She throws her arms around his neck in a powerful embrace. Stronger than any she has ever offered.

Adrian loses all sense of time. Torn between duty and need, he wraps his arms around her. Holding her to him. They stand for a few brief seconds. In a deep and joyful embrace.

For the first time, Adrian feels a sense of home.

Their blood pulses together. His heart desperately wants to lose itself in the flow of this river. To throw caution to the wind. And plunge deep into the cool and refreshing water.

But his head interrupts. Knowing this is not what is asked of him.

He pries himself from her hold. And places her a foot away. So he can, once again, get his bearings.

Gabriella's eyes drop to the ground. Embarrassed and awkward. This is far from typical behaviour for her.

In fact, this place is very foreign ground.

Speaking carefully, for fear of offense. Adrian whispers, "I am glad to see you, too."

Glad, she thinks. Berating herself for her foolishness. Glad.

As though I truly am his sister. Gabriella nods formally. Not trusting herself to speak. She turns and strides to Casmire. Gathering his reins in her palm.

She wants to ask Adrian where he went. How he came back? But she is too mortified to say a word.

Her questions will have to wait for another time. When she has regained her composure.

She is sure the events will bear some wisdom for her.

Gabriella touches Casmire's neck. Connecting to her steadfast friend. Placing her foot in his stirrup, she swings gracefully onto his back. Feeling some pride return. Knowing she is on her path again. This is where she belongs.

Not in the embrace of a man who is not her match.

She turns to face Adrian. Waiting patiently by Ginetta's side.

He watches Gabriella. Wishing he could ease the struggle. For her and for him. But this is how it must be.

Sensing she is ready to leave, he mounts his faithful steed. Turns toward Gabriella and says, "Shall we go?"

She merely nods. Awaiting his direction.

Adrian urges Ginetta east toward the mountains. Gabriella follows. Keeping a few paces behind so she can avoid conversation. Checking Casmire's urge to be at the front. Much to his irritation. But she cannot help herself.

Her pride still hurts too much to speak aloud.

Gabriella never deemed herself a beautiful girl. Hannah claimed that accolade from their early years. To be fair, Gabriella always felt grateful that the weight of beauty fell on her sister.

She was free to tumble and toss, to climb and explore, while her sister wore tight corsets and precious silks and jewels that required safe keeping.

No, Gabriella never aspired to be beautiful. Until today.

Suddenly, she envies her sister's grace. Her ability to turn any head she chooses. The gentle and subtle arts that come so easily to Hannah and are revered by men. Gabriella has no doubt that Adrian would adore her sister.

If he did not already.

Swallowing her pride, she allows Casmire the rein to match Ginetta's pace. He tosses his head in gratitude. Claiming his rightful place. At least in his mind.

The flick of Ginetta's ears at his approach reveals a different tale.

"Tell me about the Hidden Palace," Gabriella states. Keeping her intention well-masked. And her gaze straight ahead.

Adrian is startled by the request. Then remembers she has a

special purpose. Even if he is not privy to the task. Or permitted to stay once she arrives.

"What would you like to know?" he responds. Curious where she will take this chess match she has begun.

Gabriella ponders the question. Feeling the impatience in her chest. Knowing she must pace herself.

"Perhaps you could start with its size," she responds. With a tinge of derision.

Adrian has to hold his tongue. He does not brook arrogance well. Particularly from a girl ten years his junior.

And there it was again. The aggravating truth that she flew past his defences before he even realized the intrusion. Knocking him off-balance.

Adrian steadies himself. Focuses on the mountains in the distance. Allowing his mind a moment to grow calm.

"What does that matter?" he says, serenely. "You will have to deal with the size regardless of knowing the reality in advance."

"Do you not like to know the size of your enemy before going into battle?"

"I deem it irrelevant," Adrian responds.

"Why?" Gabriella asks. Curious how a man of his lithe form would not want to assess his opponent. And realizes, suddenly, that this answer may also explain the strange puzzle of today's events.

"Gabriella. Do you have faith in your abilities?" he inquires.

Startled by the question, she replies candidly. "The ones I have honed."

"And do you believe in your quest?" he continues.

"With all of my heart," she replies, softly.

He adores her honesty. And immediately quells his feelings. "Then what do the details matter? When you know you are guided and will act accordingly."

Adrian gazes at her with kindness and sympathy. Understanding all too well that a sacred path is both the simplest and the hardest one to follow.

She holds his gaze for as long as she can bear. Every time he shares his wisdom with such tenderness, she falls in love with him a little more.

Gabriella turns away. Abandoning her questions. She accepts the consolation of silence.

And reaches out to the beauty surrounding her. The steady gait of her steed. The glory of the sun. The grace of the hawk. The promise of the mountains.

Nature has always been her healer. Gabriella offers up her heart. Confident that this sacred lover will not reject her.

She takes comfort in the arms that have held her all her life.

NINE

DESPITE THE TRUTH of his teaching, Adrian must admit he resorted to magic. Beneath the ancient wisdom he shared with Gabriella, ran a gentle current of distraction. Drawing her away from the facts she sought. And leading her to the questions he could control.

Adrian glances at her elegant face. She has not looked at him in over an hour. He tries not to let it bother him. And fails brilliantly.

He touches the neck of his steady Ginetta. Reassured by her strength and her warmth. Somehow, the willing company of such a regal creature gives Adrian faith that he treads an honourable path.

He knows what awaits Gabriella at the Hidden Palace. And the longer he can keep her from the brutal reality of the place, the better he feels about taking her there.

Not that this journey is for his comfort. He knows he must guide her. And for whatever reason, he is being asked to return to that godforsaken place.

But if he were the sort of man to take the easy path, he would be riding hard in the opposite direction. And taking her with him.

The Hidden Palace is not for the faint of heart.

The Great Prince built the palace, stone by stone, to be a place of refuge. Refuge from the daily burden of running the land.

Every ruler needs one. A place to gather one's thoughts. And gain perspective on the times.

But Adrian knows that the Prince built this palace with only one thought in his mind. That he must deceive the people.

Believing that only one man knows what is best for the land. And if that requires killing and pillaging and breaking apart all who stand in his way, so be it.

Somehow, Adrian also knows the Prince can feel that what he does is wrong.

Many deem Adrian a fool for believing this cruel man has a conscience. Or, even more incomprehensible, a heart.

No matter, he thinks.

Adrian has never needed the assurance of others to confirm what he knows to be true. Like a transparent glass, the Great Prince has revealed that he carries a great burden of doubt. So many doubts, in fact, that he built a palace to hold them.

But the more time he spends, ruminating in those doubts, the darker his mind grows. Day by day. Hour by hour. The Prince inches his way toward madness.

This is where he guides Gabriella. Adrian's brow furrows.

Ginetta flicks her head, pulling the reins under his hands. Sensing the darkening of his mood. And attempting to lift him back into the present.

After all, they are closing in on the mountains.

They bear the glorious promise of food and water. But also the possibility of ambush.

With rocky crags, come excellent hiding places. Perfect for cowards and thieves.

As though picking up on his thoughts, Gabriella sits taller in the saddle. Taking in the change of terrain as they approach the foothills.

The grass no longer cracks and breaks with every step. The colours broaden from browns to greens and yellows. And the earth flexes her shape into gently rolling hills. Rather than insisting on a long, flat view.

The slight bite in the air makes Gabriella smile.

She has missed the cool breeze that comes with the company of trees. Despite being unfamiliar with this land, the colours and shapes of the ground make her think of her home.

And she is grateful for the kindness.

Adrian feels relieved to see some joy on Gabriella's face. He knows he has been hard on her. And the journey to come will only bring more difficulties.

So he appreciates any moment that reminds them of the joys in life. The more arduous the path, the more precious the tender blessings.

Casmire's and Ginetta's ears perk forward in the same instant. Concerned with hidden threats. Their riders may prefer the mountains. But they are not so keen.

The footing is more treacherous. The rocks hide predators of every incarnation.

And the opportunity for escape is limited to forward and back. This is not a route they would choose.

But Ginetta already knows a truth they cannot avoid.

There is no other way to the Hidden Palace.

TEN

DEEP IN THE HILLS, Adrian and Gabriella set up camp for the night. Gabriella lays out their bedding. And looks up at the mountains looming high above. She marvels at their size. Their dark, mysterious ways.

Adrian sparks the fire to life. Noticing Gabriella's fascination. And trepidation.

He appreciates that she takes the time to feel out the place she enters. To offer her hand. Rather than crashing through without acknowledging the spirit and creatures of the land.

She feels his gaze and turns just as he drops his eyes to the fire.

Adrian stokes the flames. Taking the liberty of enjoying a larger blaze given the ample state of the moon. If trackers want to find them, they will have an easy enough time with the natural light. As long as he keeps the smoke in check.

Proud of her accomplishment, Gabriella hands Adrian the two hares she caught for dinner. He smiles at her.

She nods back. Still awkward in his presence. Trying to walk the rope between what she feels and what is expected.

A balance Gabriella never mastered, given her propensity for speaking her mind.

She takes a seat by the fire. Watching Adrian prepare a spit to roast the animals. Somehow, she knows being denied the very thing she wants is a lesson in maturity. She can feel the shift.

Despite all she has been through over the last two years. The losses. The hiding. The constant movement. She has never experienced a denial like this one. As a child of royal blood, she is far more used to getting what she desires.

But she knows the ways of the gods. She was schooled rigorously in them by Serafina. For all the whims that humans exhibit, somehow, the whims of the gods are far more painful.

And this one has exceeded all expectations.

Gabriella raises her eyes to the mountains. Their rugged sides. Their craggy surface. The snow freezing the top reaches of their brow.

She feels comforted that the earth, too, knows the rough hand of the gods. And only hopes that the pain of her journey will make her as beautiful a creation as these sacred monoliths.

Adrian takes a seat by the fire. And Gabriella brings her gaze back to him.

"Will you not tell me anything about the Hidden Palace before we arrive at its gates?" she asks.

Her patient and resigned tone catches Adrian off guard. He looks into her eyes. Seeing only the shielded gaze of a woman with a purpose.

"What would you have me explain?" he replies, equally guarded.

Though, on his part, the guarded tone hides his sadness at realizing she has shed the soft skin of adolescence. And has donned the responsible shell of adulthood.

Gabriella sits a little taller. Remembering the stance and tone of her mother when she addresses the royal gatherings.

Until this moment, she never recognized that her mother chose every action.

Opening her hands, as a symbolic offering of trust to the person before her. The gesture acknowledged the tremendous humility required to ask for assistance. And with a simple gesture, her mother balanced the scales of fate.

Showing that a Queen and a Commoner were made equal by a simple exchange.

"You deserve to know," she offers, "that I am not altogether sure why I must go to the Hidden Palace."

Adrian sits back a little. He needs extra space to observe this new Gabriella.

"But I trust that the mission is an important and sacred one. Not just for me, but for all affected." She takes a deep breath. Steadying her energy. "I wish to know the extent of the darkness I must endure to breach its walls and resist its power."

He gazes at her in silence. Feeling, for a moment, as though their roles are reversed. That she is the Guide and he is the Follower. He realizes that he is getting a glimpse at the woman and the leader that Gabriella could become.

Never before has Adrian wanted so passionately to fall on his knees for a woman.

He folds his hands together. Focusing his energy. He must speak rationally and not act impulsively.

"The Hidden Palace is a place of great and dark power," he begins, keeping his eyes on his hands. He feels Gabriella's energy go still. She listens with her whole being.

If Adrian ever doubted it before, he knows now that she is on a sacred mission.

"Resisting its draw takes focus and purpose. All the more so if you are asked to remain there beyond a few days."

He gives words to a thought that had not occurred to him until this moment. "Do you intend to reveal yourself to the Prince?"

Gabriella waits. Holding her answer inside. Waiting for Adrian to lift his gaze. So she can speak to his spirit.

Reluctantly, he looks up from his hands. He knows the answer. But does not want to hear her say it.

"Yes," she states, calmly. "I must."

Adrian nods. "Then I will tell you whatever you need to know to protect yourself."

Somehow, this statement breaks Gabriella's heart all over again.

For in his words, she knows, he is saying that he will not stay with her. He will deliver her to the Hidden Palace. And he will leave.

And she will be more alone than she has ever been in her life.

ELEVEN

MIRACULOUSLY, they made it through the night. Adrian packs the final cooking implements into his saddle bags. He checks over his shoulder. Making note of Gabriella as she silently prepares and speaks with her steed.

The change in her is remarkable. None the less so for the speed at which the transformation has occurred.

Before him stands not only a woman. But a being of the gods. Whether she is blessed is for them to say.

He will, of course, do whatever they ask to assist her. Even if it breaks him in two.

Gabriella catches his eye and smiles briefly. Then, in an instant, the mask of responsibility covers her face. And she swings onto the back of Casmire.

She is ready and eager to go. Even if her companion has his doubts. Which, Adrian can see, Casmire clearly does.

He strokes the neck of his own dear horse. Ginetta has been through many a mountain range. She does not, however, relish the terrain. Or the exposure to large predators.

Adrian sends a thought of comfort and support to Casmire. The great steed perks his ears forward. And dips his head slightly to acknowledge the gesture.

Like his rider, Casmire goes where he is called. Regardless of the danger. And today, their path winds deep into the heart of the highest mountain range in the Prince's lands. Danger is an under-statement.

Adrian mounts his steed and quickly swings her in the direction of their journey. The sun is already showing over the horizon and they have many miles to tread.

Gabriella catches up and rides beside Adrian as long as the path allows.

He understands why she rides close. Partly out of wisdom. For to be close means they can act as a unit if attacked. This also gives the impression of being much larger than they truly are. Which should dissuade the big cats from perceiving them as a meal.

But Adrian knows the real reason. He was able to avoid the nerve-wracking depths of their conversation last night by insisting that she rest. Never mind that hearing about the Hidden Palace before bed is a sure-fire way to prevent sleep.

He can put it off no longer. She has been patient. And, even this morning, when he knows she wants to ask again, she waits. Perceiving his reluctance.

This is the greatest sign of maturity she has exhibited yet.

He knows she is not naturally patient. In fact, this is, as most weaknesses are, also her great gift. Her desire to act will surely save her people one day. And, for that, they will love her forever.

A chill rides up Adrian's spine. He reminds himself that this is only one version of the future. To get there, first, Gabriella must remain alive.

"The Hidden Palace..." he begins. Then looks at her.

Her face is eager. Nervous, but excited. She says nothing. But he senses the increased beat of her heart.

"The palace is a stronghold that was built on a foundation of paranoia," he continues. "And sealed with the mortar of betrayal. You must know this for it affects everything within its walls."

Gabriella stares at him. Expecting him to admit his melodrama. To temper his overstatement. But he does not. He simply watches the path that winds before them.

She shivers. Knowing he would never overstate the truth for the sake of scaring her. "Including my sister?" Gabriella doesn't want the answer. But she must ask.

In fact, she already knows they are getting close to the palace. Even though she has no idea where it is. She dreamt about dungeons and torture and drowning rats all night. Time is of the essence. She cannot afford to avoid the truth.

"Yes," Adrian answers, simply. He takes a deep breath. Knowing she needs more.

"How long has your sister been in the palace?" Adrian asks the question to buy time. He needs a moment to prepare for the answers he must inevitably give.

Gabriella does not hesitate. She knows the number to the second. "Seven hundred and forty-nine days."

Adrian nods. "A little over two years."

"Yes," Gabriella whispers. Already lost in thought about her sister. She shakes it off. The past does not matter. Only the present offers the wisdom she needs.

He strokes Ginetta's neck. More for his comfort than hers. Even still, Ginetta appreciates the affection.

"Then Hannah has been under its influence longer than most," he speaks honestly. Anything else is, at best, a waste of time.

At worst, a danger to their lives.

"I cannot lie to you, Gabriella. She will have been affected." Adrian looks directly at her. The flicker of compassion in his eyes causes her to flinch.

Somehow, Gabriella finds this more painful than anything he has done to date.

"Given that you are twins, I imagine Hannah is very strong," he offers, though he knows it is small comfort. "Her natural fortitude will help. But the Hidden Palace finds cracks in the thickest armour. It sneaks into the corners of your mind. And whispers lies until they sound like truths."

Gabriella winces. "Are you saying I may not recognize her? That she will be... changed?"

Adrian surveys the surroundings. Affected by the very tale he tells. He suddenly feels nervous. Like they are being observed. He checks the high ridges of rock around them to make sure they are not being stalked.

"I am sure you will know her, and she will know you," he says. "But you were raised in a home filled with love. Protected by the embrace of acceptance. And that was the last time you laid eyes on one another."

He allows a moment for his statement to sink in. Then reinforces his point.

"Have you not altered in the last two years?" Adrian asks, not expecting an answer.

He keeps his eyes on the increasing grade of the trail. Concerned he might betray how much she has affected him with her transformation in only a handful of days.

"On the outside, yes," replies Gabriella. "But I am the same person at the core. Based on all you have said, my fear is that she will appear the same to my eyes. But will be different in her heart."

Gabriella drops her gaze to Casmire. Taking comfort in the steady presence of her friend. Her life has offered little in the way of reassurance recently. And now she must face her worst nightmare. That her twin may no longer want her.

Despite her words, Gabriella silently admits that she has changed since meeting Adrian. Her priorities have shifted. She would sacrifice almost anything to have him by her side. And she has known him for less than a fortnight.

She locks her eyes on the mountains in a fierce stare. As though to protest their ever changing terrain. Their unpredictable trails. The turbulent weather. The wind picks up, blowing a response to her challenge.

Gabriella pulls her cloak tighter. And throws her inner torment to the wind, the mountains, the sky. Must her sister change, too? She cries out to the ancient ones. Why does everything in her life insist on being volatile?

She grips Casmire's reins a little too tight. He shakes his head in protest. Gabriella returns her attention to the present. Pats his beautiful neck in apology.

Adrian senses her battle but cannot ease her anguish. He can only offer the truth. So he does his best to deliver the words gently.

"Hannah may very well be different. My instinct tells me this is why you must go to her," Adrian cannot help saying.

Gabriella locks her eyes on him like a desperate woman seeking water in the desert. Demanding Adrian share the elusive treasure he withholds.

He knows he must tread carefully. For he can see things that others are not always equipped to hear. He cannot risk Gabriella misinterpreting his words.

Her need does not abate. But he cannot answer yet. For both their sakes.

Adrian feels the battle raging in his very essence. His heart wants to give everything to Gabriella. To protect and guide her. And never leave her side. His heart would have him throw himself at her mercy.

But his head knows that they walk on treacherous terrain. The Hidden Palace will test every drop of Gabriella's strength. He cannot distract her with fairy tales and wishes. Not now. Not when so much is at stake—

Enough! Adrian yells in his head. And he feels Gabriella's spine go straight. Her gaze flickers, registering the sheer force of his outrage.

He forgot how deeply sensitive she is. Others do not pick up his well-guarded thoughts. But Gabriella is not like other people. Nor does he guard himself as well around her.

She thinks she is the cause of his rage. Which, in some small manner, is true.

"I know you are called to the palace on a sacred errand," Adrian begins, speaking slowly in order to monitor every word he says. "And I have no doubt this is related to your sister."

Gabriella nods. She plays, nervously, with Casmire's reins. But forces herself to be silent. For fear Adrian may change his mind about sharing his insight.

"Be cautious, however, about assuming the Divine's reason for sending you. We can never know the full complexity of the web being woven."

Gabriella's brow furrows. She adjusts her position in the saddle. The mountain path has grown steeper. As though foreshadowing the challenges that lay ahead.

As if she didn't know, she grumbles to herself. The warrior fire sparks in her belly.

"I have a feeling," Adrian ventures, "that you have already been advised this is not a rescue mission."

Startled, Gabriella cannot help but stare. She almost asks if he saw her with Astriel. But she catches herself. Suspecting that there are some things he sees.

And some he merely perceives. Then guides the easily led to reveal the truth.

She levels her gaze at him and does not answer. Though her shock is answer enough for Adrian. He refrains from smiling.

"As horrifying as the Hidden Palace is. And as obvious as your mission may seem, allow yourself, for a moment, to think of the hundreds of people living and working in those halls. Every day, countless exchanges. Conversations. Actions. Routines. In each of those seemingly insignificant moments, a new path could open to you. Unless you stay alert, you cannot know which one matters."

Gabriella cannot help herself. She is intrigued by the world he creates.

"I know your spirit aches for your sister," Adrian continues, "And your rage burns to redress the Great Prince and all his wrongs. But you cannot know the deep and lasting effect of your presence there. Perhaps you are going to inspire a scullery maid. Or affect the future of a young noble. Or bring hope to the hearts of the people."

"But –," she begins.

"No," Adrian insists. His voice so powerful that Ginetta pins her ears back. "Never assume you know the reason behind your task. Arrogance can cause great damage. To yourself and those within your reach."

Adrian takes a deep breath. He must take the plunge. If he is to guide her in the window of time they have together, he has no choice. He must reveal his hand.

"You, Gabriella, are a Sacred Messenger. And you must bear this charge with an even greater humility than being graced with royal blood."

Her eyes open wide. Gabriella thought she understood the depth of Adrian's strength.

But the power emanating from him now is almost more than she can bear.

"You cannot possibly know the full purpose of your journey and message. Nor are you meant to."

He stares fiercely into her eyes. Knocking the breath from her chest.

She forces her legs to hold onto Casmire. Afraid she might tumble to the ground.

"Trust in the ones who guide you, Gabriella. Practise your faith in their whispers. Fall into the arms of their sacred knowledge. Accept that your path may change with the breath of the wind. Above all, believe that the Divine holds you in her hands," Adrian speaks with the voice of experience.

"This and only this is your task."

TWELVE

Overwhelmed by Adrian's revelations, Gabriella rides silently for hours. The trail narrows and becomes more technical. She rides behind Adrian. Allowing her time to process what has happened.

Casmire handles the challenges of the cold weather and the awkward terrain admirably. He takes Ginetta's lead without too much injury to his pride. For once, Gabriella notes, he acknowledges another horse may know more than he does.

Perhaps the biting wind encourages him to follow rather than challenge. The force and chill has all of their heads bent and focused on getting over the high pass.

The mountains do not spare their fiercest edge. These are trails that few are meant to find. And the sharp rocks and cutting wind make that clear.

If you dare to tread this far from the predictable path, you had best be sure. Otherwise, you do not belong on this sacred ground.

Despite the severity of the weather, Adrian feels grateful for the remote path and the decreased chance of ambush. Given the shock his guidance has inflicted on Gabriella, the last thing either needs right now is to fight off bandits or a predator.

Other travellers complain about the elements. Adrian appreciates the blessing of inclement weather. The less savoury creatures also tend to be cowards.

A fierce storm sends them running every time.

Adrian gives Ginetta full control as they cross the peak of the trail. She can feel her way better than he can guide. He glances back to ensure that Casmire is close enough to follow. Head bent, Casmire keeps within reach of Ginetta.

A wise move when other senses take over from sight.

Ginetta leads them safely over the ridge. Then down the steepest edge of the mountain face.

Steady and confident, like a seasoned climber. She understands that careful steps count for more than displays of prowess at the pinnacle of the world.

Once they reach a level gradient and the wind has abated, Adrian takes the reins. From this point, the way to the Hidden Palace is in his hands.

He must stay focused and alert.

For in stating Gabriella's purpose out loud, no matter how remote their location, he has risked whispering the truth onto the wind. A being that has been listening for an opportunity will search for them across all the lands.

And there is always a creature waiting for such a moment.

Adrian glances at Gabriella. She is deep in thought. Or perhaps she is exhausted. Either way, he is glad she is preoccupied.

She has yet to realize that her greatest peril is not found in overcoming the obstacles to her purpose. Her greatest peril lies in people finding out who and what she is.

Many have levelled kingdoms and slaughtered villages to gain control of a Sacred Messenger. For in controlling the Messenger, you control the message.

Then you can call yourself God.

A chill runs up Adrian's spine. He prays the sensation is not a premonition. Ginetta senses his dark thoughts and tosses her head. As always, she is right. They are too close to the Hidden Palace to let his thoughts run rampant.

He must be more careful.

They descend far enough down the trail that the cloud cover no longer obscures the view. The foothills and valleys roll elegantly below them, filled with farmlands and orchards and acres of live-stock. This side of the mountains is abundantly rich.

Finally, Adrian can gain some sense of their position.

He gazes out over the rugged terrain. Quickly assessing their location as deeper in the northwest than he might have guessed. He recalibrates where they must go in order to reach their destina-tion. A little further, but not such a long stretch.

Satisfied they managed such a rugged crossing and knowing well the dangers that lie ahead, Adrian allows himself a brief instant of absolute wonder.

Even as a soul that loves the ocean, there is nothing as spec-tacular as the view from the crest of a mountain. From this point, the entire world appears serene. And anything feels possible. Even flight.

Adrian's breath catches in his chest. Immediately, he knows the surprise is not his. He turns to see the beauty of their surroundings reflected on Gabriella's face. He softens. Grateful she receives this moment of bliss in the middle of so many trials.

"It's stunning," she whispers. As though offering her words to the mountains as gratitude for their majesty. For a brief moment, Gabriella allows herself to be held in the arms of these ancient lands. Their beauty is like a balm to her sore heart.

Adrian feels the mountains glow with pride and appreciation. And he realizes how limited his perception of Gabriella's gift has been.

She is not just a Messenger for humanity. But one for all of creation.

Her aware presence in these mountains has brought healing to their sacred ground. So many cross this land. So few give thanks for the passage.

Adrian lowers his head. Expressing silent gratitude for their safe journey. For the graciousness of the earth and the elements. Either could have barred their way.

And while they did not make the journey easy, they did not impair the path.

If a mountain does not want you on her back, she can crush you in a second. Every experienced climber knows this truth. And never takes the power for granted.

They arrive at a fork in the trail. Adrian brings Ginetta to a halt. Waiting silently.

The cleared ground is wide enough for Gabriella to bring Casmire to Ginetta's side. They can ride two abreast again. Gabriella feels reconciled enough to Adrian's words that she can bear to be next to him.

Besides, she has more questions. When he is ready.

She waits. If not patiently, then at least resigned to the fact that he does not intend to move. Not until he receives the wisdom required.

Gabriella is sure they are meant to take the left path. But orientation is Adrian's area of expertise. And she does not want to seem impertinent.

She smiles. Her father would be grateful to know that, for once, she has chosen silence over impertinence. She doubts he would ever have believed that this day would come.

As quickly as she feels joy in thinking about her father, grief seizes her heart.

Gabriella lowers her eyes and places a hand on Casmire for comfort. Wondering whether she will ever see her father again.

She catches herself wondering whether he is alive. But as soon as the question rises to her mind, she knows deep in her soul that he is, indeed, still living.

What state he is in or where he might be, she can not say, but she gives thanks that he is not dead.

"We are losing the light," says Adrian, breaking Gabriella's morbid reverie. "But no matter. I would prefer we ride under the cover of darkness for a few days."

"A few days?" protests Gabriella. Just like that, she is a child again. Wanting everything now. And resentful the world does not deliver according to her expectation.

"We are not far from the palace. As pretty as these lands appear, they are filled with danger. Most of which we cannot see."

"So why travel at night?" she asks, trying to calm her impatience.

"Because," Adrian adds, as he spurs Ginetta down the right path. "At least it levels the field. We cannot see them. And they cannot see us."

She does not have to ask Casmire to catch up to Ginetta. He is already moving.

Gabriella glances quickly to her left. She cannot help but wonder what lies down the other path.

Adrian answers her silent question. "That is the more direct path. And the more dangerous one."

"Why?" she asks, already guessing at answers.

Adrian appreciates that she does not expect to be fed information. She takes her mind forward even before he responds. As insolent as that might seem, he sees the instinct as the mark of a true leader.

"Inexperienced travellers tend to take that route. And impatient ones," he adds pointedly.

Gabriella rolls her eyes. "I may be impatient. That does not mean I cannot fight."

"Just because you can fight, does not mean you will win."

She falls silent. And Adrian can tell she is trying to get a sense of what he sees.

He knows she takes his words seriously. Or she would not have stopped talking. Given what they are about to face, he is grateful for small victories.

More than anything, Gabriella must learn the balance between listening to him and heeding her own guidance. The wisdom is in the choice.

He gives himself a moment to check the path ahead. They are still high enough in the mountains that the trees are sparse and the line of sight is clear.

The day is fading. They will not be targets to anyone with a strong arrow arm.

Adrian scopes the edges of the path. Sensing forward a few miles. He does not perceive anything. They should have clear passageway for at least an hour.

Good, he thinks. That gives me enough time to start the

conversation.

He turns to address Gabriella and realizes she is already looking at him. Her bright, eager eyes pierce his heart.

What he would not give to turn their horses around and run.

For the first time in his life, Adrian feels he could abandon his path. He could reject all he has become. If only to save this flame that burns in front of him.

Of course, he knows the truth. If two people on earth would never be permitted to hide, it is Gabriella and Adrian. The Fates would chase them down. And throw them back into the fire.

For that is exactly where they are headed.

Into the Fires of Hell.

THIRTEEN

"You asked me about the Hidden Palace," Adrian begins. He knows talking about the place as they ride closer risks alerting the palace to their arrival. But knowing the palace as he does, Adrian figures it is a small price to pay.

Odds are it already knows they are coming.

Gabriella needs all the preparation she can get. For the palace is unlike any place she has ever experienced. As difficult as her path has been, she has no idea what she is about to see or feel.

In all likelihood, she will desperately want to flee.

Adrian breathes in the beauty of the birch trees in the moonlight. They reflect just enough of the moon's rays to guide them. And the shimmering light gives him hope. Or, at the very least, faith.

He turns to see Gabriella watching him carefully. She takes in so much more than even she knows. Adrian holds her gaze just long enough to make her blush. But she does not look away. Adrian is pleased.

Gabriella feels the confidence strengthen in her.

Regardless of her feelings, she must meet Adrian's challenge. Or she will never be worthy of his guidance. This small act has taken tremendous courage. As her heart races, she keeps her hands and her eyes steady.

The big physical leaps have never been hard for Gabriella. She would gladly take up a sword, swing from a tree, and tackle the largest opponent.

The small, intimate steps are her most terrifying challenges. Risking her pride. Her heart. Her reputation. All to gain the acknowledgement of a suitor.

With Hannah around, the risk was never worth the possible reward. Boys sought out Hannah. So Gabriella got used to being tough. The one who teased boys rather than flirted with them.

Besides, she prefers their respect. In her experience, it lasts longer than affection.

"You need to understand that the danger of the Palace reaches far beyond its walls," Adrian states. He looks at her to ensure she is listening. Gabriella nods.

"Now that we are on the North side of the mountains, we are within reach of everyone influenced by the palace."

"You speak as though the building is alive," objects Gabriella.

Adrian keeps his sharp gaze on the path and his senses alert to every direction.

"It is alive," he states, simply.

Casmire flicks his head. Not liking the tone of this conversation at all. He wishes they would stop. Each word makes his skin crawl.

Feeling his irritation, Gabriella scratches Casmire's neck. He is placated. A little.

"Those are forest legends and country tales to frighten people into submission," Gabriella insists. "A building cannot control its people, aside from the imposing nature of its size."

"No!" barks Adrian. Gabriella's stiffens and her body shifts back in the saddle.

She falls silent. Knowing that Adrian would not jest about this.

"You forget who built that building. You forget that you have been in the presence of the Great Prince. You wanted to grab your sister and run. You even risked being insubordinate to your father when you felt the evil that entered your home."

"Yes," admits Gabriella. A shiver runs up her spine. "But that is a man."

"A man made of sinew and bone. His palace is made of stone and mortar. These materials are not so different."

"But a man is animated. He has a soul." Gabriella scoffs, even as the words exit her mouth. "Or the possibility of one."

"Oh, but buildings have souls. Trust me on this point." Adrian's gaze travels far away. Gabriella fears she has lost him.

And she may never get to the truth about the Hidden Palace.

Adrian forces himself back. To this time. This reality. And takes another approach.

"All the years you grew up in your home, did you never once feel she was watching over you?"

Gabriella sighs. She wants to think of her home and does not want to. Afraid she may grow wistful. And she cannot afford to be wistful. Gabriella has no idea if she will ever see her home again. And it breaks her heart.

"Yes," she responds simply. She adjusts her cloak. Pulling it closer against the cooling night air.

"Your home has the spirit of a Guardian. Protecting those she loves. She exudes a regal and confident air. The people of your lands loved being invited into your castle. While they were there, they felt sheltered. And safe."

Gabriella looks at Adrian with a hint of tears in her eyes. She falls a little deeper in love as he talks about her beloved home. But she does not want to hear more.

For fear she may turn Casmire around and dash back.

"And the Hidden Palace," she asks, "This place repels its people?"

"It devours them," replies Adrian.

Gabriella winces. "What do you mean? It does not... it cannot." She is at a loss for words. She cannot even conceive of what he says.

That is when they both hear it.

Movement. At the edge of the woods.

Gabriella grabs her longer dagger. Ready to spur Casmire forward when Adrian lifts his hand. Signalling for her stop. Ginetta slows and Casmire matches her pace.

Gabriella glares at Adrian and mouths, "What are you doing?"

She wants the fight. She craves it. She has been hiding and following too long. And she needs the rush of combat. To feel alive again.

"We do not know what we are up against," he speaks directly to her mind. Gabriella cannot help but stare at his motionless lips.

She breathes hard. Calming her immediate reaction to panic. He is in her mind!

"Can you hear what I am thinking?" she asks.

'Yes," admits Adrian.

"What?" she hisses out loud. In her fury, she pulls Casmire. He bucks in surprise. Gabriella clutches to his back and immediately apologizes.

Casmire comes back to the ground. But now they are both

spooked.

He paws at the ground. Adrian gently moves Ginetta closer to Casmire.

"I am sorry," whispers Adrian. "I should have warned you. I do not listen to your thoughts. That goes against all that I am."

"Oh, but jumping into my head does not? Showing up unannounced? How do I know when you are there?" she demands. Worrying what she had been thinking just before he popped up uninvited.

"I know. I handled it poorly. I apologize, Gabriella."

"Just…give me a signal," she responds harshly, still feeling vulnerable. But wanting to get on with the matter at hand.

Adrian brushes two fingers across his temple. Gabriella nods. And braces herself for having him in her mind.

"We have not had a chance to speak about direct mind contact. But I promise I do not listen to your thoughts beyond our exchange. This is a subtle skill. Once mastered, you can be select in what you listen to."

"I will take your word on that," Gabriella grumbles in her mind.

A smile flickers on his face. Pleased her spirit is intact. Then turns his full focus on the movement in the woods.

Adrian should have paid closer attention. They have travelled far enough that the forest has thickened. He needs to be more careful. Even if it drains him faster, he must keep all senses on alert.

He guesses they are within ten leagues of the palace. Anything can happen here.

As the thought enters his mind, he feels it coming. With no time to respond.

In the blink of an eye, Adrian and Gabriella are surrounded by masked soldiers on horseback. Casmire startles and Gabriella has no idea what to think.

She holds tight to his reins, keeping Casmire from crashing through their ranks. They spin around, seeing the tight formation of armoured guards.

She reaches for Adrian's mind. To no avail. Gabriella looks at him, thinly covering her panic with outrage. He feels her fear and her desperate need to react.

Adrian gestures for her to be calm. He slowly increases the power of his presence.

The guards respond instinctively – backing up their circle. Gabriella breathes easier. Adrian surveys for an opportunity to slip past this barricade.

He is not sure how they will lose twelve soldiers on horses. But he will tackle one obstacle at a time.

Then he feels the absence of hope before it arrives in physical form. Adrian stops planning. He knows what is coming. And braces himself.

The guards shift as one unit, like they are being pulled on invisible strings.

And a large gap opens in the circle.

Gabriella immediately thinks Adrian has pulled off a wondrous trick. She grins and seizes the opportunity, lunging forward with Casmire. Both thrilled to be free.

"Gabriella, no!" Adrian yells into her mind.

She reacts to the command too late. Pulling the reins. As a force works against her like a powerful wind. Through strength of spirit, she whirls Casmire around, saving their lives. As the Great Prince materializes in the gap.

Closing the circle.

Gabriella stares, disbelieving. At the man she could call her brother-in-law. Casmire paws the ground. Furious. Convinced he could have broken free.

The Prince smiles. Enjoying the beast's frustration. And Gabriella's incredulity.

He has no intention of answering her questions. That would spoil his fun.

"My dear sister," he begins, as he steps forward, holding a hand out to Gabriella, and spooking Casmire in the bargain. "We were hoping you would come to visit."

"So you sent your best guards to seize me?" she retorts. Gabriella does not bother to disguise her contempt.

"Seize," he laughs, coldly. "No, no. Merely secure. I did not want you to flee before I could greet you myself."

"You certainly make an impression," Adrian adds, riding forward to support her. "I am sure Gabriella would be delighted to know how you appeared out of thin air."

The Great Prince glances at Adrian. Barely giving him the grace of a look.

"I believe you have fulfilled your role, Guide," the Prince dismisses him like a servant who has overstayed his time. And brings his gaze back to Gabriella.

"I will escort the Princess Gabriella from here to the Palace," he adds.

Gabriella swallows hard. She does not trust herself to be alone with the Prince. Not yet. Concerned she will grab her dagger and lunge for his –

"On the contrary," insists Adrian. "I promised Gabriella I would escort her to the Palace walls. And I intend to keep that promise."

The Prince sneers and locks Gabriella eyes. "The world is such an entertaining place. Every day I am surprised. Who knew even slippery magicians can learn to keep a promise?"

Gabriella turns, giving Adrian a startled look. Magician? Broken promises?

Adrian shakes his head, solemnly. Regretting he was too careful to let Gabriella in. He erred on the side of caution. And now he will pay for his mistake.

Gabriella stares at them. Sensing an old battle. She does not know who to believe. She would like to believe Adrian.

But what does she know about him, really?

The Prince smiles. Feeling Gabriella's hesitation. That is all it takes to turn someone. A seed of doubt.

We all harbour and nurture doubt. Like a trusted, sceptical friend we keep in dark corners. Leaning in for its counsel when we are most frightened.

Life teaches us to be suspicious. To expect betrayal. The Great Prince knows that all it takes is a suggestion. A whisper. And even the strongest will fall.

He levels pitying eyes on Adrian. Smiling at his easy victory.

"Have it your way, Guide. Accompany the Princess to the palace walls," the smile falls abruptly from the Prince's face. "But do not expect to leave."

Before Adrian can react, the Great Prince claps his hands – releasing the deafening sound of thunder and a suffocating tower of black smoke.

In an instant, the path is suddenly empty. Every person. Every horse. Vanished into thin air.

THE
HIDDEN
PALACE

ONE

GABRIELLA WAKES WITH A START. Sitting up, in a spacious bed, she cannot believe what she sees.

Somehow, she has landed in a guest bedroom. In what she can only guess is the Hidden Palace. The decor in the room is luxurious. No expense has been spared.

Rich colours and fabrics. Elegant silks and bright dyes. The walls are hung with tapestries. And her bed is covered with the finest silk she has ever touched.

And yet, she can feel that it is all a trick of the senses.

If Gabriella were to ignore her eyes, she would swear she was in a prison cell. Disguised with brocade curtains and delicate furnishings.

She shivers. Jumps out of the bed. And feels something soft brush against her.

Striking a fighting stance, Gabriella prepares to fend off an intruder. Except her leg catches against a tight circle of fabric. And she tumbles to the floor.

Confused, she searches for the object that tripped her. And sees she is dressed in nightclothes. That is what she felt against her leg a moment ago. Fabric.

The realization sinks in.

She remembers being on Casmire. Outside. Facing the Prince. Still in her riding attire. How did she get into this nightdress? Who…?

Gabriella rakes the room, looking for the culprit. Someone did this. Someone took her out of her —

She refuses to continue the thought.

Feeling exposed, Gabriella wraps her arms around her body. Worried she is not alone. She searches the room. And forces herself to speak. "Show yourself," she demands. Trying to sound imperial.

"Who did this?" She looks around. "And where are my riding garments?"

No one responds to her questions.

Relieved, her courage returns. She is determined to find answers.

Gabriella searches the room. Pulling open drawers. Tossing pillows to the floor. Seizing wardrobe handles and throwing open doors. If she can just find her proper clothes, she can find…

She stops, suddenly, in mid-search. Adrian.

Gabriella is frozen. The room looks like it has been ransacked by pirates. She reaches as far as she dares within the palace. But cannot feel his presence.

Suddenly, she is besieged with fears. Where is he? Is he alive? If he is, what has the Prince done with him? Her breath stops and her heart pounds.

Her cheeks flush. And she remembers doubting him. A few cruel words from the Great Prince. And she turned on Adrian like a treacherous adder.

She breathes. Centring her energy. And regaining control of her senses. Gabriella reminds herself that she is in enemy territory.

She must be vigilant.

She does another sweep of the room. This time with all of her senses.

For now, she seems to be free. She does not sense that she is being monitored. Though she knows better than to count on that impression.

Gabriella feels that something is amiss. She may not be able to see the snare, but she knows that she is caught in a trap.

That is when she catches the edge of the trick.

Like the fleeting tail of an animal disappearing into the woods. She sees enough with her peripheral vision to trust her instincts.

Gabriella looks down at her fingernails. And sees that they have grown more than she would ever allow had she been conscious.

That is when she knows.

She has been here longer than a night. Whether by magic or some strange force, she suspects that time does not obey the same rules in the Palace. Or perhaps just her perception is different.

Either way, she has been here for at least one week. Possibly two. And Adrian has been in the dungeons. All alone.

She needs to know if he is alive. Gabriella has not used these skills since her instruction by Serafina. She has not practised. And she may not be able to do what she was taught.

But she has to try.

Closing her eyes, Gabriella breathes steadily. And weaves herself into a trance.

She roots her energy deep into the earth. Anchoring into an ancient power. A power older than anyone can fathom. As deep as she can possibly go.

Once she touches that ancient place, she slowly, delicately

pulls her energy up into the heart of the Divine Mystery. The sacred force that holds us.

She pauses for a moment, in the sacred womb. The place we were all born and the place we all go when we die. She breathes in the calm. The silence. The infinite peace.

Until she can feel that peace seep into her own heart.

Then, when she has truly found the center, Gabriella reaches out her energy like willow branches calling to the heavenly seas. Reaching far in their watery depths. Where all the secrets of the universe are held. She breathes a sigh of release.

Now, she is ready.

Leaving her physical body behind, Gabriella ventures cautiously out of her room. Attempting to find where Adrian is being held.

Stepping out the door and down the hallway, she gradually senses how vast the palace is. Bigger than its residents and workers realize. Possibly even bigger than the Prince realizes. For there are many hidden places in its walls.

And even more secrets.

She slips down the great staircase. Knowing the residents are still asleep. She must have woken in that sweet space between the night and the dawn.

The threshold of all possibility.

Though she knows that includes the darkest and the noblest possibilities. This is the moment in the night when a soul makes deep decisions. The ones that change our paths forever. For good or evil.

As she approaches the bottom of the staircase, she checks to make sure no one in the palace has stirred from bed. She can feel that she does not have much time.

The servants will awaken in the next twelve minutes.

Though, if what Adrian says is true, she should be careful. The palace itself may never sleep. She pauses. Breathing deeper.

Gabriella feels that even the walls need to rest.

Somehow, whether through instinct or grace, she has found the window of time when the palace, too, has taken the opportunity to slumber.

As her heart beats, steadily, like a slow, predictable clock, she knows her window of time is closing. There is one, at least one, in the palace who shifts gently out of the dream state. Gabriella feels her opportunity evaporating.

Eleven minutes.

Stepping off the bottom of the grand stairs, she shifts into the center of a huge space. An elegant space, intended to overwhelm and impress. This, she senses, is the core of the building – the Great Hall.

Gabriella pauses. And looks up.

The Great Hall arches high into the sky, towering above all the floors in the palace. This is the hub. All the energy of the Palace, no matter how hidden, eventually reports back to the Great Hall. The heart of the building.

If, indeed, this Palace has a heart.

Ten minutes.

From here, she could send a message that would reach every corner of the palace. It may, or may not, find Adrian. That depends on how heavily he is guarded. But if she were to send a message, this would be the moment.

She realizes this is a risk. In fact, it is a great risk.

One Adrian would warn her not to take. He would know, as she does, that in this one simple act, she risks her entire mission.

Gabriella pauses. Recognizing the seriousness of the realization.

Adrian spoke to her of not assuming her mission. Not closing off the possibilities. Or ever second-guessing the Divine.

But who is to say it is not him?

Her heart fills suddenly with a deep and profound love. The passion she feels threatens to overwhelm her. To tear her from everything else that once seemed important.

Her senses dance with the need to be near him. To touch him. To know he feels the same. And, in the rush of her feelings, she almost loses control.

Eight minutes.

Gabriella breathes. Centres. And makes her decision.

She prays for strong and powerful Divine protection. For her sake and for his. They will need it if they are to survive.

Then, in the span of a breath, she sends a swift, cryptic message.

Gabriella feels it fly through the corridors of this morbid building. Like a flash of lightning. And just as powerful.

In the instant of transmission, she prays for its swift delivery and safe protection.

Then waits.

Breathing slowly. Embracing the silence. Keeping herself in a receptive state.

Nothing. Not even a heartbeat.

Six minutes.

She breathes to stay calm. This is a strange and unknown place. She cannot expect things to work as she might expect. Truth be told, she cannot be sure the message will work at all.

Gabriella senses the one awakening is slowly shifting out of sleep. Breaching the barrier between the otherworld and this one. Not yet here, but close.

She waits.

Praying for an answer. Yet open to the revelation.

Five minutes.

She cannot stay here much longer. She must make her way back to her room. For if she is caught in trance... if someone were to find her at her most vulnerable —

Gabriella extinguishes the thought. Focus. She must focus.

She breathes. And waits.

Nothing.

No response. Four minutes.

She begins to pull her energy back in, preparing to head back to her room.

Wait! There is... something.

She reaches out again. A little further. Trying to sense what is coming through. Hoping she can feel him. Just enough to give her confidence that he's alive.

A WHOOSH of a cold, dark energy rushes down her spine. Like an icy hand has raked its nails through the core of her soft being.

She gasps! And lets go instantly.

Three minutes.

She pulls her energy back in. Enfolds herself in sacred protective light. And rushes up the staircase. She traverses the hallway so quickly, her energy blurs.

In an instant, she is back through the bedroom doorway. And in her body.

Her entire being lights up. Energy explodes from her heart centre, aligning her spirit with her physical form. And forcing out any remnants of the dark energy that connected with her in the Great Hall.

Gabriella's eyes snap open.

She whips a shawl off a nearby chair. And wraps her shivering body in the woven fabric. Desperately trying to regain some warmth.

But her body feels chilled. And her spirit feels shaken.

Two minutes.

Forcing her muscles to move, she huddles next to the roaring fire.

As she recovers from the shock of the chilling message received, Gabriella fights back tears of rage. One slips down her cheek. She swipes it away.

But her heart fills with a deep sense of dread.

Staring into the dancing flames, she knows that the Prince has placed Adrian in the deepest, darkest bowels of this place. A place so dark, she could not penetrate the barrier. She could only feel the creeping, primordial force surrounding his cell.

He is chained and alone. Slowly and steadily tortured with whispers of hatred and betrayal.

She knows it will take all of his strength to stay sane.

A knock startles Gabriella from her heart-wrenching vision. And she feels it.

The clock has run out.

She looks up at the door as it pushes open.

Gabriella has been so focused on her errand that she did not wonder who might be breaching the layers of sleep.

Who would awaken at this hour to greet a visitor?

She did not think, until this moment, how rare an occurrence guests must be at the Hidden Palace. How fascinating it might be to talk with a stranger.

Gabriella steels herself for the intrusion of a maid. Someone sent to check on her. Likely to keep tabs on her movements. And her belongings.

As the door opens without her permission, Gabriella sees a polished and self-important woman stride into her room.

A woman Gabriella should have felt coming. And yet, she did not. A smile appears on the woman's face as she reaches out her hands in greeting.

"Gabriella! You made it."

Gabriella knows she should move forward. She should be excited. She risked her life, and Adrian's, to come here.

But suddenly, Gabriella feels shy. Cautious.

And deeply guarded around this woman. Her twin sister.

Hannah.

TWO

THE TWO WOMEN STARE at each other. They have changed substantially in two years. Hannah smiles.

But Gabriella feels it is a practised smile. A smile performed for many. Now this forced gesture has become part of who she is.

Who is this woman standing before her?

Gabriella pulls the shawl closer around her body. Feeling the chill sink deeper into her bones. She commands her body not to shiver.

But still she cannot bring herself to speak.

All she can do is stare at this woman she should know. This person who shares her blood. The reason she came to this godforsaken place.

Hanna makes the first move. "Forgive me," she begins, and steps toward Gabriella. "I forgot that you must be cold."

Gabriella backs instinctively away from Hannah's advance. Catching her sister off-guard.

Hannah looks at her inquisitively. Not even offended.

Which Gabriella would have expected of the Hannah she knows. And loves.

"What makes you think I am chilled?" Gabriella asks, unable to keep the accusatory tone out of her voice.

Hannah gives her another smile. This one is kind but condescending. Clearly, she has developed a repertoire of smiles. Gabriella wonders how many she will encounter during her stay.

Hannah steps closer. Gabriella forces herself not to back away. She must regain control. She needs to figure out what has happened. What is happening.

Gabriella holds her sister's gaze.

"Only that you are not used to such thin garments for sleeping. And you are clutching to a shawl," Hannah chastises her.

For the length of the moment that Hannah's words hang in the air, Gabriella doubts her instincts. Desperately wanting to believe the honey-soaked words.

But she knows, deep in her being, that Hannah is lying.

She can sense it with the bond that is still there between them. Her sister may be able to fool the world with her newly acquired skill at deception. But she cannot fool Gabriella's blood.

And her blood knows that Hannah is a liar.

Gabriella feels her strength return. She stands taller. Casting off the shawl.

She stares her sister directly in the eyes. Defying Hannah's confidence. Claiming her stand in the truth.

Hannah's smile wavers. But holds.

"The chill was temporary," Gabriella assures her sister. "I would prefer, however, not to be dressed in this nightdress. May I ask where my riding clothes are?"

Hannah hesitates. Looking at her sister with new eyes.

For a brief second, Gabriella swears she saw the real Hannah. Like this liar is just an illusion. Or a strange apparition.

And behind it, is her true sister. Gabriella reaches out.

But her hand connects with the new Hannah. The imposter. The illusion has stolen her sister and put this facade in her place.

The new Hannah smiles. An empty smile.

An empty and automatic response to another person's gesture. With no feeling behind the twitch of the muscles in her face.

Gabriella drops her hand.

Hannah tips her head in recognition of Gabriella's request. "I will find your clothes and have a maid bring them to you. The Prince and I eagerly await your presence at our table. We have much to catch up on, my dear sister."

Hannah reaches for Gabriella's shoulder.

And Gabriella braces her body for the touch. Forcing her shoulder not to move.

Knowing that she does not want this woman to touch her but needing to play the part. She locks her eyes on Hannah's. The only way that Gabriella can force herself to take what may come with this new Hannah's contact.

Hannah's fingers land on her shoulder.

Worse than a shock, Hannah's touch does nothing. No love. No warmth. No feeling at all.

The absence is like a knife to the heart. Leaving Gabriella despondent.

She cannot show this. For her own safety. And Adrian's.

Instead, Gabriella nods her head in a formal return of this woman's gesture.

"Thank you. I am in need of sustenance. And would be grateful for your hospitality," she replies.

Hannah smiles. Seemingly pleased with Gabriella's response. And turns to leave.

Gabriella cannot tell what is going on underneath the forced expressions of this woman in her sister's guise.

Nor does she know if the true Hannah feels her prison.

And that is the most disturbing truth of all.

THREE

GABRIELLA PACES HER ROOM. She has a short window of time before the maid arrives with her clothes. Her mind races like wildfire.

What is she meant to do? Must she play this part? Be false to all she is?

She stops. Catching sight of the view out the slender window.

A courtyard of servants scurry to do their work as quickly as possible. No one stops to say hello. No one speaks to each other.

The scene breaks Gabriella's heart.

She recalls a time when she would watch the servants in her father's courtyard go about their day. Chatting and laughing and helping one another. Sharing stories.

The servants were as much a family to Gabriella as her own. Looking out for her. Instructing her. They were part of the castle. Part of the larger family.

Her home was their home.

Gabriella feels a twinge in her heart. That reality no longer exists.

All of her brethren, whether by blood or not, have been scattered to the winds. Just as she has. Who knows what has happened to them? Who shelters them from the storms? Her heart aches for their safety.

She looks again at the people in the courtyard of the Great Prince.

And cannot fathom a man who would treat his fellow beings in this way. Hold them in a grip of fear and panic. Trapped in never-ending despair.

How do they get up in the morning? she wonders.

And then she knows. Just as she does.

By necessity.

Each day, she knows, the purpose will come. And if the only purpose for that day is survival. Then so be it.

Gabriella takes in the poor souls below her. Not a word shared. Not a whisper. No one dare break the spell the Great Prince has cast upon their lives.

A lightning bolt of energy rages through Gabriella's being.

Simultaneously, she is enlightened and furious. Those are Hannah's people, she thinks. They are her souls to protect!

Never would she leave them in such a state, unless she, too, were… under a spell.

Gabriella paces. That's it!

No one loved the people in their castle more than Hannah. She would speak with each of them every day. Find out the latest happenings in their lives. Comfort them when they were upset. Mend the broken romances when they fell apart.

She was truly their friend.

And was meant to be their Queen when her parents were no longer in this world.

How dare the Great Prince take her from her people!

Gabriella slams her fist against a wardrobe. The reverberating sound brings her back to this reality in an instant. She feels the shockwave ripple through the walls.

And knows she has made a fatal error.

Not only has she alerted everyone to her presence. She has enraged the Palace.

Gabriella pulls her hands close to her body. Instinctively protecting herself. Adrian was not telling tales. Or trying to frighten her.

He meant every word.

Gabriella glances around her room. For the first time, really examining every piece of ornate furniture. Each ancient tapestry. The heavy rugs on the floor.

The Prince believes he owns every item.

But the Palace knows otherwise. The Prince does not possess the place he built. The Palace possesses him.

Gabriella slows her breathing. Forces herself to be calm.

And recalls her lessons from Claudius.

When walking in enemy territory, move slowly. Carefully. With focused concentration. Awaken your senses. And keep your weapon at hand.

Most important of all, never underestimate your opponent.

Gabriella takes a deep and conscious breath. She is in the Palace's territory now. She must use all of the wisdom at her disposal.

Panic threatens to take over. She breathes deeper.

And the air suddenly feels thick. Like it wants to crush her. Like it will drain every ounce of hope from her being. And she is the smallest creature to ever walk the earth.

Gabriella gasps. She clutches her chest.

And in the grace of that moment of contact, between her hands and her heart, she is released.

She feels the pulse of the Divine rush through her. And her body lights up with joy.

Her eyes close. And Gabriella breathes in the crisp, beautiful air.

She can sense she is protected. She is held in the palm of safety as she walks these walls.

Gabriella's eyes open. And she is no longer afraid.

She does not know if this feeling of calm will last. But she is grateful.

And, for the first time since arriving, she feels a glimmer of hope.

Within seconds, the Palace reacts. Sending a shockwave of rage through the walls. Several servants call out. Gabriella knows that sound well. It is the shock of pain.

She quickly realizes that one of the voices came from the other side of her door.

The maidservant.

Gabriella knows that the young woman was waiting. Likely leaning against the door. For what reason, Gabriella does not know.

In the instant that Gabriella dared to bring hope into these walls, the Palace struck out at anyone and everyone she could hurt.

Gabriella smiles. And gives thanks for her sacred guardians.

They led her here. To the edge of the world, where no light has shone in years. She knows now they brought her to be a beacon of hope.

Her mind begins to spin stories.

Who she is meant to help? And why? What demons will she face? And will she have the courage?

Her minds races off in a million directions. Like a wild horse set free.

Casmire!

Her mind yells his name before Gabriella can restrain her desperate realization. She feels the smug response of the Palace.

Every muscle in her body wants to lunge out the door. To search each stable and paddock to find her dear friend.

But she holds herself in place.

Though she has not spent much time with the Prince, she knows he would not waste such a valuable animal. Nor would he hurt him without a reason.

Gabriella can tell the Prince is a man of patience when he chooses to be. He has learned to wait. She can sense it.

For with patience, comes control. He selects just the right moment to cause the deepest and widest wave of suffering. Choosing the exact action to inflict pain.

And then he strikes.

Like a cobra, weaving and dancing. Each subtle motion, another wave in an ever expanding trance. Casting a net over its prey. Until they are helpless in its gaze.

Until they have lost any sensation. And no longer have the will to flee.

Except the cobra does not realize that every night, it falls asleep in its own trap.

In a basket of its own weaving.

And one day, even the cobra, must die.

FOUR

GABRIELLA STARES AT THE DOOR. But it does not move. She can sense the maidservant on the other side. In fact, she can almost hear her breathing. Realizing the woman might still be in pain, Gabriella decides she must be the one to act.

She strides over to the door and pulls it open.

Startling the young woman in the hallway. And striking fear into her heart.

Gabriella waits for the maid to say something. Do something. But the poor woman is frozen. And, Gabriella realizes, probably no older than she is in years.

And certainly much younger in her exposure to the world.

Gabriella steps away from the doorway with a gesture.

"Please, come in," she says.

But the maid only clutches Gabriella's clothes tighter. And does not take a step.

They stare at one another for a moment. Then the maid lowers her eyes.

And still, she does not move.

Gabriella sighs, frustrated. What is wrong with this girl?

All Gabriella wants are her clothes. The maid could just leave them. And she would dress herself.

Ready to make that very suggestion, Gabriella is suddenly struck with a realization. This girl has never been outside the Palace.

She may have been raised here. Never once allowed to venture outside the walls.

The Palace is old enough. The tales in the countryside claim the Prince cleared the land over twenty years ago. When he was only nineteen years of age.

Barely a year older than Gabriella and this maid are now.

That was the year the Prince lost his father. A man once great, he descended into madness in his later years. The Great King was mad for long enough to affect the most essential time of the Prince's life.

The years that bridge between childhood and adulthood.

And hence, the Great Prince was born. By the time the Prince had come of age, he was so deeply ruled by paranoia, he would not take his father's title.

Even after the King was long buried in the ground.

Gabriella had her own suspicions, however, about the reasons the Great Prince did not take the title handed to him by his ancestors.

She believed he wanted his own title. His own way.

To mark the world as his without the encumbrance of the past. By foreswearing everything that came before him, the Prince was free to do whatever he pleased.

To the detriment of all.

Gabriella sighs. And feels the girl jump.

Still frozen in place, the girl reminds Gabriella of a fawn. And her heart softens. The only way to coax a fawn is to be patient.

As much as Gabriella wants to grab the clothes from the girl's arms and send her on her way, she knows better. Or at the very least, she is learning.

Gabriella leaves the door open. And walks far into the room.

Spotting a simple wooden chair, clearly intended for being waited on, Gabriella places the chair in front of the fireplace.

She positions the chair so that, if she must wait for hours, she can spend her time observing the room. Gabriella intends to learn as much as she can about this Palace. Whether through the people, the furniture, or even the floorboards.

Every object has a tale. Discovering the story simply requires patience, stillness, and an open heart.

And Gabriella could use practise on all three.

Creak. Gabriella's gaze lifts to the doorway.

Given where she is positioned, she cannot yet see the girl. But Gabriella knows she has, at least, ventured a step. She did not expect progress so quickly. Though it may still be hours before she joins the Prince and Hannah.

A satisfied smile appears on Gabriella's lips.

She settles into her seat on the chair. Nothing would give her greater pleasure than to keep them waiting. And guessing.

Creak. Gabriella is more than pleased for the maid to take her time.

Until she recalls the frightened servants in the courtyard. Realizing that the Prince, or possibly even this strange Hannah, might take their rage out on the girl.

Fury blazes through Gabriella. Let them try. They will have to deal with her.

Besides, she reminds herself. No one gave a time to arrive. They simply said to join them.

Gabriella smiles to herself. She is confident she could outwit the Prince. Her smile fades a little. As long as she restrains her tongue. And her temper.

Hannah, on the other hand, always won their arguments. She was patient enough to wait Gabriella out. No matter how clever Gabriella tried to be, Hannah foresaw the action she would take.

Suddenly, Gabriella remembers the realization she had on the journey to the Palace. And her mouth falls open.

She knows exactly how Hannah saw her actions before Gabriella took them. Cheater! Thinks Gabriella, with equal parts outrage and admiration.

Hannah had prescience even at that young an age.

Gabriella slowly closes her mouth. As the inevitable next realization surfaces. Hannah never told anyone. Not even her.

She is wounded. Wanting to run to her sister to ask why. But she cannot. And her heart twinges for the time passed and the possibilities lost.

Until Gabriella must admit that she never told Hannah about her dreams. Or the messages that came when she wandered the woods alone.

Neither of them felt safe enough to share their most precious gifts.

And Gabriella knows precisely why.

The days when their abilities would be recognized as gifts have long passed. They are suspect. Frightening. And labelled as a curse.

Or worse. Parents convince their children that their innate and precious ability is merely a figment of the imagination. And whatever activity coaxed the gift to the surface is quickly ended.

Gabriella and Hannah were very lucky. They grew up in a privileged home. One that still revered the old ways.

Her parents knew, one day, those ways might be the only thing to save their lives. And the people they love.

And yet, even in such a supportive home, neither Gabriella nor Hannah felt safe enough to share the gifts that had appeared.

That is the power of society.

Even when the home is fortified and privileged. The outer world wields a large sword.

Creak. The sound brings Gabriella back. The girl must be close to the door by now. When another step does not quickly follow, she has to grip the arms of the chair.

Remembering her promise to be patient, Gabriella shifts her attention.

She observes the room. Inspecting the ornate, carved bed. The overbearing wardrobe with feet shaped like gargoyle claws. And the rugs imported from far away. So thick and darkly coloured, they might hide adders and scorpions.

Gabriella knows the rugs, wardrobes, and beds did not choose to be fashioned into pieces that evoke fear. Despite the shapes and patterns chosen by their creators. Possibly even commissioned by the Prince.

Like most of us, these objects merely wish to be of service. To be admired. And loved. Unless, of course, they have been mistreated.

Gabriella evaluates each piece. Though she may be impatient with people, she has infinite patience for beautiful creations like these tapestries and carvings.

For many hours of her younger years, they were her dear friends and confidants.

When Gabriella was still little, Queen Isabel was convinced

she could be forced to be as refined a girl as Hannah was naturally. After all, they were twins.

Little did her mother realize that Gabriella's wild spirit refused to sit still, look pretty, and, least of all, please others.

Though this did not keep her mother from trying.

One of the methods her mother attempted was to lock Gabriella in her room with her studies. Or with needlepoint. Or with an elaborate dress to wear.

None of which, Gabriella would do.

Instead, she spent hours listening to the tales told by the wardrobe, chairs, brushes, linen, and even the dresses.

They spoke of the hands that crafted them. The love and care poured into their creation. The harrowing journey to arrive in her land. And the merchants who carried them to town after town.

Until finally, they arrived on Gabriella's doorstep. Each precious item was carried up to her room. And into her life forever.

Or so she thought at the time.

Creak. The girl's progress distracts Gabriella from the pain of memory.

She examines the tapestries hanging on the wall. Of all the decor, these are the most riveting. And the most horrifying.

These tapestries, placed on either side of the bed, are clearly intended to discomfort and unsettle. Possibly even to keep the guests from sleeping.

Though, Gabriella knows strangers held in the Hidden Palace are never really guests. They are prisoners. And entertainment.

These tapestries are a reminder not to take on the Prince. Or to flee. Each graphically displays the fate to befall anyone who dares to defy him.

The one to the left of her bed is a scene from a land far away. A land that may not even exist. But Gabriella knows the beasts on the artwork well. Though she has never seen them, she studied many creatures with Serafina.

She leans in to get a closer look. These are lions. Magnificent and voracious. They feast on the neck of a man. The head is completely gone. And the body awaits their bloody jaws.

Gabriella sits quietly. Knowing this game well. She waits, offering her attention to the tapestry with an open and kind heart.

There is the artist's tale. Woven with threads. Graphic in imagery. Most often, a story of battle. Complete with victor and victim.

And then, there is the tale the creation wishes to share.

This is the interesting one. The hidden tale. Gabriella can only imagine that a hidden tale, in such a place as the Hidden Palace, must be quite incredible.

Creak. Now Gabriella is frustrated for a contrary reason. Should the tapestry decide to talk, she does not want the girl interrupting the story.

Quick, she whispers in her mind. We do not have much time. Tell me your story.

She can feel the tapestry's scepticism. No one is interested in my story.

Gabriella smiles. And, the tapestry realizes, this is the first time anyone has asked.

Not even the artist, who held and wove her threads for months on end, had the courtesy to ask what she had to say.

I am interested, Gabriella whispers. I want to hear what you wish to share.

The tapestry is so touched. So grateful to be seen.

She immediately pours out her heart.

FIVE

THE TAPESTRY REMEMBERS her youth well. I was forged in a time long before your birth, she begins. And Gabriella cannot help but lean forward like a child being read her favourite tale.

Those were the days of honour and kindness, the tapestry explains, with a touch of sadness. When neighbours did not hesitate to help one another.

Gabriella glances at the lions gorging on the flesh of a man.

Yes, the tapestry admits. Even in days when generosity is the norm, there is darkness. Some would say, you cannot have one without the other.

I was born of a man who believed more in the darkness than in the light. As a miser clutches gold, some beings clutch the pain. This was the truth for my creator.

He was brilliant with the thread, offers Gabriella, addressing the tapestry silently. Using her thoughts. Partly out of respect. Partly to avoid scaring the maid just outside her door.

The colours and imagery are breathtaking, she adds.

All the more painful the burden I bear, counters the tapestry. For think of what I could have been. A portrait of beauty and desire. Or courage and valour. Even a landscape would have been preferable.

Gabriella watches a gentle ripple flow through the heavy wool. Like a sigh.

Instead, I am the visage of horror. The tapestry falls silent. Her lack of words a deep reproach to the man who used her wool to evoke pain.

Creak. Gabriella jumps in her seat. Entranced by this gracious creation, she forgot momentarily about the maid.

A flash of concern strikes her mind like lightning. What if the girl can hear the conversation? It is unlikely. But still possible.

Gabriella has no idea how things work here in the Palace. What if the maid can hear? What if that is the reason she is taking so long? And she was sent to spy on her.

She reports back to her master. And Gabriella ends up shackled in the dungeon!

Unable to help Adrian. Unable to break the spell placed on Hannah. Her two dearest friends lost forever in the depths of this nightmare —

Gabriella! The tapestry speaks sharply into her mind.

Gabriella sits up straight. Snapped from her spiral of doom and devastation.

You must not listen to the whispers, admonishes the tapestry. These walls were built to evoke paranoia. They spin your deepest suspicions into lies. When you are held prisoner by dark thoughts, no bars or keys are needed.

Strangely, Gabriella is not surprised the tapestry knows her name. But she is startled that the tapestry can read thoughts that she did not project.

The art of hearing another's thoughts is a subtle and masterful process. Most cannot hear anything unless the one person consciously directs her end of the conversation toward the other.

Much like turning your head toward your companion in a noisy hall. The direction makes all the difference.

Hearing the involuntary whispers in the back of someone's mind, however...

That requires talent. And training.

How...? Gabriella begins.

Think of my existence. Hours upon hours hung on a wall. With only the quietest beings surrounding my days.

Gabriella looks around the room at the wardrobe. The bed. The dresser. The rugs. If she focuses her attention, she can feel the subtle energy of each of them. Wanting to join the conversation. Yet respectfully declining to speak.

She suddenly realizes that this tapestry is the Queen of the Room.

She dictates the rules of order. The way things are done. And the role each object may play. The fact that Gabriella is speaking with her is no accident.

Just because humans turned their backs on the ancient ways, does not mean the rest of us did the same, the tapestry states. Amused that Gabriella has finally realized that the tapestry engaged her. Not the other way around.

There are many things humans have decided are no longer real. That does not make them any less real to us, she adds.

My apologies, Gabriella says, still a little shaken.

She is uncomfortable with the notion that her thoughts are as easy to read as a book. But her discomfort does not change the reality. Nor does it keep her from wanting to hear the rest of the tapestry's story.

Pray, continue your tale, requests Gabriella. And the tapestry kindly agrees.

I was woven when the tide began to turn. From the days of joy, to the days of woe.

She pauses, unsure whether to place her burden on this child's shoulders.

No matter how kind the offer to listen. Or how long since she had last been heard by a human, the tapestry can tell that Gabriella already bears more than her fair share.

Yet she knows that, somehow, her story must be vital to Gabriella's task. Or the young Messenger would not have been placed in her room.

Under her guidance. And so, she decides to continue.

My creation was no whim. No mere outpouring of destruction onto a canvas, the tapestry pauses. Emphasizing the importance of what she is about to say. Gabriella listens carefully.

No. I was created as one of a series of spells cast on this land.

A wave of creation poured into the world to turn the people from believing in the everlasting flow of sacred beauty. By directing their gaze from the warmth of love and onto the shadows of doubt. Their hearts were forever hardened to stone.

That, the tapestry adds, is how the Great Prince has come to possess such power.

The Queen of the Room directs all her attention to Gabriella, speaking her next words with grave focus.

Unravelling the spell is the only way he can be stopped.

A chill runs up Gabriella's spine.

Creak. Gabriella's head whips to look at the entrance to her room.

And there, at the worst possible moment, stands the maid.

Staring at her.

SIX

Gabriella stares back. Locking the maid in her gaze. She forces herself not to look at the tapestry. Not to give away the conversation that has been shared.

Gabriella has no reason to believe the maid heard a single word.

And yet, her body coils. Waiting for the maid to bolt. Ready to give chase.

Complete silence hangs between them. Each woman anticipating the other's move. Neither sure what dance they have begun.

Breathe, whispers the tapestry.

Luckily, all her training and time alone prepared Gabriella to expect the tapestry's guidance. Otherwise, she would have jumped from the chair.

And who knows what the maid would have done.

Gabriella slowly, carefully, pulls herself to sit up taller. Moving in increments.

As she does so, she dons the inner cloak of royalty.

Claiming the shift from a guarded fugitive to a calm and strong sovereign. Her external expression, in body language and facial expression, morphs from suspicion to regal command.

The maid responds in kind, clearly more comfortable with Gabriella taking charge.

She looks less like a fawn ready to bolt. And more like a servant awaiting orders.

"I see you have brought my clothes," begins Gabriella.

Affecting the tone she remembers from her mother. Gabriella may as well imitate the one she admires. At least until she is more comfortable playing this role.

The maid curtsies. Still unable to speak or step closer to Gabriella.

But at least she is no longer frozen. Gabriella may end up dressed today, after all.

The tapestry chortles. Stop that, admonishes Gabriella. You shouldn't eavesdrop on my thoughts.

You shouldn't broadcast them at full volume, retorts the tapestry. Half the palace can hear what you are thinking.

Gabriella's brow furrows. She must ask the tapestry how to avoid being so loud. Otherwise, she will not be able to accomplish a thing in this wretched place.

Seeing her displeasure, the maid takes a step back. And glances at the door.

Gabriella quickly corrects her error. She dons a calm and commanding expression. As much as she wants to be kind and patient with this girl, Gabriella knows that nothing will get done unless she takes the reins.

"Step forward," Gabriella insists. "The Prince and his Lady have asked me to dine with them."

Gabriella looks at the maid, pointedly. "And I imagine the Prince does not like to be kept waiting."

The maid freezes. And for a moment, Gabriella wonders if she chose the wrong tact.

But the maid quickly curtsies. And lurches toward her like a calf that has been prodded with hot iron. Dropping the clothes in the process.

The maid quickly squeezes her eyes shut and braces for the expected blow.

Gabriella remains in her chair. Watching this poor creature navigate each circumstance while expecting only the worst.

Her heart aches for the girl. And the horrible reality of the only world she has witnessed. And yet, Gabriella knows, she cannot reveal her hand.

She must learn the ways of this Palace before she shows her true self.

For as tender and kind as this girl appears, Gabriella cannot know who is her enemy. And who might be a friend.

She must be careful.

After several moments, the girl opens her eyes. Unsure why she has not been punished. But knowing she should not delay or surely the lash will come.

The maid slowly picks up the clothes. Then steps toward Gabriella.

She does not make eye contact. Her eyes fix on the floor. As she slowly holds the pile of clothing out toward the strange guest.

Gabriella remains still. Restraining every instinct to grab the clothing and dress herself. But she must stay true to the role.

No matter how distasteful she finds the pretending.

Gabriella clears her throat to get the maid's attention. The girl looks up, startled.

"I assume you were sent here to assist me in dressing," Gabriella states, matter of factly. The girl's hands shake. But her head quickly nods.

"Then let us see if we cannot achieve that goal with efficiency." Gabriella gently takes the pile and holds the clothing on her lap.

As soon as the clothing touches her skin, Gabriella knows the items have been searched, examined, and washed.

She is grateful for the cleaning, but immediately grows suspicious.

Why are they not forcing her to dress like the Princess they expect her to be? What could be gained by allowing her to dress in the clothes that make her most comfortable?

Perhaps Hannah spoke up for her, she ventures. Though she doubts it. She would have expected that behaviour from her Hannah.

Not from Shadow Hannah.

No, Gabriella thinks, there must be another reason for returning my clothes. They may want me to feel at ease. Let my guard down. And assume that life at the Palace operates the same way life does everywhere else.

Except she knows very well that nothing at the Hidden Palace is like the rest of the world.

Gabriella shakes off the questions. They do not matter. She must get dressed and get on with her mission. Whatever that may be.

Still avoiding Gabriella's gaze, the girl takes the first item off the pile. She cannot help but stare at the strange blouse. The manly cut of such a fine fabric.

Gabriella feels the maid wondering what kind of woman wears a man's shirt? Even if it is made of soft cloth?

She senses the questions flickering through the young maid's mind. For just a moment, curiosity wins over fear.

And just as suddenly, the maid glances back at the door.

Terrified. As though expecting soldiers to rush the room. And lock her away for her insolence.

Gabriella feels the girl's battle. Between instilled expectations and an inquisitive nature. But Gabriella dare not engage the discussion.

Instead, she sits, like an expectant statue. A guise deeply foreign.

Good, says the tapestry. Nearly sending Gabriella to the ceiling. The stranger the disguise, the further the truth will be from their minds. You are right to be careful.

Gabriella keeps her gaze on the clothing in her hands. Though she desperately wants to search the maid's expression for any sign of listening.

Are you sure she cannot hear us? asks Gabriella. She is very quiet. She may well have the gift.

No, states the tapestry, she is silent out of fear. And that fear is very effective in keeping her mind from hearing what we share. To hear the whispers of others, one requires both inner silence and confidence. This girl has neither.

For the second time since the girl entered the room, Gabriella feels a pang of compassion. Though her stoic face reveals nothing.

The girl holds Gabriella's blouse awkwardly. As though she expects the strange object to scorch her skin.

Gabriella sighs. Wondering whether this girl has ever waited on a guest before.

"Hold the blouse up higher," Gabriella instructs. The maid does as she is told.

With the garment blocking the maid's view, Gabriella feels safe removing her own bed clothing without shocking her.

"Stay still," she commands. "I am going to remove my garment so that you can assist me to put on the blouse. Understand?"

The girl squeaks an acknowledgement. She lifts the blouse even higher to shield her gaze. And provide the Princess with privacy.

She dare not witness the flesh of a regal woman who wears such a manly garment. Who knows what she might look like under her bedclothes? She might have horrible skin. Or battle wounds. Or some strange disfigurement!

As Gabriella pulls off her nightshift, she notices that the girl has begun to tremble.

Whatever does she expect from her? That she might lash out like a provoked serpent? With no compassion for another person's predicament?

As Gabriella drops the shift behind her chair, she realizes that is exactly what she expects. For we only expect the ways we have been treated in the world. No less and no more.

With a heavy heart, Gabriella brings herself to speak. "I am ready."

The girl simply trembles.

"You need not look at me," offers Gabriella. "Though I would hope that I am not hideous."

She cannot help but take some offense at the girl's inaction.

Gabriella is all too used to being treated like a boy. She has always encouraged people to perceive her as capable. But this avoidance of looking at her is beginning to be insulting.

The girl quickly curtsies to avoid the impression of insubordination. But still she refuses to look at Gabriella. Making dressing her all but impossible.

"Take a step forward," demands Gabriella. The girl does as she is told.

"Now. Lift the shirt and I will guide myself into the sleeves," she instructs. "You can keep your eyes closed if you wish."

The girl squeezes her eyes shut. And allows Gabriella to slide awkwardly into the familiar garment.

"Let go." The girl quickly relinquishes the blouse. Eyes still firmly shut.

Gabriella stares at the wretched girl. Wanting to be offended. Wishing she could sustain her hurt feelings. But all she can do is laugh inside.

If only Hannah could see this. Gabriella would be the butt of jokes for months!

Gabriella smiles, until she remembers that her Hannah is gone. Or, at the very least, frozen deep inside the strange imposter that walks these halls.

Suddenly, Gabriella has no more energy for this tiresome dance.

"Please leave," she requests softly. "I will dress myself."

The maid's eyes snap open. Frightened that she will be punished. Searching Gabriella's face for some sign of rage or retribution.

But she can see no such evil. The maid sees only pain. And sadness.

She knows these feelings well.

And so, wanting to give the Princess her privacy and not wanting to risk the sudden transmutation of one feeling into another, as she has seen so often, the maid quickly turns on her heels and disappears out the door.

Leaving Gabriella alone with her heartache.

SEVEN

GABRIELLA CAREFULLY DESCENDS the stairs. She glances around the empty, cavernous Hall that she had traversed earlier in the wee hours of the morning. Not a soul can be seen.

And yet. She feels the presence.

Is that the Palace? Or something else? Could there be some force that watches every movement inside these walls?

In a land under a dark and insidious spell, anything is possible.

She steps off the final stair. And looks at the multiple hallways leading in different directions.

Knowing, all of a sudden, that this maze of corridors is part of the Palace's strength. The greater a person's indecision, the less likely she can focus on anything but fear.

Gabriella's stomach grumbles. She silently chastises her body.

Now is not the time to be insistent. Or cave to the demands of hunger. I must focus. And refuse to play victim to the Palace's tricks. Otherwise, she will know all it takes to secure my defeat is entrapment with the scent of food.

She falls silent. Clasping her hands together. Regaining control.

Gabriella can feel the Palace watching. Carefully, guardedly, she focuses on Hannah. Wondering whether the connection to her twin still guides her.

Though the sensation is faint, she feels the distinct energy pattern of her sister.

Gabriella opens her eyes. Deliberately turning to her left, she tightly restrains any sense of victory. For fear of provoking a reaction from the Palace.

Feeling the Palace's rage, Gabriella moves quickly to counter the negative force.

And promptly strides down the hallway that leads to the main dining hall.

She can hear the whispers of servants in the walls. Keeping their voices tight but needing to speak to complete their tasks.

Gabriella cannot escape the pervasive fear. She feels the weight. The urge to stand still and pray no one sees you. And the counter-urge to run like the wind.

Neither is of help to her in this situation.

She must hold her mind steady and move forward with grace and assurance.

Suddenly, she realizes, the whispers were not from servants. She is hearing the whispers of the walls.

Gabriella places one foot in front of the other. Continuing to move forward. She cannot help but be horrified and curious.

Are the stones whispering? Are there spirits in the walls? Has the mortar captured the conversations from all the years people have lived in the Palace?

Is she meant to listen? Or ignore them?

Gabriella stops. Closes her eyes. Holding herself still.

She cannot be blown by the wind. She must keep her centre or all will be lost.

The force of the whispers feel like a cyclone whirling around her. Blowing her clothes and hair. Trying to distract her from her task.

There – in the middle of the cyclone – she finds the calm.

The eye. The quiet space. And, in that gap, she reconnects with her source. The Love that protects her. The force that even the Hidden Palace cannot impede.

And the whispers stop.

Gabriella stands in the hush of silence. As though the walls have never experienced peace. And are stunned by its existence.

She opens her eyes. Looking at the ancient stones. Wondering whether to engage them. Would they even know how to speak the truth anymore?

Gabriella knows that all stone is born in honour. They are the children of the earth. Solid. True. Dependable.

But like any porous being, they absorb the atmosphere where they are placed.

If they are surrounded by doubt and hatred and conniving, they forget their true nature. One of honour and strength.

They cannot help but join with their community. They are born to support.

If they are asked to hold lies, they hold lies. If they are asked to hold grief, they hold grief. Gabriella cannot help herself.

She reaches out and touches the stone. Deep compassion and sorrow in her heart.

A shiver waves through the mortar. And as much as she wants to pull away in fear, she does not. She holds her palm of compassion to the stone.

Wanting the ancient structure to feel her love.

They waited centuries to be pulled from the earth, only to be placed in these walls. And filled with hatred. What must that be like?

Her heart breaks for these determined souls. Holding together for the sake of the one that put them here. Yet completely unappreciated.

A sudden noise distracts her. Gabriella instinctively pulls her hand back; ready to defend. Searching the hallway for the approaching opponent.

Then she knows. The Palace spoke. Scaring her from expressing kindness.

The cankerous heart does not want her interfering with the dark power. For as much as dark power consumes, killing the one who wields it. Power is power.

What could have been the strongest force in the universe, nurturing all that is good, has been turned to a force that burns. Consumes. Destroys.

And yet. Gabriella is struck by a brilliant insight.

She wants to dance. To leap. To sing joy to the walls.

But she pulls the insight close and tucks it in her heart.

Gabriella cannot risk the Palace hearing this brilliance. She cannot let the secret slip away into the darkness. Never to be heard again.

She must hold it close. Nurture and protect it.

So that when the dragon of truth has grown and is ready to be unleashed, the winged creature will be strong and ready for battle.

She silently thanks the heavens for this gift.

Gabriella resumes her walk down the hall. Conscious of the amazed and perplexed silence that surrounds her.

She wonders whether their silence is deep annoyance. The whispers have stopped so they can watch her. Track her.

And keep her from disturbing their familiar ways.

No. She realizes. They have stopped to take notice.

For though stones are known for being stubborn, they are excellent listeners. They sense the shift in the earth. And know when to ready themselves.

For though the change sometimes takes years, they are always the first to sense a new tide. They have to be. Since their transformation takes so long.

But the stones in the Palace can feel the time has come.

The time to change. And adapt.

EIGHT

GABRIELLA EXITS THE DARK HALLWAY. Stepping into the brilliant light of the Dining Hall. Like a child exiting the womb, she feels as though she has entered another world. She stands, amazed, taking in the sudden shift of air, light, and décor.

The walls are several stories high. Built of stone and lined with huge beams of wood. The beams arch all the way up to the roof forming a dome like in a church.

Most beautiful of all, held between each beam, is a pane of stained glass. Bearing artistic renditions of life in each of the twelve main kingdoms of the Great Lands.

Shafts of brilliant sunlight careen through the glass down to the centre of the room. Caressing a long and elegant table with the faint glow of soft colour.

Despite being raised as a child of royalty, Gabriella has never witnessed such a display of opulence. Massive candelabras line the centre, ablaze with dozens of candlesticks. As though competing to outshine the sun.

Nestled around the golden objects are branches of elder and cedar and mistletoe. As though this were a day of great celebration. And the sacred trees must give branches to show gratitude for her arrival.

Gabriella looks up to see her sister at one end of the excessively long table and the Great Prince at the other. She suddenly realizes she must have been standing and staring for several minutes.

Each looks at her with an expression of amusement.

For a fleeting second, she feels like the child who, lost in a world of beauty, has once again forgotten the social graces. Though she never understood why nods and curtseys and formal words were more valuable than pure, expressed joy.

Then she realizes. She has been manipulated.

The Great Prince wanted to impress her. To show off. To make a display so ostentatious that she could not help but be overwhelmed.

Gabriella levels her gaze at the Prince. Steeling her nerves, her bones, and her eyes. Letting her armour settle as she prepares for battle. No matter that she is not actually wearing chainmail. Her methods of protection are more powerful.

The strength she bears is in her soul. Let the Prince play his games. She is ready.

Doubt flashes in his eyes.

And that is all she needs. Gabriella turns from him. Strides toward her sister. Face aglow and arms held out.

She has come here for Hannah. Not the Prince.

Gabriella is not deceived for a moment by this Shadow Hannah. This mirage. She is here for the true one. And she plans to find her.

Hannah stands. And responds, in kind, with her arms held out to Gabriella.

Pulling her close, Gabriella cannot help but hope she will feel their connection. Their heart to heart bond.

But she does not.

Hannah pulls away, smiles. Gesturing for her sister to sit by her right hand. Gabriella pauses. Recognizing the slight.

Sitting at the right hand of her sister implies she is her humble servant. Her advisor. Nothing more than a support to the Queen.

Gabriella forces herself to nod, graciously. And takes her seat.

She glances at the chair that she should occupy. In the centre of the table. The one she would be offered in a kingdom that had an intention of a kindred alliance. The centre chair implies she is of equal rank to her sister. And the Prince.

And is the one place at this table without a setting. Or a seat.

Gabriella smiles inwardly. At least the rules of the game are clear. And just as fast, she wants to break them. But that would not be the way to proceed. Not yet.

She must walk this tight rope with caution. And care.

The Prince is cunning. She must respect that trait. At least while he has two of her loved ones in his clasp.

Gabriella's heart squeezes. She receives an image of Adrian in her mind.

Blindfolded and bound in a dungeon. Surrounded by death and torture. Trapped with only his thoughts. And Gabriella knows how treacherous thoughts can be.

Enough! She must focus. Thinking of his plight does not help. She will move forward. Only action leads to freedom.

Gabriella turns to her brother-in-law. And nods. Secretly, she wants to take her knife and hurl it down the length of the table into his heart.

But she does not.

Instead, she folds her hands in her lap. Awaiting his response.

Courtesy requires that the King, or Prince, announces that the meal can begin. The Great Prince smiles. Satisfied that his wife's sister has remembered her manners.

He stares at her a moment longer. Knowing it is inappropriate.

The Prince enjoys making her uncomfortable. Almost as much as he savours her dislike. And her sister's jealousy. The combination is intoxicating.

And completely wrong.

He feels Gabriella's fire. Her powerful, rebellious spirit. And craves her passion. His wife is demure and beautiful. Every inch the correct political match. And utterly boring.

He wants Gabriella. He craves a woman of equal strength and passion. That is why he demanded she be brought to his Palace.

So he could possess her within his walls.

Gabriella shifts in her seat, feeling the intensity of his attention.

She wants it to stop. Feeling awkward in front of her sister. But the warrior in her will not drop his gaze.

The Great Prince stares a moment longer. Recognizing his match. This is what he deserves. What he wants. A powerful woman. A Queen.

With a Queen by his side, he would be a true King.

He forces his eyes onto Hannah. Vacant and numb. Mirroring his gestures. Nothing but a fragile doll next to her fiery sibling.

The Prince curses the political manoeuvring and vanity that drew him to marry the elder sister. Then raises his opulent gold chalice.

"I give this feast in honour of the beloved sister of my wife," the Prince begins, shifting his gaze back to Gabriella. Drinking her in. Wishing he could consume her instead of the feast now being carried by his army of servants.

Plate after plate of sumptuous dishes. Filling the length of the table. Roasted pheasant. Candied fruits. Seasoned vegetables. Bottles of wine. Carafes of sauce. And a full-length roasted swordfish placed at the centre.

The Prince relishes Gabriella's awe.

She has never seen such sumptuous plenty. So many pleasures in one sitting. Certainly, she has never laid eyes on a swordfish.

All of it his.

The Prince waits for the silence to force Gabriella's gaze from the culinary treasures back to him. Trapped by convention, she awaits his speech. And must accept his stare.

She does not flinch. And he wants her all the more.

"Welcome to our palace. May you indulge your every desire. May you discover your deepest power. May you honour us with your continued presence. And may you never wish to leave."

The Prince lifts his chalice higher, indicating that Gabriella must return the gesture. And she does. Sending a chill down his spine.

Gabriella knows his blessing was, in truth, a challenge.

She can feel the Prince's desire. She sees he wants to possess her. To hold her forever in his domain. And secure her as yet another prize.

Gabriella is not fooled. She does not take his attention as flattery. Or anything special. She spent too many years, watching suitor after suitor want, need, beg to own Hannah.

She knows the Prince is only interested in possession. Little does he realize that, in fact, he is the one possessed. As she recognizes the truth, Gabriella feels the rush of power. The desire to control him. The intense pull to use his need against him.

And she sees the Prince respond. Looking up from his plate. Like a puppet responding to the tug of a string. The rush of power flows between them.

Gabriella drops her gaze. Breaking the connection.

She immediately focuses inside. On her self. Relinquishing the power that rushed over her. She reaches deep into the earth. And touches something much bigger.

The source so deep it has no words. Only the ever-flowing expression of all that is. A power older than anything on this planet. Any being she can touch.

Suddenly, she is calm.

And remembers that no creature truly holds sway over another. No matter how powerful the person seems. No matter how much he has. Or who he is in league with, each and every being is free.

For millennia humans have created myths about a force that can steal our souls.

But when you study the stories, every time, the person is given a choice. Every time, the human gives their soul freely in exchange for Power. Control. Money.

We have created vast mythologies about being duped, victimized, swept away. Somehow, we have convinced ourselves that we are innocent.

The truth is we choose to be possessed.

Gabriella lifts her gaze. Looking directly at Hannah, eating her meal with precise movements. Playing a part. Completely void of feeling.

Vacant of her soul.

Gabriella's heart breaks as she realizes the truth for the first time. She wants to scream. To curse. To throw her plate, smashing the china into a thousand pieces.

Instead, she forces herself to pick up her gold utensils from the elegant setting. And surveys the delicacies arranged on her plate by the servants.

She cuts into the rich, dark pheasant meat. Places a bite in her mouth. And chews.

Gabriella feels the weight of silence. The vast expanse between the two lovers at either end of the table. Two souls woven together in marriage for all time.

She wants to curse Astriel. Though that would not be fair.

But she is sure the angel knew what Gabriella would come to realize once she arrived. That, as much as Gabriella wants to believe Hannah is the victim of a spell, she realizes that Hannah is the one who selected this fate.

Her sister chose to be imprisoned. And her sister must find the key.

The warrior inside Gabriella rebels. This is why I came! This is my sole purpose!

She skewers a candied plum. Raises the catch to her lips. Bites it. Frustrated. Infuriated. Still, she chews.

Until suddenly, she stops.

And realizes she played a part in Hannah's story. She insisted on being the strong one. The rescuer. The knight in shining armour.

What role was left for her sister but to play the damsel?

Gabriella clutches her cutlery to keep the tears from rolling down her cheeks.

And whispers a silent apology.

NINE

DEEP IN THE BOWELS of the Palace, Adrian can feel Gabriella's pain. This is the true torture.

Not the dark. Or the stench. Or the dripping water. But the overwhelming wave of her anguish. And the fact that he can do nothing.

He rails against his chains.

Knowing full well all the anger does is cost him his strength. And entertain his captors.

The game of imprisonment is a test. One that requires careful and studied movement. Much like chess. Except this is a challenge of the soul.

Losing touch with himself is the cost.

Each distraction is a trick. An illusion. A lure trying to pull him from the truth.

He sits on the cold stone floor. Focused on his precise location. Focused on the sensation in his body. If he can stay present to where he is, to the feeling in his muscles. He stands a chance of staying sane.

Adrian is no stranger to the tests of the mind. His master put him through many trials in his training. And this is not the first time he has been deeply grateful.

He recognizes that the tests, designed to build his fortitude and focus, were acts of love. Adrian wants to weep. But his body has no water to spare.

When he was undergoing the trials, he thought only that his master was asking him to become strong. To put his soul in the fire. And find the gold at its core.

Each act that Adrian thought was pure torture was, in truth, an embrace of love. Preparation for the day when a creature, such as the Prince, would enact the same gestures out of hate.

But the gesture is what matters. Whether motivated by hate or love, the gesture is the act of transformation. The gesture is the catalyst.

As an Alchemist, Adrian must always be grateful for the catalyst.

He suddenly realizes that in every catalyst is the very seed of love. The element that gives itself to transform another is the deepest act of generosity.

Adrian takes a deep breath.

He is present again. Feeling the metal against his skin. The cuffs around his wrists. That are connected to a chain that is bolted to the floor.

He cannot see the cuffs or the chains or the bolts. The wretched, coarse material wrapped around his eyes blocks out every ounce of light.

Not that a dungeon holds much light anyway. Nor can Adrian feel light on the surface of his skin. He knows that he is deep under the earth.

That is the first mistake his captors made.

They assume by placing him deep in the bowels of the Palace that he is deprived of power. That he cannot feel the light of the sun or sense the water deep in the earth. And that is where they are wrong.

Dead wrong.

The second mistake was placing a blindfold on his eyes.

For an Alchemist's talent is reinforced by blocking out the distractions of the everyday world. Rather than tormenting him, they naturally placed his focus inside. Activating his power.

Adrian focuses on the sensation of the metal cuffs. He savours the feeling. The cool edges. The smooth material. The circular flow of the opening.

In a world devoid of light, the feeling of the metal against his skin is a gift.

The metal is his friend. Keeping him company. Whispering to him in the shadows of the Palace. He does not choose to feel the cuffs are his enemy. Or his captors.

He feels the cuffs are his closest allies. His informants. A way out of this treacherous place.

Adrian flows all the love in his being to the cuffs. The fiery love pours from his heart, down his arms, into the metal around his wrists. Heating the essence of the steel. Releasing the material from its static state. Allowing it to bend and flow and change shape. Each component of the metal dancing with freedom.

The flame unites them. Adrian. The metal. All are one.

As they dance together, in the ecstasy of love and creation, Adrian feels the metal bending, softening, beginning to burn his skin.

That's when he shifts. Pulls the fire back. And sends a fierce and sudden chill.

In an instant, he hears a sharp CRACK! And the cuffs fall from his wrists.

Adrian breathes a deep sigh. And sends gratitude to the elements.

He slowly reaches up and unties the material knotted around his eyes.

His fingers are tired and tense. And take several moments to understand the feel of the ragged fraction of a sack that is wrapped around his head. Finding the edges that have been pulled into a knot.

Finally, his fingers feel the small gap that can loosen the material. He wedges the gap open, breaking the knot into two separate strips of fabric.

He removes the cloth. Keeping his eyes shut a moment longer. Lifting them open with tender care. Not wanting to shock his body or make any unnecessary sound.

And the blindfold falls into his lap.

Adrian conscientiously keeps his heart quiet and calm. As much as he wishes to express his joy and gratitude, he must stay balanced to keep from drawing the attention of the Palace. And by extension, the guards.

He cannot hide the fact that there has been a shift.

But he can keep from lighting emotional flares that provoke the Palace. And send the guards running to his cell.

He takes another deep breath. Opens his eyes fully. And looks around.

The sight of the cell makes Adrian want to close his eyes again. The stones weep with grime. The cracks are void of any creatures.

The space is deeply stagnant and neglected. Filled with the tears and agony of innumerable people. No wonder even the Palace does not wish to claim this space. This is the abandoned cell of shadows.

No one wishes to remember this place. Not even the Prince.

Though he may play at being proud of these dungeons. He does not spend any time here. He does not wish to think of the prisoners. Nor does he want the world to know this space other than to feel the threat of it.

But that is not the same as claiming a place. And knowing it belongs inside his Palace. No. Adrian realizes. In fact, the Prince is deeply ashamed of the Dungeons.

And that is his fatal mistake.

For the Dungeons feel his shame. And the more rejected they feel, the more they want to be seen. Now, the Prince has put an Alchemist Wizard into the bowels of his house.

And what is a Wizard to do but to bring the light of the gods to the darkness?

That is his calling. That is his way in the world.

He must summon the lightning.

Adrian hears the response. Thunder. Crashing over the Palace.

The soft edge of a smile rises on his lips.

Crash. The Thunder calls. Then draws even closer. *Crash!*

Adrian closes his eyes. Rising, slowly to his feet. Using the stones as support. He has not been on his feet for days. And his legs are weakened.

Crash! The sound of the thunder gives him strength. And he releases the wall.

Adrian looks deep into his being. And calls to the lightning. Visualizing the ragged bolts ripping through him. Lighting up the sky of his heart.

Immediately, he knows. He feels the power.

The same bolts have ripped through the sky outside. Adrian

feels the charge run through the Palace. And hears the screams of the villagers fleeing for shelter.

A sheet of rain pours from the sky. And the Lightning and Thunder gods play.

Every hair on Adrian's body feels electrified with the charge in the air. The smile on his face broadens.

The storm provides the perfect cover. Quickly, he seeks the door of his cell.

Adrian senses that the guards have clamoured up to the level that affords them a view of the spectacle outside.

He can hear their laughter. Echoing from a few floors above.

Another gift of being deprived of all sensory input for days on end is the sharp perception of every sense once it is set free.

Adrian hears the claws of the rats. The scurrying of the beetles. And the laboured breathing of the other prisoners.

He pauses. Wondering for a moment whether he is meant to set them free.

Not yet. The message comes. He cannot risk the attention.

Nor can he carry them all to freedom. If he were to try, he would only bring about the death of every person.

He must move forward. Quietly. Discreetly.

And without provoking the guards. Much as he would love to toy with them for all of their vicious acts towards the others that Adrian was forced to witness.

Adrian pauses to compose himself. Knowing that the guards, in their malicious role, deliberately chose to torture the other prisoners within earshot of him.

They must have been instructed that to torture Adrian would only make him stronger. Or give him an opportunity for escape.

The weak-willed are always a doorway for the powerful.

But when the weak torture the innocent, that is true pain for the strong of heart. Made worse because he feels every lash taken out on another. Every anguish of one lover listening to the torture of the other.

Adrian feels the desire for vengeance. Lets it course through his veins long enough to give him strength. Then sends it to the gods.

He cannot afford to be distracted by a fool's errand. He must seek his Messenger. And make sure she is safe.

Even as he prays, and takes each step with his aching muscles, he beseeches the gods not to torture Gabriella.

Because if they do, he will wage war. No one will cause her pain. Not if he has strength to fight.

Adrian gasps and reaches for the wall. Steadying his starved and tired body.

Oh dear goddess, help him. He has fallen in love.

Adrian swears he hears the angels laughing. He forces himself from the wall. And up the stairwell. So glad I entertain you, he thinks, annoyed.

And begins the long process of climbing the dungeon stairs.

Knowing in his heart that he cannot leave without Gabriella. That he must help her in any way she needs.

For he is now her servant. Her love.

Even if he may never utter the words.

TEN

Hannah sits in her chamber. Staring in the mirror. She cannot feel a thing. A prisoner in her own body. Somehow, she knows she is trapped. And yet…

She does not know what to do.

Like she is watching a strange tale unravelling before her and has no power to impact the telling. Even though she appears to be the star.

How did she get here? What is happening? Did she truly see Gabriella? Or did she imagine it? Could she be asleep in her parents' home? Is this insanity only a nightmare?

Gripped, suddenly, with deep panic. Hannah knows she cannot tell the difference. She has lost the ability to tell dream from reality.

She resists the urge to scream at the top of her lungs. Somehow, she knows it will bring no good. Instead, Hannah forces herself to stand. She walks to the side table and reaches for the bell. Ringing for her maid.

As she waits, Hannah presses her fingernail into the flesh of her index finger.

Nothing.

She cannot feel her own fingertips. What strange existence is this? How did she get here?

She presses harder. Insisting that her hand respond with sensation. She stops when blood breaks through the skin and, still, she cannot feel.

Hannah looks around. Examining the strange furniture. Wondering whether she should have a connection to this place. She cannot remember ... anything.

How is it possible that she does not remember how she got here? Or how long she has been in this place? Is it her home?

Hannah is seized by a deeper panic. A sense that something is very wrong.

She whips around and runs to the door. Stopping abruptly, to keep from running into the startled maid.

"Are you all right, my lady?" The maid queries.

Hannah realizes the young woman looks at her as though she is mad.

The truly terrifying fact is that Hannah does not know. Perhaps she is. She cannot recall anything about her life. Her whereabouts. Or even what has transpired in the last hour.

The maid approaches her like a spooked mare. "Are you having another spell?" she asks. Gently guiding Hannah toward the edge of her bed.

"Best that you sit for a while until you recover your bearings."

Hannah wants to smack the imperious girl for treating her like a three year old.

Until she realizes, she is a three year old.

Unable to speak. Unable to remember. Unable to make decisions.

What on earth has happened? Someone has stolen her will!

The maid swings Hannah's legs up onto the bed. Cooing to her.

"There, there. Be calm now."

No! Hannah screams in her mind. Do not do this! I must leave! I must find —

Her mind goes blank. Who must I find?

Hannah is suddenly lost in a fog. She can see no landmarks. No bearings.

Grasping for a direction. Hannah is confused. Where is she? Who is she?

She stares blankly at the maid. Lying on the bed like a corpse, as the young woman pulls a blanket over her.

"Shhhh," the maid whispers. "Do not worry. This is where you belong. And this is where you must stay."

Hannah finds herself mesmerized by the sound of the young woman's voice. Watching her lips. She is not even sure she hears words. Only the murmur of a sound. Like the wind brushing through the trees.

"The Prince adores you. The Palace must have you. There is nowhere to go."

The maid smooths Hannah's hair. Until her eyelids flutter and close. And her breath steadies.

"That's the way," the maid whispers, in a voice as soothing as a song. "Stay here until someone comes for you."

The maid steps quietly toward the door, whispering, "You belong to us now."

Hannah falls deep, deep down. Landing in a forest. She stands among the trees. And feels the roots under her soft feet. She is comforted by their texture.

She does not feel lost. She feels very much at home. Here. In the middle of the woods. With no one around.

Just her and the glorious cedars. Strong. Regal. Beautiful.

This is her family. She is safe here.

Hannah settles herself against the strong trunk of an ancient grandmother. Curls her legs under her skirt.

And leans back. Safe in the embrace.

She falls asleep.

ELEVEN

GABRIELLA SITS ON THE BED in her room. Feeling the pull of the forest.

The power brings her to tears. She misses the trees of her home deeply. And is not sure why they have suddenly come to her mind. She knows in her heart that the feeling is connected to Hannah.

And she wants to weep for joy.

The connection means she has not lost her sister. Though, the connection is faint. Gabriella knows she has found her sister. Yet her sister is the one who is lost.

Ah. Serafina. She can hear the voice of her teacher in the paradox.

Clearly, there are many connections awakening. All of them woven in the web that leads back to home. Her source. The place where all love resonates.

Gabriella sighs. And feels the pull to sleep. To lay her head down on the bed.

And never wake up.

"Who said that?" She leaps to her feet. Searching the room before realizing that the voice came from the tapestry.

Never listen to the whispers, child, admonishes the tapestry. Must I say it again?

Gabriella lowers her head in deference. Apologizing silently.

No, no, the tapestry adds. I was not scolding. Well, perhaps I was. I simply cannot help myself with humans. You are so resistant to teaching. I imagine, however, the resistance is to listening. Not to the lesson.

So I apologize to you, sweet child, she offers. For you do listen.

Gabriella cannot remember ever meeting a being with such honour.

"What were you saying —" Gabriella begins.

Stop! The tapestry insists with a force that knocks Gabriella down onto the bed.

Speak to me in your mind, she explains quickly. Though the communication is still accessible, there are fewer beings who hear our exchange. And, indeed, barely a handful of humans who practise that skill.

Our conversation is much safer if we speak thought to thought.

I understand, Gabriella replies. Shifting forward, but still leaning against the bed. As though settling in for a long conversation. She returns to her query.

When I felt the pull to go to sleep, you said, "And never wake up." What did you mean?

Ah, the tapestry muses. Now we touch on the true power of the Palace. A dark and strong force that draws on secret desires. The wishes hidden deep in the human psyche. The very secrets that, if they were unearthed, could bring freedom.

The longer they lay buried, she continues, the more they mold and fester and become unruly. Pulling the strings of each person. Keeping them trapped like a weak puppet. And the Palace understands those strings. She reaches for them in each of us. And she always finds them. For she is well practised in the search.

The true question is … When she pulls, will you answer?

The tapestry falls silent. As though waiting for Gabriella to reply.

But Gabriella knows this is not an answer to speak out loud.

This is a query to her soul. A question she alone can ponder and she alone must discover her true reply. As every person must.

The tapestry has been gracious to light the way. But Gabriella must choose the path.

Thank you, sacred one, Gabriella says. I am honoured by your challenge. She pushes away from the bed. And knows immediately that she must act.

And grateful for your teaching. Gabriella lowers her head in reverence.

As she lifts her eyes, she looks directly at the horrific images woven into the tapestry's face. Like scars on a burn victim. The twisted display means nothing.

Only threads woven in a tortured design.

The true beauty of the tapestry is not marred. Nor is her light dimmed. She shines regardless of the images piled on top of her true essence.

She is beautiful. She is loving. And she is not confused.

Oh, how we humans mistake the surface for the essence, muses Gabriella. Imagine if we could look past the shell, no matter how stunning or twisted, and see the true essence.

That seeing would change the world.

And that, she thinks as she strides to the door, is precisely what I intend to do.

TWELVE

ADRIAN PAUSES AT THE EDGE of a long, dark hallway. He catches his breath.

The endless days in the dungeon has taken a toll on his energy. He can bear the lack of food and even the lack of water. But the lack of light has robbed him of strength.

He is unsure how long he was down there. For time in the Palace warps. Leaving him with only a guess of how many days he might have been imprisoned.

What feels like weeks may only be days. And what he is sure has only been a day, may have been a month. No matter, Adrian thinks. The time has gone.

All that is of concern is where he is now. And where he is about to go.

He breathes deeply. Getting a sense of where he is in the Palace.

Adrian lets the whirl of a dizzy spell spiral through his body and release out the crown of his head. Then breathes deeply into the bottom of his stomach.

Finally. He can feel the depths of his body.

Accessible to him in a way he has not known for weeks.

He pauses. Allowing his consciousness to sink down into his

feet. Gaining sensation in his toes. Such a long time sitting in chains had him lose touch with the function and feeling of his toes.

For the first time in days, a slight smile edges Adrian's mouth. He is amused. The smallest of parts on his body. And, yet, so essential for balance and movement.

Even in the depths of darkness, there are gifts of awareness. Or perhaps, that is always the offering available in the dark. We must choose to see it.

Slowly, he opens his eyes.

The hallway has little light. Even with his practised night vision, all he can see are shadows. He knows now why the guards walk with torches. For illumination.

And other purposes.

Adrian shivers. Remembering the screams. He closes his eyes again. Focuses his attention on the present. And explores the hallway with his mind.

Carefully. Sensing the length. And whether anyone awaits.

The space is empty. Not abandoned. He senses a presence. Just not a human one.

He is being watched. Monitored. So he must choose wisely.

Adrian feels the Palace has a game in play. Moving people like chess pieces. She has all the time in the world. And yet.

He feels her impatience.

Adrian pauses. Fascinated. What would make a master player impatient?

Ah. He sighs. Then quickly disguises his pleasure. He cannot risk raising the ire of the Palace. Her rage is easily sparked. Needing minimal fuel to stay lit.

Then she will smite them all.

There is only one thing that can irritate a practised and arrogant player. The unpredictability of youth.

And no one embodies rash, unpredictable behaviour more than Gabriella.

Adrian restrains a smile. Centres himself. For fear, he might bolt down the hallway desperate to find her when he does not have the energy.

Even if he did, he would not risk it. But that is exactly why Gabriella is the player that has thrown the Palace.

Valiant yet bold. Honourable yet rash. Subtle yet obstinate.

She is volatile.

If the Palace is palpably frustrated, Gabriella must be in play. The watchful energy of the walls is focused on the one player that can change the game.

Making this his perfect opportunity to escape.

Adrian's breath catches in his chest. The moment has come. Which will it be? Does he leave the Palace as he swore he would do? Or does he stay to find Gabriella?

He promised to protect her. But which is the way to do that?

He cannot assume that being at her side is safer for either of them. It makes them twice the target. And might make them more vulnerable if they are distracted by their feelings.

Yet, the power they have together. Adrian feels the strength even in the thought. His mind counters the argument. Wielded incorrectly, such power leads to death.

Enough! He scolds himself. And angrily pushes away from the wall.

No more predicting the future. He must act. He must move.

Or he will die where he stands.

As long as the Palace does not feel he is interfering in her game, he can play his own. And then we will see what happens, he muses. Careful to shield his thoughts.

Adrian takes a silent step forward. Listening to the guards below, still entertained by the lightning and thunder. Still amazed by the unseasonable storm.

He senses one of them beginning to question the fantastic display. Only a few thoughts away from wondering whether the show was provoked.

Adrian has just enough time, before they discover he has escaped. He must hurry to the higher floors of the Palace.

By then, he will be out of reach of the dark pull of the dungeons. And will have regained his strength. Now if only he could find a scrap of food.

Moving gently in the darkness, he can tell the walls monitor his movements. They are not concerned. The stones sense his weakness. And do not feel threatened.

Not that he means them any harm.

Blaming the rocks that make up the Palace is the equivalent to blaming his muscle and sinew for moving him forward. They may hold his sword but they do not force him to kill.

No. Adrian does not begrudge the stones their ill-fated location. He feels sorrow for them. As he would for the unfortunate man who finds himself in the fanatical crusade of a zealot.

These are the souls that pay the price. And yet —

Adrian stops in his tracks. They are also the souls that overthrow the unjust. A chill flashes down his spine.

Suddenly, he feels the hallway grow quiet and observant.

Perhaps the stones are just alert to the presence of a revolutionary idea. A notion unlike any other that has occupied this space.

Adrian wants to pause. To whisper to them. To find out what they might know.

But he cannot take the risk. Not now. Not yet.

He is suddenly aware of another source of quiet. The guards downstairs. The laughter has stopped.

He is only moments away from being discovered.

Despite the pain and exhaustion in his limbs, Adrian pushes forward. Running down the hallway. Covering as much distance as he can before the guards find his empty cell.

He turns a sharp corner. Realizing he has no idea where he is. But he can feel the elevation. The fresher air. He is heading in the right direction.

Or the wrong one. Depending on your perspective.

Adrian knows that he has leapt from the fire into the blaze. Time will only tell whether he will come out alive.

But leap he has. And fight he must. For there is only one reason why he is here.

And she is still many floors above him.

THIRTEEN

Gabriella does not have a plan. Only an instinct. Somehow, her feet have brought her to this spot. This place. Outside the Great Prince's salon.

She can feel the energy pulsing from the room. This is where the Palace speaks to him. Whispering words of power. Asking him to be the voice of domination.

Her mind screams for her to run. But her feet force her to stay.

She glances to her left. Then her right. No one is within earshot. No one even dares to enter this space.

For fear of losing their heads.

As warm as the flickering torches in the hallway look and the decorated walls feel, she senses the abandoned ache of the space.

So little love has walked these halls. Her heart breaks for each tile. Each stone. Each elegant sconce holding a regal flame.

Someone cleans them. For they are void of dust. Yet they are neglected. Whoever tends them must come in the middle of the night. And leave as quickly as possible.

Gabriella wants to stroll the hall. To whisper words of appreciation.

She sighs. Turning her gaze back to the formidable wooden door.

Her mission lies behind this entrance. Not in the halls.

Silently, she whispers a promise of return to the torch bearers. Gabriella swears she feels them brighten. Knowing, one day, she will pay them their due.

After a deep, rooting breath, she raises her fist. And pounds on the door.

Chills rush down the hallway. Carrying whispers of shock and wonder. Who dares make noise here? On that door? Is she lost? Is she mad? She must not know what happens when you rap on the regal door —

A sudden hush falls.

Gabriella waits. In silence.

The door yanks open. Before she sees his face, she feels the wave of rage. And hears his unprotected thought: Who dares disturb me here? I will wrench his head from his neck and place it on a spire for all to see.

Gabriella stands strong. Knowing her power. Feeling her purpose.

The moment the Prince sees her, everything changes.

His rage shifts to lust. Gabriella braces herself deeper.

His curse morphs to a smile. She can tell that he believes she is the fly and he is the spider. How fortuitous that she has come right to his web.

Let him believe he is in charge of the trap.

He does not realize that the roles are reversed. He is the one being watched. She is the one with razored talons and a sharp beak.

She is the Raven. The Owl. The Swallow. Positioned above a prize beetle.

Waiting.

Unlike the Prince, Gabriella feels the power of the web. She relies on it. But she does not pretend to be its master. That is the flight of arrogance. The downfall of every man who forgets his true place.

The Great Web is infinite connection of all things. When you follow the threads, mastery and humility are discovered. And there is only one outcome.

True Power.

"Gabriella," the Prince offers, speaking in as gentle and enticing a tone as he can. A far cry from the whispers of his mind.

He opens the door wide, showing her the heart of his lair.

"Please. Come in."

Her mind screams one last time, "Run, you fool! Run for your life!"

But Gabriella has practised ignoring her mind and its fear. All of her teachers share the same philosophy. The mind is a tool and she must wield it. Or it will wield her.

The mind guides you to a target, emphasized Claudius. Keeping your aim true. But never let it make the final decision. That is for your heart, and your heart alone.

Gripping her shoulders so she would never forget, he added: The mind is a sword. Your heart is the hand that wields it.

Gabriella steps inside. "Thank you, kind Prince. I am grateful to be invited."

He is speechless. Kind Prince? Never in his life has he heard this name. Who is this young woman? Suddenly, he realizes his error in judgement.

And what is she capable of?

Gabriella gazes gently at the Prince. Awaiting his acknowledgement.

As host, he must direct her where to sit.

Then she feels the shift in energy. His sudden change from arrogant confidence to suspicious concern. He has pulled back a little. But is none the less entranced.

This is the moment she must be most careful.

Not of the Prince. He is only becoming aware of her power. No. The person she must watch is herself.

Gabriella feels the overwhelming pull to control. The need to turn the Prince's fear against him. The thirst to dominate.

She can feel her strings. And the Palace, reaching for them.

Gabriella centers. Breathes. Roots herself in the Great Mother of All Things.

The Mother is all powerful. And all emptiness. Gabriella is a vessel. She carries the water. The flow. The immensity. But Gabriella is not the Source.

Gabriella sighs. Content. Aware of where she belongs.

She looks up at the Prince. Waiting for his response. For a sign of action. But he only stares at her. Torn between throwing her out and pulling her to him.

Gabriella feels them growing entwined. Sensing their fate about to take a strange turn. And she knows the Palace is at the root of this evil.

She turns, abruptly, breaking their connection.

Gabriella strides to the edge of the room and sits on a divan. Only once there is substantial distance between them, does she look at him once more.

"I have come here to discuss affairs of state," Gabriella begins. Spoken like a Queen that has already ascended the throne. For a moment, she wonders at the source of this elegant speech. Then quickly pushes the thought from her head.

This is not the time for questions.

The Prince turns, staring as though under a trance. Knowing that Gabriella is meant to be here. Is meant for him. But he does not know what that means.

Gabriella continues, under the influence of grace. "Great Prince, you have ruled in one manner for the extent of your term. You have taken what is not yours. You pretend to own land that cannot belong to any one. And you wield this power with a fist of terror."

She watches the conflicted emotions on his face. Enraged that she speaks this way to him. Yet in awe of her courage.

"You know this cannot be sustained," she adds. "The people cannot bear it. And the effort wears on your soul. The time is coming for a great change. I beseech you to embrace the honourable path. And seek the wisdom of the old ways."

She stares into his eyes. Piercing his heart. "Or you will, inevitably, be dethroned."

Fury rushes through the Prince's body. How dare she? Declaring the end of his reign! Questioning his tactics! All while seated casually in his personal domain!

Gabriella holds still. Bearing up admirably in the face of his rage. Blowing like a gale force wind directed at her.

She can feel the Prince's torment. Unsure how to act in the face of this treachery. This treason!

And yet… he wants to use this. This is the reason to make her his Queen. To have such courage, such power, at his side!

He quakes at the thought. Filled with overwhelming emotion, the Prince paces. As though searching for an answer by moving, back and forth, across the carpet.

Gabriella stays calm. Watching him. Using the rhythm to weave peace in her heart. She cannot lose her nerve.

Remembering the last few weeks, she sees that this mission was the natural evolution of her path. Each step. Every challenge. Led to this very moment.

To doubt that would be to doubt her path. And that would be real treason.

Gabriella continues to watch the Prince. Caught in the snare of his mind. Attempting to force his way out of the ever-tightening trap.

A flare of concern rushes through her. If the Prince winds himself into a corner, then believes that she is the one who put him there…

She immediately stops the thread.

Gabriella knows she is in a powerful state. This moment hanging between her and the Prince is like fertile soil.

Any thought she fosters could be just the seed to sprout into reality.

The Great Prince stops in his tracks. Stares at her.

He is torn between believing Gabriella is an evil sorceress. Or an angel from Heaven.

The Prince softens. His body released from the stranglehold of his tortured mind.

He has not thought of Heaven in many years.

The Gates of Paradise seemed lost to him the moment he plotted against his father. Regardless of the events that led to his choice. He was the one to send the Great King into the mountains. Leading to his inevitable death.

And still, the Prince does not feel worthy of the title his blood declares is his to own. Despite his accomplishments and acquisitions, he has never – not for a moment – felt like a King.

Yet this young woman, sweeps into his salon. And declares that he must change his ways. That this land was never his. That he acts without honour. And now — now – he feels like he could be worthy of the title, Great King.

Faced with the very woman who could bring him to his knees and cast him off the throne, he suddenly feels the potential of true power.

His legs quake. Unsure of this ground.

Of this feeling so contrary to everything that he has built. Everything he has chosen until now.

His mind screams – Traitor! His heart whispers – Faith.

And he does not know which to heed. Which path to take?

The Great Prince has reached a crossroads.

THE
GREAT
PRINCE

ONE

THE YOUNG MAID HEARS the Palace call. Scrubbing potatoes in the scullery, she pauses. Like a slave that senses her master's wish. She stops breathing and awaits instruction.

She likes being in the back kitchen. The other maids laugh and call her simple. But Syrena knows better.

The scullery gives her peace, quiet, and moments such as this to converse with the true ruler of the house. Not the foolish servants tasked with folding linens and bossing around young girls.

Syrena only talks to the real power. The lifeblood that courses through the veins of the stones and mortar. The spirit that determines the shape of each life within its walls.

She knows that by doing the Palace's bidding, one day, she will be a leader. She will dictate the rules. They will all bow to her. And then they will know fear.

The rush causes Syrena's head to spin. Close to passing out, she catches herself. She feels the knife in her hand. And lays it gently on the table. Forcing herself to breathe.

Breathe in. Breathe out.

Gripping the wooden table edge, she slowly regains composure. When she can feel her feet and stands without the assistance of the table, she returns to her task. Picking up the knife and peeling tubers for dinner.

She has to remember her place. For now.

After all, she needs to eat. So she does not want to raise the ire of the current rulers. They could sweep in, arrogant and false, and accuse her of anything they wish. Purely for the power of the accusation.

They never need a reason to take out their frustration on the youngest in the ranks. She learned that quickly enough.

Since she came to the Palace, they claimed that this was her new family. But they are no better than the family she fled at the tender age of six. She shivers. Recalling the terrors she knew until she became an orphan. By her own hand.

She grips the knife. As her mind wanders the dark hallways of the past.

"Syrena…," the Palace whispers. "I have need of you."

"Yes, mother," Syrena responds without making a sound. For she has long decided that the Palace is her true mother. The one who looks out for her. The one who listens to her deepest desires and promises that they will come true.

Syrena loses herself in a moment of fantasy.

Dressed in a regal, floor-length gown, she ascends to the palatial throne. She turns, gazing down at the many faces, standing below. Some filled with adoration. Some filled with fear. Their expressions send a chill down her spine.

But none thrills her as much as the look on the Great Prince's face. She gracefully claims her seat beside him. He regards her with adoration. Wondering how he ever lived a moment without her by his side. She gifts him with a smile then turns her gaze on her people —

"Syrena!" The voice of the Palace snaps the young maid from her reverie. "The Great Prince is in danger."

Listening intently, Syrena is immediately ready to act.

"What do you need?" she responds, desperately. "I am your humble servant."

"But of course, you are," the Palace whispers, like a voice from the depths of Syrena's being. Somehow, the Palace always knows what she wants. Lulling her into obedience with whispers of belonging and acceptance.

Syrena bends like a pliable tree. Ready to do anything.

"Go to Hannah's room. Wake the princess. You will need her for this errand."

Syrena stiffens. She abhors the Princess. The one they call the Prince's bride. As though that woman could ever be Queen!

"Why her? Hannah's mind is weaker than the babes in the nursery," she grumbles. "I will take care of the Prince. Let me go to him."

A wave of anger pulses through the walls. The Palace resists the urge to send a pile of rocks tumbling onto the girl's head. Impudent creature. Insisting on her agenda. She is lucky she possesses the gift of trance. Or the Palace would crush her like the bug she is.

But not yet. Not while the Prince is in danger of switching sides. As long as his heart is vulnerable, the girl still has a purpose.

"Little one," the Palace coos, sending Syrena back into a suggestible state. "The time is not yet ripe to give yourself to the Prince. First, we must use the one he has chosen. For by the very nature of that choice, she has a hold on his consciousness."

Syrena listens. Her free will suspended and her desires in the

Palace's full control.

"Go to her room. Wake her gently. And dress Hannah in her most alluring gown," the Palace dictates. "Once you have done this, I will give you further instruction."

Syrena turns abruptly and abandons her post.

Leaving the scullery behind, she walks straight through the kitchen. Past the startled kitchen hands. And ignoring the vigorous protests of the cook.

"The Princess needs me," Syrena says, simply. And keeps going.

The kitchen servants exchange a look. Syrena always made them nervous. The girl was strange from the moment she arrived at the Palace, with a wild look in her eyes and a bloody butcher's knife clutched in her hand.

The cook's assistant sighs. And gestures for the young girls to return to prepping the feast. The assistant remembers the terrified child that arrived that day. And the months of coaxing before the girl would sleep without a weapon by her side.

Despite her soft spot for Syrena, the assistant is sure something evil has her in its grasp.

She reaches for a clasp of sage. Brushing her heart with the protective herb and whispering a prayer under her breath.

No matter how she feels. Dinner must get made. The assistant chastises the gossiping servants. And turns her attention to the hens on her table, stuffing them with bread and herbs and butter.

"When the Princess asks for Syrena, the girl must go," she insists, using as firm and annoyed a tone as she can muster.

The girls silence their talk. Resuming their tasks. But the cook's assistant can feel that the entire kitchen has been unsettled.

And she cannot blame them.

For in her bones she knows that something very bad is about to happen.

TWO

SYRENA STANDS OUTSIDE the door to Hannah's room. Grumbling. She must go through. She can feel the impatience of the Palace, like walls closing in on her.

But, in this moment, her jealousy is stronger than her fear of punishment.

The young maid's fingers curl and uncurl. As though sensing Hannah's life pulsing on the other side of the door. Knowing, all it would take would be one quick and crushing motion. And the Princess would no longer be an obstacle.

Giving in to the fantasy, Syrena feels the rush of power flood her body.

The world without Hannah. What a beautiful thought. She could accomplish so much with her gone. A whimper of pain escapes from inside the room. At first spooking, then satisfying, Syrena.

She smiles. Putting her hand to the door.

Syrena considers acting against the Palace's wishes. Showing her mother what she can do. What she is capable of. And that it is always better to act now.

Syrena pushes the door open. She sees the fragile, sleeping Hannah, and knows this is her moment. Her gift.

She takes three confident strides into the room, then stops. Startled.

Hannah has suddenly bolted upright. Sitting on the bed. Staring directly into Syrena's eyes with a fire that knocks the young maid backwards.

The Princess stands. Her eyes locked on the maid. Hannah moves forward. Full of fury and seeking vengeance. She advances closer and closer to the maid.

Syrena backs toward the wall. Slowly. Steadily. Keeping her eyes on Hannah. Until she bumps into the stones, with nowhere left to go.

Hannah steps right up to Syrena. And hisses in her ear, "Did you think you could just sneak into my room and strangle me in my sleep?"

She feels the maid quake with fear. And Hannah smiles. An evil and powerful grin. Unlike anything Syrena has seen on her face before this moment.

Frozen with incomprehension, Syrena cannot speak. All she can do is stare. Wondering whether the Princess has been possessed.

That is when she realizes…that Hannah is possessed. Syrena's eyes widen.

The Palace is using her like a marionette made for its bidding. A marionette filled with the strength of a warrior and the venom of a snake.

The realization fills Syrena with a fear that threatens to crush the breath from her chest. As though sensing her victim's acquiescence, Hannah leans in. Considering whether to snap the young maid's neck.

"That's right, little one," whispers Hannah. "I see the blackness of your heart. I know what you were ready to do. One sharp movement and I will rid your body of life. Sending your soul into the pits of Hell for eternity."

Syrena closes her eyes and turns away. A tear drops down her cheek.

She has tempted fate too many times. And knows the words she speaks are true.

All Syrena has left is to pray. Please, please, Great One, just let me live. If she could only be lucky enough to live, she must… she will… always, do as she is told.

As though Syrena spoke the precise words to release a spell, Hannah crumples to the floor. A marionette without strings.

Syrena stares at the Princess.

Not knowing what to do. Hannah lies in a crumpled pile. Unconscious.

The young maid crouches down. Examining Hannah. Taking her in for the first time. She has never taken a moment before this one to truly see the Princess.

Until now, Syrena has only seen an obstacle. An enemy. A woman who had everything that she wanted. And Syrena only felt hatred for her.

Now, she cannot help but feel pity.

Syrena pauses. Her breath catching in her chest. She has never felt pity for anyone before now. Anyone other than herself.

Her back slides down the last few inches of the wall. And she sits, propped against the cold stones. As though they are the only things keeping her upright.

What is this feeling? Syrena does not like it.

Her world feels shaky. Uncertain.

She cannot afford to feel pity for another if she is to attain what she desires. And yet. Here she is. Gazing at the unconscious Princess. Not wanting to trade places with her for all the gold in the world.

Hannah groans. And Syrena pushes back towards the wall. As though Hannah has a contagious disease. And she dare not come into contact.

Syrena should move. Run. Find any other place to be.

But she cannot. She feels compelled to stay here with Hannah. To watch what must unfold between her and this young woman.

And, in that moment, as one realization after another flows through her, Syrena finally realizes why she is so unnerved.

She and Hannah are mirror images of one another.

One raised with privilege. One raised without. Both here, in this room, trapped.

Hannah groans again. Syrena holds her breath. Staring. Knowing that the Princess is surfacing. Coming back to consciousness. Perhaps for the first time in months.

Suddenly, Syrena knows what she must do.

She must get the Princess out of the Palace. She does not know why. Or how. Or where she will take her. But Hannah cannot wake up in this room. Or they will both be doomed forever.

Syrena acts without thinking. Drawing on a familiar strength. Trusting her instinct, as a warrior relies on her sword.

She scoops her arms under Hannah's. And drags the Princess toward the door.

Pulling. Heaving. Breathing.

As Hannah drifts closer and closer to the surface.

No, whispers Syrena, from her mind to Hannah. Stay where

you are. For a few more moments. We are almost safe. But you must wait. Please.

Glancing over her shoulder, Syrena can see the door an arm's length away. She pulls the young Princess closer to their escape. Praying that she makes it to the heavy wooden portal before the Palace checks on Syrena's progress.

Hannah whimpers. Her eyelids fluttering.

Syrena pulls with all her might. Throwing the two of them through the doorway.

And into the hall.

Landing with a heavy *thud* on the floor. Splayed on the polished wooden floorboards.

Hannah lifts her head off Syrena's stomach. Confused. Staring at her surroundings as though someone transported her halfway around the world. And she has no idea how they got her here. Hannah looks completely dazed.

Exhausted, Syrena remains flattened on the floor. Staring at the ceiling. Wondering what she has done. What insanity took hold of her to put her here? In direct conflict with the demands on the Palace.

A force that could end them both.

Hannah stares at the maid on the floor. Then looks around. Trying to comprehend what events could have possibly landed her in this scenario.

Turning back to the maid, she asks, "What... what are we doing here?"

"That, my lady," Syrena responds, not moving from her prostate position, "is an excellent question."

Hannah stares at Syrena. Awaiting the answer.

Finally, Syrena relents. And sits up. Staring at Hannah with equal bewilderment.

"I wish I had an answer for you," Syrena begins, "though I suspect my explanation would only cause you grief. So I will not share it."

Hannah blinks. Looking at the young woman. At their position. Then at the door.

With her mental faculties coming back to her, Hannah recognizes all the signs of being in the chaotic outcome of an adventure gone wrong.

Or, in this case, deep danger.

Growing up with Gabriella taught her that lesson. More times than she could count. Hannah turns to the young maid, whose name she cannot recall.

"Syrena," the maid replies, as though knowing her thoughts already.

Hannah decides that is a conversation to broach when they know one another a little better. And are no longer in imminent danger.

"Thank you," she offers, with all the kindness and nobility that are true to her nature.

Looking at her with deep gratitude. "Thank you, Syrena, for saving my life."

Syrena has no idea how Hannah knows this. Or how, with such speed and grace, she has brought a miracle into Syrena's life.

Genuine, heartfelt gratitude.

Syrena's eyes well up with tears. She has never tasted the sweetness of such generosity. And it overwhelms all her senses.

Syrena nods back. Hannah takes her hand. Squeezes it with

understanding.

"And now," Hannah commands, "we must run."

Hannah and Syrena spring to their feet at exactly the same moment. Each knowing that danger is imminent. Hunting them down. They flee, hand in hand, racing down the hallway. As though a pack of wolves were on their heels.

Whatever instinct took over, their lives were saved in the whisper of a breath.

For in the instant they leapt from the hallway, the ceiling stones gave way.

Crushing the wooden boards below.

THREE

THE GREAT PRINCE STARES at Gabriella. She stares back. They have been caught in this truce for many moments. Neither ready to speak. Neither ready to acknowledge the connection that flows between them.

Gabriella is unsettled by the strength of their attraction. Raised in a sheltered family. Always focused on training, rather than on men. She does not know what to do with this attention. Nor the sensations in her body.

Never mind that she believes this man to be her sworn enemy.

How is it possible that her mind is on guard, yet her body wants to cast off her clothes and sleep with any man that stirs her passion?

She knows the Prince is equally unsettled. For precisely the opposite reasons.

He is very comfortable taking any woman he deems attractive; then casting her aside once he is bored. But the fact that she has captured his heart?

That terrifies him.

No wonder men and women fit together so perfectly when they are mirror images of one another. Frightened by opposite shadows. Lured to opposite flames.

Gabriella senses that the Prince weighs a great decision. One she cannot rush.

Knowing her life hangs in the balance.

Though she would be loath to die, she has trained every day for this moment. She is ready to make the sacrifice.

The more frightening prospect is to face the messiness of living.

What if the Prince decides Gabriella is the woman who could make him a Great King? What does that bode for Hannah? For their family? For… Adrian?

Gabriella blushes at the thought of Adrian. Cursing her body for its transparency.

The Prince raises an eyebrow. Wondering what has provoked this reaction.

Sensing the future is in the balance, Gabriella forces her mind onto the Prince. On his muscular and powerful body. His strength. His flattering attire.

As she suspected, her body responds. And the Prince cannot help but smile. Assuming that her girlish behaviour is the result of being in his presence.

Gabriella realizes she must be vigilant with her thoughts. And her physical energy. She immediately runs a barrier around her mind. Walling off her thoughts from her physical responses.

Only then is she confident to think of Adrian. To wonder where he is. How he is. And whether he is alive. All while wearing a mask of polite interest for the Prince.

She thinks of their travels. Each night together under the stars. Each silent moment in common understanding. Every second feeling like infinity.

Her heart melts. Calling for him. Her true match.

Against all her instincts for safety, she feels his response.

His heart calling back.

Gabriella cannot help but feel the irony in her life.

Here. In the darkest shadows of the land, she finds love. A love that she cannot act on for fear they will both be imprisoned. Or worse.

She faces the choice between a Great King and an Alchemist. The path of service and the path of contentment. Must the two always fork in different directions?

As though sensing her distraction, the Great Prince moves closer to Gabriella.

Forcing her to focus on him. To feel his presence. To know, as he knows, that she belongs to him. The Prince feels their belonging in the marrow of his bones. No one can question him. No one dare.

Not because they fear him. Or because he claims anything he wants. No. This is unlike the past. As the day is unlike the night.

This was written before they were born. Gabriella and The Prince.

Their meeting. Their connection. No one would deny it. The Great Prince steps closer to Gabriella. Feeling her pull.

The intertwining of their fates. The very fabric of time and destiny reweaving as they stand here. Aligning them together.

To lead the Great Lands down a new path. A new way. A fresh beginning.

He takes another step. His heart softens as he gets closer to her.

The Prince feels himself becoming another man. Gabriella is capable of changing his Fate. She is born to lead him from imprisonment to freedom. This woman is the one he is meant to choose.

The Great Prince takes the final step keeping them apart.

He gazes down on Gabriella. Savouring the angle of her face

peering up to him. For he knows the natural angle, the way they must lead this land in the future, is with her gaze only and forever level with his eyes.

The Prince sinks to one knee. Taking her hand and looking up to her.

Gabriella gasps. Not expecting this action. Not so soon.

Her heart beats faster and faster. Calling out to Adrian. Desperately seeking its mate. Its true home. Pounding in Gabriella's chest as though to protest the prison she is about to choose.

And yet. She must. For all her people.

Gabriella knows her duty. She came to the palace to free her sister. To rescue her land. To be the one that made the difference.

And now that difference is being handed to her. On bended knee.

Who is she to choose her heart over her duty?

Gabriella gazes down into the Prince's eyes. Seeing the change. Knowing that she is the one responsible for the shift.

As the responsible one, she must ensure that the transformation takes hold. And ripples out to every corner of the realm.

"Gabriella," he begins, for the first time in his life, unsure what to say.

Sensing his uncertainty, she knows, as any true Queen, that she must be the one to hold the strength. For both of them.

"Yes, my Prince," she offers. "Speak your heart."

The Great Prince takes a deep breath. And launches his quest.

"Two years ago, I chose your sister as my bride," he begins, "and that was wrong. I knew then, in my heart, what my mind is now able to acknowledge. That you are my true Queen. That you are, and have always been, my Destiny."

The door to the Salon creaks open.

Causing the Prince to turn as though caught in the act of making love. He is both furious and humiliated all at once. Ready to kill or to flee.

There, in the doorway, stands Syrena.

With Hannah by her side.

FOUR

HANNAH STARES AT THE PRINCE on his knee. He holds Gabriella's hand tenderly. Speaking words she has never heard from a lover.

Let alone her husband.

And now, she is faced with her husband declaring them to her sister. Her twin.

She does not know which one has betrayed her more deeply. Who to hold in more contempt. Or who has truly broken her heart.

For though the Prince has been a cruel and strange husband, she could not help but fall in love. After two years of living together. And being forbidden to see any other men. Aside from the ones placing food on her plate. Finally, she relented.

Perhaps this was only vanity. Or confusion. For the simple reason that he is the one man who did not give her attention. And refused to declare his love.

And now she sees why. He held his heart in wait for her sister.

Hannah has never known this kind of pain. The pain of being in the shadow of Gabriella. One she adored but always assumed would walk in her shadow. The fates chose that path. On the day they were born. She came second.

Now, her younger twin, has outshone her. Gabriella is the Star.

Hannah wants to flee and hide her shame. Reject them both and force them to seek her out. Begging for forgiveness.

She reaches for Syrena's hand to run. When something stronger and more evil seizes hold of Hannah. A thought of revenge.

Cruel. Punishing. Immediate.

Syrena feels the shift. And knows. The storm brewing in Hannah's mind is a destruction unlike any witnessed in these walls.

She clamps her hand over Hannah's hand. Holding her hand tight with a powerful grip. Syrena pulls Hannah, willing her in the direction away from the Salon.

Hannah glares at her. Pulling back with equal force. Syrena simply shakes her head. Speaking directly to her mind. Don't do this. Please. You will undo us all.

But Hannah cannot relinquish the need for revenge. Her craving to cause them unspeakable pain. This husband and sister. Traitors. Each promised her love, whether in speech or in deed.

And betrayed that love the moment they had two minutes alone together.

Hannah steps into the Salon. Dragging Syrena behind her. Pulling the reluctant young woman. As she urges Hannah, silently, to stop.

Giving up on Hannah. Syrena's gaze finds Gabriella.

As the women lock gazes, Gabriella knows she is in the presence of a telepath. Not as trained or as skilled as Adrian. Yet impressively strong and adept.

Syrena shares everything in seconds. Communicating the terror about to come if Hannah continues on this path. Knowing only that someone must stop her. For the sake of everyone in the Palace.

Gabriella acknowledges the message with a gentle nod.

Releasing the young maid of her duty. Run. Save yourself. And thank you.

Syrena holds Hannah's hand a second longer. Wishing in her heart that she had met these two sisters at a different time. In a different place.

Knowing that she belongs with them. That she has much to learn from them. And would have been a much different woman under their care.

But Hannah has entered the darkness. Or the darkness has entered Hannah.

The quiet, powerful one with the Prince at her knee speaks the truth. Syrena no longer cares about the Prince. Or the romantic fantasy she created like a little girl wishing to prove her worth to all who had wronged her.

Hannah treads that pathway now. Syrena sees this way leads only to destruction.

The powerful one is right. She must run. Syrena releases Hannah's hand. Gazing quickly at Gabriella. Then fleeing out the door. Before the terror is unleashed.

Gabriella watches as her sister steps up to the Prince.

Watching him like a cat surveying her prey. Circling the two of them. As the Prince refuses to relinquish his place in front of Gabriella.

Though she can feel that the Prince is fighting his urge to put Hannah in her place.

For Gabriella's sake, he fights his old patterns. His trained instincts. And instead, waits and watches. Hannah bides her time. Provoking him. Taunting him with her mocking smile. As though to say he will never possess what he truly wants.

Gabriella cannot help but feel compassion for this man. For the love that has entered his heart. Battling the old fear with a new possibility.

Choosing again and again to lay down his weapons. Hatred. Cruelty. Revenge.

Her heart breaks as she bears witness to these sharp swords in her sister's hand. Her beloved twin. Hannah. She deserves to be revered and loved and placed on a throne. She was trained for that role from her cradle.

And now. Destiny has torn that dream from her. No wonder she seeks revenge.

Except… A chill shoots down Gabriella's spine.

Hannah is not the one who wants revenge.

The true Hannah would have grabbed Gabriella's hand and fled this place. She would have shed the Prince like an ill-fitted coat. And run off to find adventure and love and knights in shining armour. Laughing the whole way.

Gabriella swallows hard. Realizing that her sister is being used. Again!

Pulled and prodded by the real jilted lover: The Palace.

Hannah. Gabriella tries to reach her sister's mind. Feeling only darkness and fog.

Fighting shadows of betrayal and ghosts of humiliation, Gabriella cannot reach her. The true Hannah – filled with compassion and kindness. Instead, her sister's mind is a pageant of horrors.

No wonder she paces around them like a wild cat. Hannah is chased by shadows.

Shadows created by the Palace. Dancing in front of Hannah's

eyes. But they mean nothing to her sister. They are only a dark play. Keeping her sister distracted. And entranced. Caught in a dark spell.

Gabriella watches her sister's even pace. Winding around the two of them. As though she is waiting for something.

An opportunity. A moment. An opening.

Finally, the Prince can take no more. Kissing and releasing Gabriella's hand, he looks into her eyes, declaring his intention to end this charade.

He rises to his feet. Towering over the petite and willowy Hannah.

Instantly, his gaze hardens.

"Speak your peace, Hannah," the Prince states. "You and I both know our marriage was not consummated. Making our bond incomplete. And easily broken in the eyes of the land. Seek your happiness elsewhere. For you never found it with me."

This stops Hannah in her tracks. She levels an insulted look at the Prince.

"I acknowledge that this is an unfortunate sequence of events," he continues. "That you should have been released from our contract before I approached your sister—"

Hannah resumes her pacing, round and round. Staring at Gabriella as though seeking an answer. Or perhaps a weakness.

Gabriella cannot help but feel like her sister is weaving a spell.

Like an invisible hand holds her as the spindle, moving in and out. Seeking and searching. Buying time for some unknown end. What is the Palace after?

Used to strange and uneven tactics, Gabriella simply watches. On guard.

The Prince is, however, less practised at others playing games with him.

"Stop your pacing, woman! You cannot deny the Fates. Release our bond! Your sister is my natural Queen."

Hannah stops. Glaring at him. Ungrateful traitor.

The one she nurtured from the cradle and protected while so many wished him dead. Knowing the fate he would bring to this land if placed in a position of power. Who ensured that throne? Who whispered in his ear to send his father into the wilds. So he could take hold of his people and their loyalty?

Where is his gratitude? Where is his love?

How quickly the ungrateful children forget the one who gave them life. The one who made them what they are. Built them into beings capable of ruling the world.

When she just as easily could have thrown him to the wolves!

She will get his adoration back. She demands it! No one comes before her. No one.

Hannah's face goes blank. Her body stands rigid. Like a living creature suddenly struck into stone. No light in her eyes. And eerily still.

The Prince falls silent. He does not know what to make of this strangeness.

Except that he feels like a target in his own home. Vulnerable. Exposed. And not at all the Master.

A foreboding sensation slices through Gabriella. Like cold steel piercing her stomach. Taking her breath away.

On her feet before she can think, Gabriella reaches for her sister. Touching Hannah's arm. Hoping the connection will bring her back in one swift motion.

And knowing, in that instant, that she has done exactly what the Palace needed.

She gave her access to both sisters at once.

Somehow, through the magic of their connection, their history, their shared secrets. The Palace reached what she needed from Hannah.

Gabriella's touch allowed Hannah to feel safe for the first time in over a year. Connected. Protected. And able to open the very gate keeping the Palace from their most precious and guarded information.

Her instinct to protect and love her sister, has exposed them both to betrayal. Gabriella gasps. And pulls back her hand. As though a lightning bolt just ran through her.

She knows it is too late. The damage is done.

The Palace found what she had been seeking. The secret locked safely away that she could not reach … until Gabriella handed her the key.

The Prince looks at her with concern. Ready to leap to her aid.

When Hannah suddenly comes to life. Like a clockwork toy leaping into action.

He stands alert. And on edge. "What's going on?" the Prince asks, furious.

Hannah gazes at him with the expression of a condescending mother. As though he is too stupid to realize what is happening. Too slow to understand the big picture. So she must spell out the rules to him.

The Prince holds still. Feeling uneasy. This scene is vaguely familiar. Like he lived this already when he was very young. And is only now sensing the influence he has been under his whole life.

A manipulative power that constructed his fate.

He looks quickly, and desperately, at Gabriella. Knowing, in his bones, that she is his only way out. His saviour. His Queen.

Knowing, too, that what is about to happen will steal her away.

The Prince wants to drop to his knees. Take Gabriella in his arms. And never release her. But he cannot get his body to obey.

Something has him in its clasp and he cannot get his knees to bend.

Hannah steps up to him. Cruelly grabs his face. Forcing it away from Gabriella. Holding it with incredible strength in her direction.

The Prince is struck with awe.

What has possessed Hannah. Why do her eyes gleam with malice? How does she suddenly claim the strength of twenty men?

She pierces him with her eyes. Weaving a spell. Holding him prisoner. And reaching deep into his mind and soul.

Do not fight me, little one. I laid claim to you many moons ago.

I will not relinquish my prize. You and I are meant to rule this realm together. I am the only one you may love. I am the only one you may worship. You belong to me!

The Prince gasps for air. Feeling like a hand is crushing his heart.

He knows he must close his eyes. Break the connection. Keep her from accessing his mind. But he already feels the shadows sweeping in. Blocking out the light.

Gabriella, his Star, becomes more distant. Her clarity. Her hope. All fade behind the dark storm clouds flowing back into his mind.

The Prince's heart beats faster. Fighting the control. Protesting this invasion.

He does not want this. He struggles to close his eyes. Clutching the love he discovered with Gabriella.

But he knows, in the pit of his stomach, that the words Hannah is about to speak will shatter his happiness forever.

Pushing him off the cliff. Careening into the depths of darkness.

"You, my Prince, cannot leave me. You will not leave me," Hannah commands him. "You can play with this little toy beside you. But you cannot worship her. Or treat her as an equal. No. You must own her. "

Hannah indicates Gabriella with a snap of her eyes. While holding the Prince's jaw firm in her steely grip.

"You do not realize what she is. Her treasure is much more valuable than a mere Queen. A figurehead."

A sharp, icy sensation sweeps up Gabriella's spine. She senses the message about to come through the hollow shell of her beloved sister. A message that will send her life deep into the abyss.

Hannah turns back to the Prince with a spiteful grin. "Your instincts are right. She is a precious gem. One we will lock deep in our dungeons. So no one else can find her. Only we will use her. Bringing her out whenever we have need."

"She, in fact, wields the power we have always wanted. The power we crave. She will secure our reign forever and a day."

The Prince has fallen deeply under the sway of the Palace. Lulled by her words. Gabriella feels in her heart that she has lost him. The connection is gone.

The Palace knows it, too. The Prince is firmly in her clasp. Ready for her revelation.

Hannah smiles. Kissing his lips every so lightly. The Prince barely responds. Only blinking his eyes.

She turns his face toward Gabriella. So they can look down on her together. "This little creature," Hannah whispers with venomous delight, "is a Messenger."

Hannah takes his hand. Clutching his fingers in hers. Sealing their fate together.

The Prince's eyes light up with dark power. Gleaming at Gabriella.

Knowing, precisely, what that means.

FIVE

RUNNING DOWN A HALLWAY, Adrian suddenly doubles over. He gasps for air. Like someone knocked the wind out of him. Down on his knees, he can think of only one thing that would bring him to this position.

Gabriella, he whispers in his mind. And he knows.

Her secret has been discovered. The gates of treachery have been flung open.

Gripping the stones with his fingers, Adrian pulls himself back upright. Leaning against the wall. Feeling the cool, ancient rocks against his skin. His breath slowly descends back into body.

Any need to run has been relinquished. Guards or no guards. The chase no longer matters. They, too, will soon discover that the entire world, as dark as it has been, is about to get much darker.

Adrian glances down the hallway. One direction. Then the other. Getting his bearings. Though he must evade capture, his bigger problem now is a plan.

Closing his eyes, Adrian focuses in on his position.

Sensing the dungeons far below. Adrian knows he is several floors above ground and nowhere close to Gabriella. She is deep in a hidden nook of the Palace.

One kept hidden for a reason. Most likely, the Prince's private chambers.

Adrian's eyes fly open. A surge of jealousy rages through him. Like a wildfire set loose by a bolt of lightning at the height of summer.

The revelation follows. Striking just as hard and fast.

As clear as the stones under his feet. He sees the Great Prince, on his knees, holding Gabriella's hand. Claiming her as his Queen. And Gabriella, tears in her eyes, ready to acquiesce.

Adrian slides down the wall. At a loss.

He cannot fathom Gabriella in the Prince's arms.

His mind reels from the sting of torture. Imagined torment far worse than anything they could have done to him in the dungeons. Gabriella wed to the Great Prince. Sharing his throne. His Palace. His bed.

No! And yet, his heart breaks. Feeling the truth of the vision. Telling himself, she would only agree to be with such a man for the sake of the Kingdom.

Adrian cannot allow it. He rails in his mind at the Fates. How dare they make such a match! What could come of it? What cruel games do they play?

A quick flash of Hannah at the Prince's door. With a maid at her side. Frightened. Pulling Hannah away from the scene with the Prince and Gabriella.

Adrian clutches at hope. At the possibility that they are not together. The feeling disturbs the vision. Keeping him from seeing the whole picture.

But he clings to the hope. Knowing, in his heart, he would not feel called to help Gabriella had she accepted the Prince. Something has happened.

Sliding back up the wall, he feels the deep chill sweep through the Palace walls.

Placing Hannah's fearsome visage in front of him. Unlike the Hannah he met years ago. This was a corrupted and vicious version under the sway of a malicious force.

One that would never allow the Prince to be stolen. For he is the linchpin to the Kingdom. He is the rightful owner of this structure. A building constructed by his ancestors. Filled with their history. Their decisions. Their legacy.

Adrian suddenly realizes that if the Prince were no longer willing to do the bidding of the Palace, the inverse would hold true.

She would have to relinquish him. Making him the free and open ruler of the land.

Adrian's heart is crushed by the next, inevitable realization.

If the Great Prince were free, and he chose a strong and valiant Queen; the Great Lands would be held in a sacred and loving embrace.

Unlike anything the people have known for centuries.

Through his training, Adrian has connected with the beauty of the old ways. The peace and community that once existed in these lands.

A time when every Kingdom and Queendom shared resources. Engaged in open conversation. Scoffed at the need for protective walls or weapons of war.

Days when each and every person held the other in their hand. Understanding the meaning of responsibility and community. A feeling that has not been held in the land for many, many years.

And one, he knows in his heart, Gabriella could bring back.

But that vision does not aid his broken heart. As much as

his soul wishes for peace, his heart lays claim to Gabriella. She belongs to him. And he belongs to her.

The Fates be damned!

Thunder crashes outside the Palace walls in response to his call.

Adrian does not care. He will pull down the Palace stone by stone to prevent such a union. This is not the way it is supposed to be! Despite all of his training, Adrian does not care anymore about being careful. Or detached. Or staying hidden.

His despair is too deep. The pain is too profound.

He opens his mouth and yells to the skies. Howling with the fierceness of a wolf slain within reach of his family.

Echoing through the hallways of the Palace.

Thunder and lightning crash outside in reply.

SIX

GABRIELLA FEELS THE HOWL in her soul. Her heart squeezes. Adrian. Do not despair. And yet, faced with her shadow sister and the dark Prince, she cannot help but feel anguish herself.

All is lost.

No. A voice whispers to her. Faint but clear.

All is not lost. When the darkest hour arrives is also the time that the Star appears. The moment of the night when sailors rise from their bunks to take the wheel. And farmers leave their houses to tend the fields.

This is the sacred hour.

In the darkest soil, the seed finds a home. Burrows deep. And waits. Knowing that the sun will call her forth to burst into freedom.

Gabriella holds her breath.

Within inches of the Great Prince and Shadow Hannah, she does not want to reveal that she has received wisdom. That there is any hope.

Her greatest safety in this moment is their belief that she is a prisoner. Alone. With no one to guide or help her. They must feel assured they hold all the cards.

Cautiously. Quickly. Gabriella sends a thought. Who speaks?

For that, you must wait. Play the scene in front of you. Be true to yourself. I will be here when you need me most.

I need you now! Gabriella cannot help but exclaim.

Though much good it does her. The voice is gone and the Great Prince has gripped her arm. Pulling her to her feet.

His lustful look is back. The tenderness stripped from his eyes. He only sees the power she holds for him.

"You have been keeping secrets from me, little Messenger," the Prince whispers in her ear. "But no longer. You are my mouthpiece now. My conduit to the gods."

"And as soon as the people know I possess a direct channel to the Divine," he continues, "those who once harboured thoughts of rebellion will quickly fall into line."

Gabriella offers a silent prayer to give her strength and remind her from whence her true power comes. Then levels a calm gaze at the Prince.

Even in his possessed state, he notices that the young woman he seized on the back roads is gone. Replaced by a strong and capable adult.

"Do what you want, Prince," she begins, "But do not pretend to control me."

She closes her eyes. Channelling all her power. Pulling fire through her veins.

He watches, amused. Until his hand grows hot. He holds her arm tighter. Thinking this must be imagined. His palm begins to burn.

Transfixed, he cannot believe what he feels. This must be a trick!

The Prince yells in pain. Throwing her arm from his clasp. Staring at her like she is a demon witch. Hannah shakes her head and grabs his palm. Ready to scold him for being a child.

When she sees the burnt flesh, she holds her tongue.

Gabriella opens her eyes. The display took precious energy. But the effect was worthwhile. Both the Prince and Hannah regard her with more caution.

"Lock me in your dungeon. Starve me. Torture me," she states, serenely. "No matter what you do, word will leak out. And the people will come to my defence. Their work may take years. And I may not even be alive when they come. But never underestimate the connection between a Messenger and her people."

The Great Prince admires her passion. Her strength. Her need to oppose him. But he cannot let her think she has the upper hand.

"You are powerful," he replies. "And I applaud the display." He leans in as though to kiss her. Gabriella does not flinch. He hovers, close to her lips.

Then reaches, just as quickly, to snap his burnt hand over Hannah's arm. Crushing her forearm. She screams in pain, causing her knees to buckle.

All without losing eye contact with Gabriella.

She breathes in, sharply. And the Prince looks satisfied. Gabriella gave the very reaction he expected. And wanted.

"You forget I have been doing this a long time," the Prince explains. "I know you better than you think."

Looking at Hannah, he crushes harder, bending her arm back to a painful angle. She calls out again. And her knees sink deeper.

He turns to Gabriella. Watching her face go pale with silent fury.

"You could withstand any pain I cause you. So why would I bother? Perhaps for sport," he shrugs. "Or to make a point."

He pulls Hannah's arm harder until he hears a crack. Hannah yells. A tear streams down her cheek.

The Prince releases her, and she falls to the floor.

"The path to your compliance is causing pain to those you love. No matter how foolish your compassion may be," he sounds almost bored. "You will bend when I threaten their lives."

He glances at Hannah on the floor. She tends her arm. Looking around the room, then at Gabriella. Confused about where she is. And how she has become the target of torment.

Gabriella desperately wants to hold Hannah. To make this all go away.

In the middle of cruelty, she is able to feel her sister's presence for the first time. Only to be faced with Hannah's broken heart.

The Prince watches Gabriella. Enjoying the show.

Gabriella pulls her attention from her sister. And turns it on the Prince. Watching him silently. Calming her reaction. Until she finds perspective.

She remembers that he, like everyone in the Palace, has become a puppet. Playthings used by a malicious force.

A force that grew over generations of panic, greed, and desperation. Years of famine and war and neighbours pitted against one another.

A force that has existed so long that everyone within its walls believes this is, indeed, the way all creatures behave. That there is no other way to be. When in truth, humans knew many millennia without war.

Gabriella watches the Prince. Adjusting her gaze. Waiting for insight. Until she finally detects a white filament. Hovering around him like a fog.

A haze of confusion. Keeping them from connecting.

She tilts her head, slightly. Sensing that when she gets just the right angle … just the right alignment … a window opens. A pathway.

There! Right through the haze, she can see it! A direct connection to the Prince.

The true Prince. Underneath the panic and confusion and desperation. Underneath the Palace's control. Gabriella can see him.

Valiant. Powerful. Generous.

And in that moment, she knows. This is indeed a Great King.

The man who took to his knees before her was no act. He is truly the man that is under a strange spell. He could lead her homeland to freedom and reunite the Kings and Queens who once ruled the territories of the Great Lands.

This is the King who could bring peace.

And with peace, her family could return from exile. Take their lands once more. Ruling with kindness, compassion, and responsibility. The gifts she was given from the moment she was born.

Gabriella's face lights up with joy.

Except, when she shines that light onto the Prince's face, all she sees is torture. Murder. Decades of slaughter and starvation. She is hit full-force with the pain that has riddled this land since his great-great grandfather took the crown.

Suddenly, Gabriella sees the history of King after King. Each thinking he was in control of the force that led him down this path. Thinking he was the ruler. When in fact, he was being used. As the force grew in power.

The Palace used each of them. Building her strength. Feeding off the ever-expanding suspicion and hatred. Letting the kings pretend but always knowing what was hers. Her territory. Her people. Her control.

No single person can stop the force now.

This will take a community.

And Gabriella has absolutely no idea how to make that happen.

SEVEN

Running down the hallway, Syrena hears the man's tortured howl. She stops. Listening carefully.

Syrena does not know who he is. Or where he is. But she suddenly knows she must find him.

Not to save his life. To save Hannah's.

As soon as she heard his voice, she knew. This man has power. Between her knowledge of the Palace and his abilities, they can save the only person to show her true understanding.

Syrena does not care about anyone else. Not even the kitchen staff who she knows are kind, but are still afraid of her. She takes a sharp turn past the lower servant's quarters and leaps up another set of stairs. Taking them two at a time.

Syrena lands on the fourth floor. Stops.

This floor is the bridge between the ground floors of the servants and, below that, the underworld of the dungeon. This floor connects her to the higher realm. The floors with the visiting guests, the regal dignitaries, and, of course, the permanent residents of the Palace.

She pauses only because she knows that she must be more cautious about her movements on these floors. Not because she believes the inhabitants are more important or more valuable than she is, but because they believe they are.

Syrena has always been more aware than they think.

They seem to look down on her. When she is the one that pities them. For they are under the illusion they are free.

And Syrena knows now, that they are as much a prisoner as she is.

They have finer dresses and more silver and gold. Giving them the ability to travel a greater distance from the Palace. But their movements, their expression, and even their feelings, are far more limited. Like her, they are all prisoners.

Which is why she must find the howling man.

She takes a moment to tune in to the pulse of anguish. Aware that such clear expression means he can only be an outsider. Everyone raised in this place was strictly taught to silence their feelings.

No. Not taught. Forced to crush them deep into the ground. Never to be understood again. The only acceptable emotion in this place is fear.

She pauses. Realizing the gift of being offered a sensation other than fear.

Syrena breathes in the man's anguish. Savouring the feelings flowing from deep within the palace halls.

She smiles. Letting her body feel every ounce of the intense emotion. Knowing this is the precise reason so many deem her strange. Standing still at the top of a staircase savouring anguish. What kind of child does such a thing?

Syrena sighs.

A child raised in a place where feelings have been outlawed for so long, that anguish tastes like an exotic dish. Served by a stranger from another country.

She savours every nuance. Every note. Every precious flavour. Her body relaxes. The smile deepens. And Syrena feels just a little more human.

That is when she knows.

For the first time in her life. She understands that she is not strange.

Syrena knows in every dancing element of her body that she is, in fact, alive. She has sensed a gateway, a portal, where others have denied anything exists.

And she – she! – is the one who must fling it open.

In that instant, Syrena knows exactly where the howling man is located. Propped against a hallway on the far end of the fourth floor. How he managed to get there from the dungeons, she does not know.

But he must have been in the dungeons until now. Or she would have felt his presence! That or —

She holds the thought. Not wanting to allow the Palace to sense it. But she knows this man's pain. And why he howled through the walls. And, for what feels like the first time since she was a small child, Syrena feels great compassion.

As much as she wants to allow the colours and sensory expression of these feelings to wash over her, she knows time is of the essence. If she does not reach this man soon, all will be lost. And she will be thrown into the dungeon with him.

If she were that fortunate.

With that thought, she releases her swift and agile feet. Flying along the ancient stones of the Palace. Every stone she touches sends whispers of hope and freedom as she passes.

For though the force that took over the Palace may be malicious and malignant, the stones themselves were quarried from the ancient reaches of sacred earth.

As each being awakens within the walls of this ancient structure, that awakening light shines into the hearts of the stones. Sparking the memory of their origin. Of the blessed earth from whence they came.

Strengthening the essence of beauty and power within the Palace once more.

Lighting the fire of love.

If only those with courage in their hearts could sustain the flame. The stones will hold the fire. Allowing it to grow until all creatures feel its warmth.

As has been done since the beginning of time.

And could be done again.

EIGHT

ADRIAN FEELS HER IMPENDING arrival. He pushes himself up the wall. Steadying his body. Standing firm on his feet.

Grounded in this reality once again. No matter what he feels. Or what may have happened to his future, he must be ready.

He believes she is a friend. But he must always be ready for a foe.

His memory wants to reach back into the Prince's private salon. Seeking out Gabriella. Desperately wanting to pull her to him. To save her. Or have her save him. No matter the method. For them to be together.

He shakes away the thoughts. Curses them as cobwebs, blocking him from the present. Even as he hears the footfalls heading in his direction. Still, his mind only wants to be with Gabriella.

That is when he sees the shadow. Around the corner.

Adrian feels more like himself than he has in several days. The rush of fear awakens his senses. Lights his eyes and brings weight to his feet.

Finally. He has landed in the present. Ready to fight.

The woman rounds the corner like a bird on fire. Flying toward him without thought, hesitation, or concern for her well-being.

Not until she sees his form right in front of her, does she stop. And catch a breath.

Adrian is taken aback.

For this woman, unlike any other, reminds him of the ancient Phoenix. The bird so many believe does not exist and, yet, he has had the privilege to see.

Though many would not call the sighting a privilege. For when you see a Phoenix, you know that you are being called to walk the path of death. You can never tell whether you will come back to this world. Or transition to the Otherworld.

That is the gamble you make when you acknowledge the Phoenix. That is the path of the Shaman, the Shapeshifter, and, in his case, the Alchemist.

For you cannot bend the rules of this world until you have experienced the rules that exist beyond – above, below, and in the infinite nothingness.

And here, he is faced with the human incarnation of the Phoenix.

What could it mean? How is he to address her? What does she want of him?

Adrian casts the questions from his mind and gathers himself.

He bows deep and with great respect to the woman.

Holding his head bowed until she acknowledges that he is worthy of interaction, Adrian stands completely still.

Syrena stares at this strange man. This man whom she knows is one of great power and knowledge.

This being who has clearly trained with masters and knows the ways of worlds far beyond her imagining. Let alone her experience.

And here he stands, in a pose of contrition, waiting for her to speak.

"Please," she whispers, "say something."

Syrena can barely speak. For fear he has mistaken her for

another. And may decide not to help her.

Adrian raises his head. Gazing at her for a long, quiet moment.

His eyes shine, as he recognizes a kindred soul. "Welcome, dear one," he says, finally. "I have been waiting a long time for you to arrive."

Syrena smiles and throws her arms around him. Shocking Adrian to the bottom of his feet. Feeling the rush of her compassion and gratitude. Unsure how to react, he simply allows her to hold him. Receiving the kindness.

After a moment's hesitation, he wraps his arms around her. Returning the embrace. And the gratitude.

He pulls back. Looking at the young firebrand. She beams at him with the full force of the sun. Set to pull him on her quest.

"What is your name?" she asks.

He hesitates. Knowing this is a risk. A very substantial risk to give a Phoenix his true name.

He also knows — for him — there is no other path. He chose a long time ago to take the chaotic and unpredictable road of truth. Through fire and fury.

This is the way of his soul. "Adrian," he states simply. Ready for anything.

Syrena offers her hand. "Syrena."

When he places his hand in hers, she wraps her warm fingers around his palm. Looks directly into his eyes. And says, "Now we must run."

And with that, Syrena is already in motion.

Pulling him with her.

They fly together like the furies on a mission for the gods.

NINE

The Palace can feel it. Her control is slipping. There is chaos in her walls and she will not allow it. Just when she finally retrieved her Prince, others change their minds.

Like the insolent maid. Pretending she is anything more than a pathetic orphan. Saved from the grips of a rageful father and a weakling mother. The girl meets a few strangers and, suddenly, believes the world is hers for the taking.

She will discover there is a price for turning her back on the one that has kept her alive. The one who has held the cruel forces at bay. People who would as soon snap her neck for a crumb of bread than ponder whether she is worth anything.

For though there may be a new light in the Palace walls, there are always weak minds for the taking. All it takes is gathering enough of them to overwhelm the ones who believe they have her cornered.

No one understands the game of winning like she does. She has studied it for generations. She is not about to relinquish the reins of power now.

Foolish ones have entered her walls before. She threw them over the barricades to break their necks on the rocks below.

Always they believe the tide has turned. Only to discover that she is the ocean.

She has the force of history on her side and they must fight wave after wave of established beliefs. Changing the tide is never as easy as people think.

Inevitably, after fighting the waves, their limbs tire. Their breath falters. And under the swell of water they go.

She will out wait them. Out last them. Out manoeuvre them.

Let the little ones attempt to take her down. The thought that moments ago had her upset, now entertains her.

All she has lost is a maid. Why she was concerned, she cannot even recall.

Even if they manage to take her off guard, she has the one they will never see coming. The one that each of them has underestimated. The one who appears quiet and unassuming. But can ruin them all.

After a brief moment of upset, the Palace is now deeply amused. Let them come.

She will unleash a force unlike anything they have imagined.

For hell hath no fury like a Palace scorned.

TEN

GABRIELLA SITS PATIENTLY in her cell. She recognizes the sights and sensations from the flashes she received when searching for Adrian. She almost finds it amusing that she is now in the dungeon and he is free. Except…

She does not know where he is. And Gabriella fears, deep in her heart, that he has fled the Palace. And she will never see him again.

Though, truth be told, she would be grateful.

For even if she is never meant to see his face again, she could live with herself if she knew he were free. And alive. Even as she considers the notion that he is far, far from these walls and getting farther away with every breath. She knows.

He is here. And he is searching for her. A thought that almost breaks her in two.

Adrian cannot be captured for her sake. He must flee. He must teach others and raise an army to defeat the very force that keeps their land imprisoned.

And yet.

Perhaps this is exactly where they both must be. In the depths of evil.

For how else can one roust the shadows than to be in the dark where they live? How else can they expect to break the force that pits them against one another except by banding together?

Gabriella takes a deep breath.

She must not allow the dungeon to dictate the direction of her thoughts. She realizes she is unpractised at solitude. Even all those months in hiding and on the run, she always had Casmire.

Her heart clenches at the thought of him. Wondering where he could be. Whether he is safe. And cared for. Hopefully, he has managed to tear himself free of any ropes they used to hold him and has run far away.

Gabriella sighs. Knowing that, too, is unlikely.

For she seems to have a talent for picking men who stay by her side. Even when it assures their death.

Fury rages through her. Knowing that if she has the audacity to inspire such loyalty, she needs to be worthy of their trust. She must be the one who leads them to victory. Not the one who hides in the shadows expecting some kind of rescue.

Then she stops. Recognizing that this is the rash voice of youth. Filled with potential for leading her followers down a dark path.

She has been given this time in the dungeon for a reason.

Gabriella stands. Even with the shackles on her feet, she can move a little. Enough to take a prayerful pose and calm her mind. She needs to reach deep within to the Great Well.

Breathing. Quieting her mind.

She becomes aware of the patient drip of water in her cell.

Persistent. Insistent.

Gabriella focuses on the simplicity of the water. The calm, steady flow of each drop. The timeless effort of the water. And suddenly, she knows.

The quiet here is the gift. For though she is still in the walls of the Palace, the force that monitors every corner of this building does not bother with the dungeon.

She is not sure why. Perhaps, there is too much other activity to watch and the dungeon offers so little. Perhaps because the souls kept here quickly lose heart and fall into the depths of despair. So the Palace has no need to watch them.

Gabriella smiles. This is indeed the gift of the dungeon.

In the darkest corner of the Palace, she has found safety. A place where she can, without detection, ponder the plan to reclaim her homeland.

She gives thanks to the chains. To the walls. To the steady drip of water intended to drive her mad but, instead, giving her exactly the company she needs.

She considers the paradox of being locked in a cell yet knowing she is the source of freedom. Gabriella smiles. That is when she realizes the truth that has eluded her since she arrived.

She is not the source of freedom. That has been her misunderstanding.

The Source is Freedom.

Gabriella's knees buckle from the weight of what she has just been given. She sinks to the ground. And cries for the first time in years. Knowing that she is not the one who needs to figure anything out. She is not the key. She is not even the saviour.

She is the Messenger.

And the message has been given.

ELEVEN

ADRIAN STOPS MIDSTRIDE, overwhelmed by a wave of power. Syrena immediately knows the footfalls that were so evenly matched to hers are no longer moving. She stops and turns. Looking at Adrian like he is mad.

"We cannot stop," she whispers, urgently.

Looking around to ensure they are not being watched or followed. "We must keep moving. The only safety is in movement."

Adrian smiles. Patient and calm. Knowing she mistakes his serenity as evidence of madness. Do you not feel it? He asks, directly to her mind.

And waits for her answer.

Syrena tosses him an annoyed glance. Not due to the intrusion into her thoughts. She finds this intriguing.

No. She is annoyed by the implicit challenge. Despite his calm, amused manner.

She cannot help but accept. Though, she is more comfortable with the action of fire than the peace of water. Still, this is why she respects Adrian. He takes bigger risks than she can fathom.

Syrena forces herself to breathe. And look inward.

As much as she wants to deny the feeling, she senses a shift. Like a fresh wind has entered the Palace. A cool breeze making its way through every wall. Every crack in the mortar.

Freedom.

Eyes wide, she stares at Adrian. Incredulous. "What does it mean?" she asks, out loud. Still unable to communicate with him using silent thought. She is not sure why he is different than the two sisters. Maybe she fears his power. Or his judgment.

Adrian is confident she can master the skill. But understands why the idea is discomforting. Syrena does not like that there is a direct channel to her mind. She is too new to this land of hope and possibility, to want anyone entering her head.

Even though he assures her that, out of respect and honour, he cannot listen to her thoughts. Syrena does not want to take the risk.

There are too many years of darkness rattling around in there for her to invite anyone before she has cleared the rooms of dark, rotting furniture.

Gabriella has found the way, he answers.

"The way out?" she asks, hopeful but apprehensive.

Adrian shakes his head. Much more than that, Syrena. She has found the way to freedom. Not just for you. And me. For all of us.

What Adrian offers flies in the face of everything she has ever known. In Syrena's world, the rich will always be rich. The powerful will always be abusive. And no one can hope to stop them.

All the small people can do is make the best life with what they have been given.

That is more than Syrena even hoped for in this lifetime. So she is happy to take it and run. Not believe fairy tales about young women in dungeons suddenly being able to overthrow the most powerful man in the Great Lands.

"That is not possible," she whispers. Looking around as though expecting a bolt of lighting to come from the ceiling and smite her to dust. "No one overthrows the Prince. We are stuck with him. He was born to this life. And the Palace will ensure he dies with it."

Ah, Syrena. Not only is it possible, it is happening, he states simply. The only reason it has not happened before now, is because we have all invested our lives in believing the impossibility. Rather than the miracle.

Syrena stares at Adrian as though he has declared that the sky is green.

"That is fine in fairy land," she scoffs. "But here…" Syrena glances around, frightened at the words she is about to speak.

For by saying them, she commits treason.

"There is a darker force than you can imagine," she insists. "A force that controls everything inside these walls. That has been in our minds since we arrived and plays us like puppets. You and I are lucky we have escaped its attention this far. And if we want to live, we must escape. Let the others fend for themselves."

Syrena grabs his hand and pulls him forward. "Please. Use your magic. Let us find Hannah and escape this place forever. The others can live the lives they have come to expect."

Adrian looks at her with patience. Can you truly wish that on them after Hannah showed you a different path? After feeling, for the first time in your life, the balm of kindness from another human being?

His tone makes her furious. "That is exactly why I must repay her. By freeing her from this place."

And we will, he assures her. Realising, suddenly, that Syrena does not need to understand. Everything will become clear when the time is right.

She is right to keep moving. "Take me to Hannah," Adrian says out loud.

Overwhelmed with relief, Syrena forces herself not to hug him. She did not wish to fight Adrian. Especially because she knows he is crucial to their escape. But she was willing to take him on if he did not come back down to this world.

Much as she admires the magically gifted, she cannot abide how quickly they throw aside the practicalities of life. And right now, running is one of them.

Glad Adrian is being reasonable, and not wanting to risk a change in perception, she quickly shifts into motion. Leading the way up a staircase.

Adrian follows Syrena. Grateful she knows the way. Gabriella needs us together, he thinks to himself. As much as he wants to instruct Syrena, her actions will lead to exactly what Gabriella requires.

Enlivened by a freshly stoked faith, he takes the stairs swiftly and easily. Leaping up them with the energy of an exuberant child.

He keeps close to Syrena. Contrary to her belief that he is drifting up in the clouds, he is highly alert. Using all of his senses to ensure their safe passage to Hannah.

Rest assured, sweet Gabriella, he addresses her directly, whether she can hear him or not. I will gather us all. Every one that could be of use to you.

For when the moment is right, Adrian knows.

The Messenger will need every last one of us.

TWELVE

Adrian and Syrena arrive at the Great Hall. Startled by the long and winding parade of visitors.

Syrena glances quickly at Adrian. Though she is unable to transmit her thoughts to him, they are written all over her face.

What is happening? He shares the sentiment.

Keeping her at his side, and just out the way of the large doors, he takes in the spectacle. A flood of people pours steadily into the Great Hall. Reaching from the front gates, though the Palace entrance.

The mix of people comes from every corner of the Great Lands. Dressed in vibrant colours. Clothed in black. Rich fabrics. Tattered rags. The crowd blends together all walks of life. And every means… or lack of means.

Syrena is overwhelmed by the sheer variation. Adrian, on the other hand, is cautious. Then concerned, as something feels very familiar.

"This is not possible…" Adrian speaks the words out loud. Knowing the noise from several hundred people overwhelms the sound to everyone except Syrena.

"What is not possible?" she asks. "The Prince has simply arranged some kind of… community gathering."

Even as Syrena speaks the words, she realizes they sound ridiculous. The Prince never gathers people at the Hidden Palace. He has other abodes for his public endeavours. Never this one.

"These people… I have seen them before," Adrian's memory requires only a fragment of a second to bring to mind the time and place that feels so familiar. A day he could never forget. The day he met Gabriella.

"The Annual Pleading," he whispers. Completely perplexed.

"The what?" Syrena asks.

"A single day in the year when anyone can make a request of the Great Prince," Adrian explains, staring at the flow of people entering the Hall.

"They are not guaranteed anything," he continues, "other than an opportunity to ask for what they desire most. The Prince often says no. Yet they still walk or ride — thousands of miles for some — to make the request."

"That is utterly stupid," Syrena sneers at the strangers now. Deeming them foolish. Or maybe even dangerous. "Why put yourself through that kind of torture when the outcome is almost certainly a rejection?"

"Clearly, you have yet to fall in love," Adrian laughs, his voice touched with a hint of regret.

Syrena blushes and avoids his gaze. Irritated by her involuntary display of emotion, she snaps. "Do not assume you know everything, mystery man."

Adrian regards her with curiosity. For a moment, concerned that he might be the object of her affection. But he quickly surmises, to his relief, that is not the case.

Much as he wants to tease Syrena about the source of her

embarrassment, the abating flow of pleaders brings his attention back to the matter at hand.

What are these people doing here? Why did the Prince allow them to come to his Hidden Palace? Adrian forces himself not to broadcast the next thought – especially to Syrena. What is the likelihood that the Prince will let them leave?

Unless. Adrian suddenly knows: the Prince brought them here without revealing the Palace location. They have no idea where they are.

So they would have no way of finding the Hidden Palace again.

But that is a tremendous risk. Especially for one as paranoid as the Great Prince.

As the last of the people enter, filling the large room to its capacity, Adrian ushers Syrena past the door. They cannot help but be in awe of the sheer mass of people.

Behind them the Royal Guards close the immense hall doors. Making Syrena nervous. Adrian places a hand on her forearm and sends her calm thoughts.

Much to her amazement, she quickly relaxes. Knowing that she has Adrian on her side, the Guards barely seem like an obstacle.

Taking Adrian's cue, she allows herself to look around. Take it all in. She has never witnessed such a gathering in all her years. Never mind the mix of strange people in beautiful clothing. Each one looks like a rare gem, no matter how roughly hewn.

Is this what the world has to offer? Could this be what awaits her outside the Palace gates? Syrena suddenly feels like a five year old presented with a long table of desserts. The array of possibilities is overwhelming.

Adrian, on the other hand, cannot shake a foreboding feeling that the Prince has an ulterior motive for allowing these people into his most sacred of spaces.

Even a man as vain as the Prince would never want this mass of humanity in his Great Hall. He does not have altruistic leanings. Nor does he have any interest in what these people want.

More likely, he wishes to make a point. A very dramatic and unforgettable point.

Adrian prays he is wrong. As he examines the raised stage with two regal thrones, positioned at just the right height for all to admire the Prince and his new bride.

The thrones are left empty while the people get settled.

Partly for the commoners to remember their place. And partly so the entrance of the Regal couple is that much more dramatic and appreciated.

Trumpets on either end of the stage sound the call. And the room falls to a hush.

All eyes watch the doorway to the far left. The doorway with the deep red velvet curtains. They wait. And wait some more.

Until a hand parts the curtain.

Much to the shock of everyone in the Great Hall, through the curtains steps…

Gabriella.

Looking radiant. As though a thousand suns shine from her heart.

She strolls to the centre stage. The entire room holds their breath. Staring at her as though they have never seen such a creature in their lives.

Completely rapt and awaiting her words.

Every soul, including Adrian, seems to have forgotten that they came to see the Prince. For in this moment, they are sure that the reason they are here is for her.

Gabriella stands directly in front of the two thrones. Taking in the crowd. Knowing that these are her people. They belong to her. As she does to them.

"My dear ones," she begins, and the crowd hushes to a silence. "I have come here today for you."

She gazes on them with deep love. And no apparent concern for her position.

"We are all prisoners of these times. Hearts caught in webs of hate. Minds caught in nets of desperation. I am here to tell you that those days are over."

All attention is on Gabriella. Even the Royal Guards listen intently. As though in a trance. Only Adrian seems to notice the two very empty throne chairs behind her, awaiting the guests of honour.

"Each of us holds the key to our freedom," Gabriella continues, looking directly at Adrian. As though sensing his concern. She beams at him with such intensity, he cannot resist her. And has to force himself not to rush the stage.

"Behind me are two thrones," she states the obvious, and the room gasps, suddenly remembering the Prince and his bride. Wondering where they could be.

And what will happen when they arrive.

"But do not believe that they have power," Gabriella's voice booms across the Hall. Sending the people into deep reverence. "They are but two chairs. Made of wood. Carved by hands. Fashioned to impress."

"They mean nothing without you," she gazes at them with intensity. "You are the power of this land. You are the force behind every structure built and every crop harvested. You inhabit, nurture, cherish, and cleanse the land."

She raises her hands high. The room fills with electricity. Like a lightning storm has been unleashed inside the stone walls.

The crowd is amazed. In awe of the sheer force weaving all around them. Winds blow round and round. Holding them all tightly bound together. Like the comforting, yet powerful shield of a great set of wings.

They barely notice when the Great Prince steps on the stage. Fighting the sweeping winds inside his Hall. Yet determined to take his throne. He turns back to Hannah, expecting her to be at his side. Instead, she clutches a beam to keep herself safe. Winds whipping her hair and her skirt.

Yelling without effect, he commands her to join him with a fierce gesture. Hannah shakes her head. And stares at Gabriella. Loving and fearing her sister, all at once. Far more than she ever loved or feared the Prince.

Grabbing beams and stones, the Great Prince pulls himself toward his throne. Against the crescendo of wind, he yells at the guards to seize Gabriella. But the sound of his voice is lost in the howling air.

Gabriella smiles, calmly, at the centre of the storm. Miraculously, when she speaks, her voice carries easily to the people listening.

"Take the hand of the person next to you," she instructs. Every being in the Hall, including Adrian and Syrena, follows her guidance.

Syrena locks eyes with Hannah. And calls to her with her mind. Desperate to reach the one that she loves with all of her heart.

The power of her focus breaks through her misgivings.

Conveying a message directly into Hannah's mind.

Come to me, Hannah. I will keep you safe. You belong with me.

And with that calling, Hannah releases the beam. Braving the wind. She rushes to Syrena and Adrian. The crowd parts easily. Making way for her to reach the one she suddenly knows has always been waiting for her.

Hannah throws her arms around Syrena. Planting a kiss on her lips. Syrena blushes from head to toe. Adrian laughs heartily into the howling wind.

Hannah clasps Syrena's hand. And turns her attention to her sister.

"Together, we are the source of freedom," Gabriella continues. "Together, we birth the change that this land desires."

Arms outstretched, she rises above the crowd. Adrian feels as though his breath is being pulled from his body as he watches Gabriella take flight. Sending a wave of transformation through the world unlike any felt in centuries.

Every person in the room feels their immense power. Every one knows their gift.

Lighting flashes above them all. Yet no one, except the Prince, feels worried for his safety. Gabriella gathers the lightning in her hands. Sourcing the light and power in her palms before sending it through the network of connected hands.

"Sing the world into being," she instructs. "For with our locked hands, we bridge the distance between the past and the future, the present and the new millennium."

Gabriella shines like a star. Guiding the way. "We are the gift-givers. And with this light, we birth the new way of being."

An explosion of light bursts through the Hall. Like a thousand suns imploding.

Crouched on his throne, the Great Prince closes his eyes tight against the force of the blast. As he holds them shut, he realizes, that he is the only one in the room not holding another person's hand.

The brilliance abates. He opens his eyes. Stunned, by what he sees... or does not see.

The Hall is empty.

Every soul is gone.

THIRTEEN

GABRIELLA AND ADRIAN LAUGH, running with their hands locked together.

They stumble down the dirt path, just ahead of Syrena and Hannah. Crashing through the cedar trees and dodging slippery rocks.

Casmire and Ginetta gallop freely ahead. Racing each other. Occasionally glancing back in the direction of their family. Keeping them in sight.

Gabriella still cannot believe it worked. As much as she knew the Divine would not fail her, right up until the moment she took flight, she had no idea whether she would, indeed, be able to fly.

Let alone free every person in the room.

She leaps over a rock and throws a smile in Adrian's direction. Squeezing his hand as the joy rushes through her veins. He cannot take it a moment longer.

Adrian pulls Gabriella off the path, deep into the trees. And kisses her.

Knowing that this may be the only moment he gets to have Gabriella for himself. That after this, he may have to relinquish her forever.

But here, in this forest, she is his and his alone. He pulls her close.

Gabriella returns the kiss with a passion held in for far too long. She does not care about the future. She does not think of anything else. Except Adrian.

They pull apart. And stare at one another. Unable to believe this is happening. Not sure if it really is.

"Get out here, love birds," yells Hannah, amused and exasperated, at the same time. "We have no time for a secret rendezvous. You know the Prince will be sending his hounds and guards after us in minutes!"

Grabbing Gabriella's hand, Adrian leads her out of the trees. Still unwilling to relinquish his hold on her. At least until she is called to find her Mentor.

Which Adrian can feel is coming.

Hannah shakes her head at her smitten sister. "I never thought I would see the day," she teases. Then quickly takes off, running down the path to avoid being caught by an embarrassed, and much faster, Gabriella.

Drunk on the air of emancipation. No one dares speak the truth.

That it is just a matter of time before the Palace winds the Great Prince into a frenzy of paranoia and hatred. Seeking the very person who not only defied him. But lit hundreds of souls in that room on fire with her message.

A fire he must drench before it takes hold in every village across the land. Each village represented in that Hall.

For once the fire takes hold, he cannot stop the future coming his way.

A future ablaze with freedom.

GRATITUDE
My great, big, heartfelt thanks to:

My oh-so-lovely reader & editor, Kathryn Cottam. Your passion and guidance are inspiring.

The dazzlingly talented Roberta Cottam for her elegant cover design. I would be lost without you.

My gracious and lovely map illustrator, Vanessa Mayville. You are abundantly gifted.

The generous Won Ng for her proofreading skills. Your precision is amazing.

A second round of big, mushy thanks to Roberta Cottam for her patience and brilliance in completing the paperback layout.

Sweet hugs to my friends & family for your abundant encouragement on this ever-winding path.

Gracious thanks to my readers for your generosity and support.

Special love to my insightful husband, Kevin Corkum, for being my dedicated partner on this journey.

And ever-flowing thanks to the Divine for trusting me with this tale.

ABOUT THE AUTHOR

During a career in reporting, screenwriting and short fiction, *Messenger* lured K.M.Tremills into the magical world of novel-writing, asking her to write the exploits of Gabriella, Adrian and the Great Prince.

Kate lives deep in the charmed realm of British Columbia, gathering inspiration in the woods. Her East-coast Canadian heritage inspires the poetic style found in both the *Great Lands* series and her second series, *Fated*. Kate also spends time in the United Kingdom and the United States, where she researches, writes and weaves a little magic.

Kate loves hearing from readers! Connect with her at www.katetremills.com

In times of great darkness, wisdom lights the way home.

GABRIELLA PACED THE CLOSE COTTAGE, restless from hiding too long.

She needed time to think. And assess her choices. In the three years since her flight from the Hidden Palace, Gabriella trusted few places. This hideaway was one of them. Due to its location and the discretion of its owner.

Even better, the cottage was shielded by spells.

She stopped and peeked out the heavy, brocade curtains. They were designed to block the sunlight and most certainly the Moonlight.

But now, she needed the comfort of the night goddess.

As she stared into the far reaches of the sky, Gabriella was relieved to see the Moon. Shining at her, the nocturnal deity whispered,

I have watched over your world for countless nights. And have hidden my face for limitless days. The tides wash in and out. The birds rise in the morning. And the owls call in the evening. No matter how many men wreak havoc and how much blood soaks into the earth, creation will go on.

"Yes," Gabriella replied. "But you are not called to tumble such men from power. Causing innocent lives to end before their time. Threatening the wellbeing of more. And asking citizens to risk everything in support of a cause that may fail."

The Moon shone bright and said,

That is true, my daughter. But you agreed to this path with no assurance that the way would be peaceful. Though you were chosen to shine, never assume the path of a star is an easy one.

Burning bright one evening only to discover the fuel for her fire dwindles the next. Then her sister star is chosen to take her place in the firmament. Such was ever the way of life, and so it will ever be.

Gabriella tilted her head and drank in the Moon's words. In years past, she would have been infuriated by the lack of clear direction. But since leaving her childhood behind, she had learned that the stars and deities spoke in the language of mystery.

She had come to appreciate the subtleties of the Goddess. The quiet guidance of the angels. Her path was more often whispers and nudges than blazing signs. When she heard loud, demanding sounds, they were words spoken by men. Despotic ones.

The stars have immeasurable time, thought Gabriella. So they speak softly and guide with metaphors. They do not need to rage or stomp. Millennia are but a blink of the eye in comparison to the turning of the spheres.

But she did not have thousands of years. Nor thousands of days.

Gabriella felt the mounting impatience of the Great Prince. His actions grew rash, and his judgment was compromised. She could not afford to wait until he razed every village and destroyed every forest in his search for her.

If people were to die from his obsessive quest, Gabriella thought, she was determined they be given the choice. Though the outcome may be the same, choosing your death was far more powerful than being cut down as a pawn.

She growled at the thought of her people being slaughtered, whether in their beds or on a battlefield. Gabriella wished she had the power of magic that could shield them as she took on the Great Prince. Though she knew that would take too much strength.

This was their feud, not the war of ordinary people. At that thought, the Moon shimmered and replied,

Ah, but that is where you are wrong, daughter.

These are the days of the small ones rising to topple the mountain. Though they would be grateful for you to fight their battle, we cannot expect the structure to hold when only one has the strength to bear the weight.

You must allow them to stand with you. To share the burden of the load. They will whisper gathered wisdom in your ear. Just as you respect the guidance of the stars, so must you listen to the collected discernment of your people.

"Does this mean the days of Kings and Queens are over?"

Asked Gabriella, wishing the Moon would say yes.

She had no desire to climb a throne or place her sister back on such a high and targeted post. From the time of her birth, Gabriella had only witnessed the throne to be a heavy burden. Not a prize to be coveted.

No, my sweet girl. Leadership and wisdom are still very much required. Your parents taught you well when they offered shelter to the meek and food to the hungry. But they carried too much on their own shoulders. And did not allow their people to hold them, as you must do.

"But we have all grown accustomed to hiding," replied Gabriella. "How will they respond when I ask them to step out into the open and lay down their lives? The lives of their children? All for the slim hope that we can defeat a tyrannical force who will stop at nothing to rule?"

Gabriella did not say the force was the Great Prince. Deep in her heart, she held hope that he was the good man who once knelt before her and asked her to be his Queen. As wrong as his offer was, given he was sworn to Hannah, Gabriella longed for the Prince to win the battle for his soul.

This is where the path of trust opens. You have grown accustomed to walking alone, my daughter. Relying only on the forces beyond the veil. And growing too comfortable bearing a sacrifice that belongs to others.

Now, you must learn to believe in others. No longer is this the battle of one. This is the war of many. Women and men define their character in the side they choose and the actions they take. You are being asked to lay that challenge at their feet. And to allow each person to choose their way.

Gabriella dropped her gaze to the grass rippling outside her window. She focused on the light dancing across the blades, willing herself to be at peace. But rage gathered in her fists. And she gripped the heavy curtains, crushing the fabric, resisting the Moon's guidance.

She had been raised to fight for others. She was taught to defend the weak. Not place the battle at their door and expect them to wield weapons they did not own. This was an outrageous demand, thought Gabriella.

"This cannot be," Gabriella said, not trusting herself to say more. The Moon's light cascaded softly to the earth.

Tell me your objections.

Gabriella lifted her fiery gaze, burning as bright with rage as the Moon shone with patience. She was grateful to be protected by magic or she might have led the Prince's army straight to her door.

"These people do not know how to fight," exclaimed Gabriella. "They have not been trained. Nor should they be expected to take on a battle that was started by kings! You cannot expect them to shed blood for a feud that is not theirs to bear. That is cruel and archaic reasoning. And I will not stand for it!"

She could not ask this of a farmer, a cook, or a blacksmith. They chose honourable professions that upheld life. They were needed in their villages. She was a different beast altogether. An outsider. A loner. One who preferred her steed to people. And the wooded trails to the gossipy court.

Gabriella fell silent in her fierce anger. Pulling on the curtains, until they threatened to tear from their hangers. Waves of anger rolling off her like steam from a hot spring.

The Moon waited, as though knowing that Gabriella would

quell her roiling blood. Loving her chosen daughter, as deeply for her outrage as for her committed heart.

"I was raised for this task," Gabriella said, finally. "I accepted the challenge. When the angels came to ask whether I would carry the torch, the risks were made clear. I was ready to lay down my life then and I am willing to lay down my life now. But you cannot ask me to demand that of my people."

And why not?

"For all the reasons I have stated!" retorted Gabriella. "They do not deserve to die!" The Moon shone with the deep understanding of the stars.

And you do?

Gabriella's breath caught in her chest. Her fists unclenched. And her cheeks burned hot with discomfort. Never in all her years of service had she asked that question. Never had she wondered why she was the one who felt called to lay down her life.

And yet, somewhere deep in her heart, she knew her answer. Yes. Gabriella believed that she deserved to die. Why else would the gods have called her to this task?

As she considered the question for the first time, her heart broke. She, the daughter of nobility, with a sister that bore the soul of an angel, and a family that served only with the kindest of intentions, believed her sacrificial death was justified.

Not once had Gabriella paused to consider the other path. The one most other young women walked. A journey of love and family. The choice to live. To thrive. To build a legacy beyond death.

Her heart pounded in her chest. Gabriella's thoughts drifted to Adrian.

Once when they lay together and he thought she was asleep,

she heard Adrian whisper to her. A secret wish. His desire to leave behind all that was asked of them and, instead, choose their own path. Together, without the burden of the world.

She held her breath that night. Gabriella did not trust herself to turn, to move, to look him in the eye, for fear that she would abandon her promise to the angels. She blinked back tears, choked down her own desire, and let Adrian fall asleep with his wish dying on the cold night air.

A tear fell down her cheek, as Gabriella watched the myriad of stars appear in the sky. She allowed herself a moment of wistful sorrow. Rarely did she have the luxury of feeling. Survival chased tender moments away. Fear of discovery held sway over any occasion to reflect on her choices.

But tonight, cradled in the safety of her shielded refuge, she gave herself leave to wonder. What would happen if she abandoned her mission? The earth would continue to turn. The stars would rise each night. And the angels would find another Messenger.

That may be so, but there might not be another Messenger for thousands of years. At which time, the world will be unlike any we recognize.

"But there is another," Gabriella countered. "You spoke of a star, a sister star, to take the place of the one that lost her fire."

Yes.

Gabriella sighed, realizing her error. "But you speak the language of the universe. Not in the timeline of human history."

Precisely. Stars alight and descend over thousands of years. And your world, my dear one, affords not that luxury.

Still, Gabriella wondered, whether the Moon's words spoke

of prophecy. Would Gabriella's star burn on the battlefield, while Hannah's ascended in the palace?

Gabriella released the curtains and stepped back. Fatigued from years of sacrifice. She allowed the wave of exhaustion to roll over her body. And the sorrows to press on her heart.

Perhaps the time has come for Hannah to carry the mantle of leadership, she mused. If I can knock the Great Prince from his throne, my task will be complete. And Hannah would be crowned the Great Queen.

But if Gabriella were to follow the Moon's instruction, she must find a way to lead her people into battle.

How am I to do this? She asked. Throwing the desperation of her heart to the skies. You must help me see the way. Or I fear I will follow the familiar path unknowingly.

And with her heart-wrenching request, the curtains swept apart, and a Moonbeam pierced her brow like a bolt from the sky. Gabriella was brought to her knees. Struck by a vision...

A GLIMPSE INTO

HELEN STEPPED OFF THE ELEVATOR. She wasn't sure what drew her here. She had followed an instinct. Luring her up sixty-one floors to the top of this glass sky rise.

She stood for a moment in the entryway.

Gazing around, she absorbed that no man's land between elevator and business. Imagining how many people passed through this space. Matching what they wore to the finest details of the wallpaper, the door frames, the frosted glass. She smiled. Knowing these were the tiny specifics most people blurred past in their day.

For Helen, each detail was a clue. A fascinating mystery to be solved. She knew that someone had chosen each item, no matter how banal, to give an impression. To set a mood. Every thing selected to intimidate or welcome, depending on the business at the end of this passage.

Helen knew she stood on a bridge between worlds.

On her last birthday, Helen had created a game to follow any pull her instinct presented with enough force. No matter where it took her or how much talking she needed to do. She promised to follow.

Usually it involved picking an unsuspecting business or event, seeing how far she could get and how much she could find out. She gathered as many clues as she could before she opened their door, then kept the game going as long as possible. Other people went to movies. Helen invented her own little plots.

She knew Manhattan had millions of people, but it could be a lonely place at the best of times. Never mind expensive. So she created a fun source of entertainment to get to know the city, while meeting people she would never run into in her normal life. Not that Helen was remotely normal.

She had been on her way to a housewarming party with no intention of detouring into an Upper West Side skyscraper. Helen strode extra fast when she was forcing herself to a destination. She didn't like parties much, especially ones where she had to bring a home-oriented gift, but she reluctantly admitted they were a place to meet friends. Or potential job prospects.

She would have gone straight past the building had she not spotted the Logan & Associates logo. The moment she saw it, she felt a spine-tingling chill, and stopped in her tracks. The chill was her sign that there was something special about the place. Something mysterious.

Helen couldn't explain it. But she suddenly had to know who Logan was and why he needed associates.

She found herself pulled into the lobby by a curiosity so strong she would have sworn someone was tugging her blouse. The building was remarkably quiet. She looked around but did not see a soul in the lobby. Even the security guard was strangely missing from his desk.

Helen didn't question her luck. She headed straight for the elevators, quickly checking the building's directory for Logan & Associates before disappearing through the elevator doors.

Now that she stood in front of their logo, emblazoned on the wall, Helen wondered what could have possibly enticed her up sixty-one floors.

Their conservative emblem announced their importance like a law firm yet with too much flair to be such a practical enterprise. Sparkling silver, the logo's material implied expensive services and the size laid claim to the entire floor. Yet the name was so banal, she would almost assume they didn't want anyone making the trip.

What kind of company offers high-end services to a limited clientele, Helen wondered as she moved her gaze from the logo to re-examine the entryway. She suddenly picked up on the missing washroom. And the lack of art on the walls.

They aren't looking for exclusive clients, Helen thought, *they don't want clients at all. Or, at least*, she corrected herself, *they don't want anyone who isn't invited.*

Helen smiled. Jackpot! And the chill shot up her spine. Just like when she saw their name. If she needed any confirmation, she had it. There was something mysterious about this place. Which made her game all the more exciting.

As she turned her gaze to the office behind the glazed glass, she wondered how to play this. The best approach was to let the receptionist take the lead. Helen preferred to be in charge, but when the dance was this unscripted, she knew to follow where other people loved to show the way.

Luckily, she had dressed for the party. Most days, she would never wear pants that required an iron, let alone a blouse discreet enough to be worn to a job interview. She glanced down at her flirty blouse, and shifted the shoulders back to adjust the plunge down her chest. Well, almost discreet enough.

Helen shook off her doubts and pushed open the glass door. She wasn't surprised to see the waiting area empty. But she had expected a receptionist. Not seeing anyone at the front desk, she moved lightly yet confidently into the quiet space.

As she moved past the simple, modern furnishings and the non-descript glass table, she was no closer to figuring out what this place was. Luckily, she spotted a pile of magazines in the far corner of the waiting area.

Helen was a pro at figuring out a business within five minutes of seeing their reading material. She walked straight past the front desk, around the edge of the waiting area, and reached toward the stack tucked in the corner. As though no one expected them to be read at all.

"May I help you?" a voice asked in an unhelpful tone.

Helen practically jumped out of her skin. She whipped

around to see the receptionist leaning out from behind an absurdly large computer monitor, looking far from amused. Helen wondered whether this woman was really a receptionist or a guard dog with her finger poised on an alarm button.

Helen smiled effortlessly and stepped toward her opponent. She didn't actually care what the woman's real job was. Helen reveled in the challenge. Hostile receptionists were like a rite of passage. If she hadn't piped up, Helen would have been disappointed to move past so easily.

"Why, yes," Helen began, approaching the front desk.

Helen's eyes swept over the clean, sharp lines of the white barrier between her and the reception area. The chest-height obstruction said much more than anyone else might imagine. Discretion. Restraint. Secrets.

Where others noticed simple elegance, she saw protection and suspicion. Logan & Associates didn't want anyone sneaking up on their receptionist and catching a peek at her work. Helen smiled innocently and leaned in to create an air of intimacy with the cool guardian of the front desk.

"I have an appointment with Mr. Logan," Helen said, glancing over the barrier at the immaculate desktop. Not a sheet of paper in sight.

The receptionist gazed back without flinching. Then asked, "Which one?"

"Senior," Helen responded quickly.

She had no idea where that answer came from. Helen cursed her fast tongue.

Why did she say Senior? She should have opted for Junior. Helen always had better luck with younger men. Between her playful tone and complete lack of interest in their opinion, they couldn't help but be drawn to her.

"Your name," the receptionist demanded.

"Helen," she replied. "Helen Troy."

"Take a seat, Miss Troy."

As she perched on a white leather chair, Helen was nervous, but excited. She had secured an invitation inside this secret place. Not only was she going deeper into the labyrinth but she was officially rescued from her party.

Who knows, she laughed to herself, *she might even get a job out the deal.*

While she waited, she picked up one of the neatly stacked magazines. Intrigued to find an interior design magazine on the top. She glanced around surreptitiously as she flipped the pages.

No way this is a design firm, she thought. *Not a stitch of art. No minimalist yet pretentious furniture. No discreet yet oh so obviously placed awards for clients to notice.* She gazed down at the magazine. *Unless this is meant to distract me from whatever horrible problem I have by gazing at harmless, pretty pictures.*

Helen looked up, trying to catch a glimpse of the inside workings of Logan & Associates. No one walked by. No one showed up for appointments. No one called. She was alone with the sullen receptionist.

She began to wonder if anyone worked in this place. The more she wondered, the more the quiet grew unsettling.

Helen's mood shifted. She no longer felt excited. She felt vulnerable. She was alone in a strange office with one exit. If anything went wrong … she glanced up at the door. Thinking about how quickly she could get to the stairwell.

Wait. Had she seen a stairwell? Or just the elevator? She wondered. *Skyscrapers had to have a fire exit. It must be code. But she couldn't recall seeing the door. Or the bright red Exit sign that lit the way in case of fire.*

Helen admonished herself. She was getting worked up over nothing. She must have missed it. Her instinct had never steered her wrong. That intuitive pull had landed her all kinds of amazing jobs, apartments, and even the occasional fun affair.

But she couldn't shake the feeling that this place was strange. Like whatever they did here was definitely *not* a game. And that feeling clashed with her reason for doing anything.

By her twenty-seventh birthday, Helen decided she'd had enough drama to last several lifetimes. That night, after many drinks, she swore on an invisible stack of bibles that she was never taking anything seriously again. Not love. Not money. Not even life itself.

As far as she could tell, life was some elaborate game played by the gods. Where dice got tossed and you had no say in the numbers that showed up. Helen had lost that toss too many times in twenty-seven years.

She was playful by nature. But she decided it was time to up the stakes — so her game was born. If life was a crapshoot, she was going to have as much fun as possible. Helen wanted to play life full-tilt, following her intuition. Life was for living. Not for getting attached. And definitely not for staying in one place too long.

Nope. Helen was about as far as you could get from every other twenty-seven year old on the shores of Manhattan. Most twenty-somethings with enough chutzpah to get to this island,

and afford the rent, were filled with more ambition than one human being had the right to carry. The very thought of it made her nauseous.

They were determined. Helen gave them that. Determined to climb any and every wall presented. To what aim, she had no idea. Their pathological need to prove themselves seemed just as random, and infinitely less fun, than her decision to let her intuition take her wherever it damn well pleased.

When she committed to her game, Helen was so excited she made the mistake of telling people at parties. She loved the idea of letting life lead the way! Pure adventure. Letting go of the reins. She was sure people would be inspired or at least intrigued.

Not so. The response she typically got was horror, confusion, or a blank stare. Not one ounce of curiosity. Not one person wanting to tag along and give it a try. She had expected more of people in New York. Especially the artists.

Somehow, her lack of ambition did not make her intriguing. Helen discovered that it made her suspicious. Like she made the whole thing up just to trick them and steal their gold when they weren't looking. Though she had ancestors who might have done that, she was still insulted.

Helen felt a twinge. Someone was staring at her. She turned to see a young associate waiting. Eyes flitting from Helen to the floor then back to Helen. She cradled a pad of paper in her arms like a shield and had a nervous energy that made Helen think of a startled fawn.

The jumpy associate did not ease her fears. Helen figured the young woman was naturally twitchy. But for some reason, Helen had a feeling she made the little fawn extra nervous. And the longer she waited, the more uneasy the associate grew. Helen had to decide. Either she was in or she was out.

They stared at one another for a very long moment.

When Helen thought the young woman was poised to bolt, she stood up and smiled. Then gave a quick nod.

The associate sprang forward down the hall without as much as a glance back. Either she had no interest in an introduction or she figured she would never see Helen again. Helen wanted to ask questions, to gather as much information as she could before getting launched into the interview.

But the fawn kept a far enough distance to discourage conversation. Helen shrugged off the awkwardness of being led without a word and used the time to look over the unusually silent surroundings.

She walked past stretches of secluded cubicles. Not so unusual, though Helen found herself a bit surprised to see people. She half expected the place to be as deserted as the lobby. Despite the number of diligent employees at their desks, not a peep was made. Only the hushed rhythm of keys tapping and papers shifting.

When she tried to make eye contact, not a single head glanced up. Every face stayed glued to the task at hand. Her presence was of no interest. Or they had too much work to worry about the new recruit.

Giving up on human contact, Helen caught sight of the tall windows above the cubicles, displaying the sun falling over the skyline. No matter which way she turned, her view was filled with light gleaming off elegant skyscrapers and landmarks. From this height, the city took her breath away.

But then, she had fallen in love with New York at first sight.

A fact that might have worried her … for a few reasons. First, she had promised never to fall in love. And second, she was no romantic. As nostalgic as she sometimes felt for eras like the 1930s with their sensual approach to life, she knew romance was a fantasy. Even with a city, love affairs brought trouble. Setting you up for overblown expectations and crushed dreams. She preferred to follow the whims of her heart. Not someone else's.

Lucky for her, New York never stood still. If a place could be more restless than Helen, it was Manhattan. The city was always shifting, always changing. She had picked the perfect relationship. Like being with a new lover every night.

The associate stopped abruptly. Catching Helen off guard. She stopped as the young woman stepped aside, to the right of a heavy-looking wooden door. Helen waited. Thinking the fawn might lead the way.

But the young woman just stared. Blinking at Helen, like she should know what to do. Helen smiled and stepped toward the door. Glancing at her guide for any clue she had guessed wrong. Nothing.

So Helen reached her hand out to grasp the doorknob. Turning slowly. Wondering, for a brief second, whether she really wanted to go through with this.

The latch clicked. And the associate bolted. Springing away in the flash of an eye. Leaving Helen alone.

Fair enough, she thought. *Into the deep end we go.*

And she pushed the door open.

www.ingramcontent.com/pod-product-compliance
Lightning Source LLC
Chambersburg PA
CBHW061559190726
48288CB00007B/2102